MY HEART
HEMMED IN

Other titles by Marie NDiaye available from
Two Lines Press

Self-Portrait in Green

All My Friends

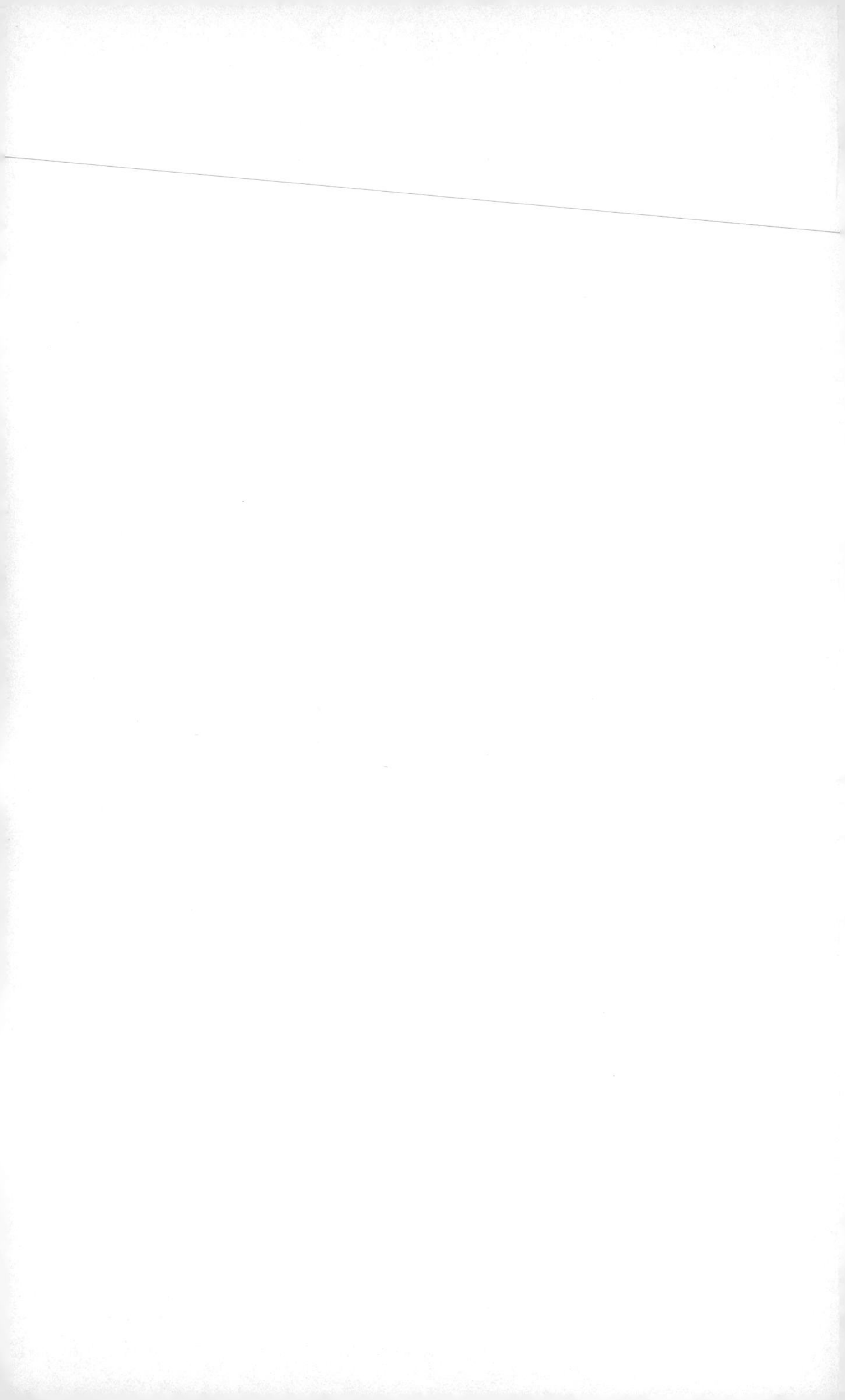

MY HEART HEMMED IN

Marie NDiaye

Translated by Jordan Stump

TWO LINES
PRESS

Originally published as: *Mon cœur à l'étroit* by Marie NDiaye

Two Lines Press
582 Market Street, Suite 700, San Francisco, CA 94104
www.twolinespress.com

ISBN 978-1-931883-62-7

Library of Congress Control Number: 2016962014
Cover design by Gabriele Wilson
Cover photo by Federica Landi / Millennium Images
Typeset by Jessica Sevey

Printed in the United States of America

1 3 5 7 9 10 8 6 4 2

Cet ouvrage, publié dans le cadre d'un programme d'aide à la publication, bénéficie de la participation de la Mission Culturelle et Universitaire Française aux Etats-Unis, service de l'Ambassade de France aux EU.

This work, published as part of a program of aid for publication, received support from the Mission Culturelle et Universitaire Française aux Etats-Unis, a department of the French Embassy in the United States.

This project is supported in part by an award from the National Endowment for the Arts.

1. When did it start?

Now and then, at first, I think I catch people scowling in my direction. They can't really mean me, can they?

When I summon my courage and mention this to Ange, at the dinner table, he pauses for a moment, sheepish or troubled, and tells me he's noticed the same thing with him. Looking into my eyes, he asks if I think his students have some grievance against him, or if through him they're aiming at me, knowing I'm his wife.

That question leaves me at a loss. What could I have done, and to whom?

I see deep concern for me in Ange's eyes. He wants me to tell him his students' hostile stares are intended for him and him alone, as are even the dark glances my students give me, meant for him and no one else.

But what could Ange have done, and to whom? Isn't he a beloved teacher, isn't he a discreet and perfectly honorable man?

We finish our meal in silence, each aware of the fear gnawing at the other but neither daring to speak of it openly, because we're both used to peace and serenity, an untroubled understanding of everything around us, and so, in a way, our own fear offends us, like something unseemly and out of place.

2. We don't know

The mothers press their red-faced children to their bellies when I appear in the schoolyard. My students' tormented stiffness makes my heart ache. What sort of wickedness are they suddenly believing in, I ask myself, that they don't even dare to look up at me, when we once got along so well?

Disturbed, I wonder: What have people been telling them?

I've always believed that no disgrace is ever completely unearned, and that, however excessive or obtuse or cruel a reaction to a dubious reputation may be, its cause can rarely be questioned.

You always have some idea, I thought, of the wrong you're being blamed for. You always have some idea, I thought. But now I can only confess—knowing it's stupid and presumptuous of me, my brow burning with shame—that I cannot begin to imagine any reason why Ange and I should have become pariahs at our school.

It's impossible. God knows I try. God knows Ange tries, all night in bed, tossing one way, trying some more, then tossing the other, when he should be deservedly enjoying the sleep we require for our responsibilities as patient, faithful, tireless teachers. I sense that Ange can no more find a comprehensible motive than I can, but we never bring up the subject, fearing our words might endow it with a terrible reality.

We're convinced of our innocence, but ashamed all the same.

3. So many happy years

We've been working at this school for fifteen years. We love the smell of the hallways in the early morning, when we open the doors to our orderly classrooms with no one around and the clean blackboard, the gleaming floor, all those faithful, persevering things quietly waiting, all that tranquil constancy rushing forward to meet us, in a way tenderly reminding us who we are.

We've been working here for fifteen years, first as colleagues, then married, by which I mean that Ange is my husband and I, Nadia, am his wife.

We teach in neighboring classrooms, and we very naturally came together, not rushing into it but never pretending to forestall what would have happened anyway. We love our school with a passion that only a handful of our fellow teachers can understand. Is there perhaps a little too much pride in that passion, I ask myself, beneath its veneer of devotion? Isn't that a thing to be chastened, stifled, and then shrunk down to a more ordinary fondness for our jobs?

This, I tell myself, not quite convinced, this might be

what's causing the violent aversion Ange and I inspire in our students, in their parents, in the principal, in our neighbors. We weren't sufficiently humble. Our own good intentions had blinded us.

But is that really so terrible?

4. Nothing to do but keep on

I walk past a little man shuffling along the edge of the sidewalk, paying him no mind.

"Nadia!" he feebly calls out.

It's my husband, Ange. He has his schoolteacher satchel under one arm, carefully clasped to his torso. We walk on together to our apartment building on Rue Esprit-des-Lois, and I realize I have to slow down if I don't want to leave Ange behind. We say nothing. We no longer dare ask each other if we had a good day, knowing perfectly well we can't have. And so we keep silent, we walk with our heads down, our eyes on the ground to make sure we see nothing that might hurt or upset us, any sort of offense, which we will react to, we know, with only a pained silence, even more unpleasant to hear together than alone.

It's cold out. Come on, hurry up, I'd like to tell Ange, but I keep quiet. His jacket is hanging loose, in spite of the cold. His top shirt buttons aren't fastened. It's not my husband Ange's way to be careless with his appearance, or his actions. Nonetheless, I keep quiet, for fear of drawing attention.

Over these past few weeks, with the behavior of everyone around us mutating so intensely that it's turned from respectful goodwill to a sort of contemptuous hatred, I've developed a certain sense of the situations liable to set off that behavior in one way or another. In the street, then, I'm convinced nothing will happen to us as long as we keep silent. Yes, we attract overt, venomous stares, like scavenging dogs that are so ugly they can only be looked at with loathing, but that's all. People simply look at us and despise us like wretched dogs.

I discreetly turn to Ange and say, under my breath, "Hurry up, it's so cold out."

He seems to be breathing heavily. I see sweat on his forehead in spite of the cold. He clutches his satchel tighter and answers only with a grimace, making no attempt to speed up.

"Are you afraid someone's going to snatch that away?" I say, nodding at the satchel.

A tall young man coming toward us hears the sound of my voice. His face is so pleasant, so perfectly sympathetic that at first I don't think to be on my guard. I even begin to break into a vague smile, merely taking care not to look him in the eye. Only Ange can I now look at straight on, though I do so less and less because of the unease that comes over us both at the sight of each other's frightened eyes, those other eyes mirroring our own panic and walling us off from all consolation, prevented from giving it and unable to take it. Even my little students I peer at from one side, looking at their neck or their ear as I speak.

The man stops short when he draws even with me. He begins rubbing his hands on his thighs, and he barks, "What? *What?*"

"It's all right," I say.

The cold air seeps under my collar. I feel it flowing down my back, I feel myself wincing. A sudden urge to urinate tenses my bladder. He then says, "You looking at me? You smiling at me? What right do you have to smile at me, you filth?"

To my surprise, I read apprehension in his pretty almond-shaped eyes. I'm not relieved to see it. On the contrary, my fear only grows.

"I don't know," I say. "I'm sorry, I'm sorry. Really," I say, "I don't know."

"Oh sure, you don't know," he says.

He takes a half step toward me. His lips are blue with anger and cold. A dense steam streams through them, and I can feel its warmth on my face. He leans back, then abruptly snaps forward and spits on my forehead. I wear my hair in bangs, and now they're damp with his spittle. It's nothing, I tell myself, just a little wetness on my hair, it's nothing.

I press my legs tightly together, careful to look no higher than his chest, and I see that chest rising and falling in his snug red sweater, stirred by a fear scarcely less violent than my own. What's he afraid of, I ask myself, what's he afraid of? Slowly the chest backs away, then disappears from view.

I hear footsteps behind me, my husband Ange trudging forward again. So, I tell myself, Ange stopped. He waited for that incident to be over, I tell myself, that altercation, whose cause escapes me but whose effect I can feel on my cold forehead, with that boy in the simply knit sweater, the kind I used to make for my son, to swathe my son's shallow chest in loving, warm red wool. Ange was right, I tell myself, to keep out of it. What good can come of confronting the fury and fear of square-shouldered, brutish-handed young men?

I start off again, not turning back, acknowledging our shared shame. It's cold out. I remember that Ange's jacket is open, his top shirt buttons undone, in spite of the cold.

We live on a quiet street, populated mostly by retired teachers Ange and I have come to view with a certain arrogance, because we find deep fulfillment in our work, and the idea that anyone might blithely settle for an existence deprived of that work surprises us and strikes us as suspect.

"Poor people, poor people," he whispers as I walk past his window, on our building's ground floor.

He whispered those very same words just this morning, when Ange and I set off for our school. I stop and say, "What is this?"

And then: "Really, how dare you talk to us like that?"

This man's cloying, ostentatious sympathy grates on me, this man we hold in such low regard. Nonetheless, I stay where I am, cold or no, staring sternly at my neighbor's cheek. Ange has caught up with me. He's gasping for breath. I say to him, "He won't explain why he thinks it's all right to pity us morning and evening, it's irritating."

"Oh, what does it matter?" Ange pants.

And as the old man gazes on him with a pity so overblown that his eyes brim with tears, Ange squares his shoulders and gravely sets his lips.

"Oh, poor people," the man repeats, his compassion seemingly roused by the effort Ange is expending to quell it.

Without nodding goodbye, I open the front door and climb the two floors to our landing. I can hear Ange's loud, labored breath far behind me, and I tell myself I should have waited and helped him up the stairs, carrying his satchel and holding his arm, but the fear of finding out what it is that's suddenly weakened the unfailingly sturdy, robust man that Ange is keeps me from coming to his aid.

Ange doesn't need anyone, I tell myself. It's cold out, and he hasn't even bothered to button his jacket and shirt, I tell myself, because he has a constitution like iron.

I begin bustling about our cozy little apartment, pretending I have things to do, and when Ange finally comes in I don't look up at him. I can only hear his quick little breaths, and a wheeze of the sort that punctuates a snorer's sleep. Ange drops into an armchair. The satchel slips to the floor. He spreads his arms, gingerly lays his head against the chair's back.

"So," I say, frightened, "what's the matter?"—dimly sensing what's wrong, or the nature of the disaster that's befallen us, but doing my best, with questions and gestures ("What's the matter?" I say again, slowly raising my hands to my cheeks), to put off the moment when I can no longer pretend I don't know, pretend I haven't seen.

I spot a rip in Ange's shirt, a blood-soaked hole more or less over his liver.

"My darling," I say, "my darling."

I'm a taciturn and reserved person by nature, and I'm not in the habit of saying such things to Ange. But I say again, "My darling, my darling," pressing and kneading my cheeks, wanting to go to him but powerless to move my legs, managing only to say once again words I ordinarily never speak: "Ange, oh, my darling."

5. How could I not have known?

"You've got to come over," I say.

Which they immediately do, practical, efficient, both of them tall and husky like Ange but animated by a vivacity that I assume must be continually refreshed by the sway of the long, tinkling Indian skirts they've been wearing since they were teenagers, indifferent to changing fashions. Their faces are much alike, and I often mix up their names.

They kneel down before their father, concerned and watchful but showing no shock or surprise, as if, I tell myself, bewildered, this were a situation they've already foreseen, already thought through, almost studied. They must have trained for this moment, I tell myself. But how can that be, when I had no idea, when I saw nothing?

In hushed tones, I tell them that Ange refuses to go to the hospital—that's why I called.

"It's not reasonable," I say, with a perplexed little shrug.

"On the contrary, it's perfectly reasonable," says the one who must be named Gladys.

"The hospital is out of the question," says the other, possibly Priscilla.

She gives me a surprised, very slightly offended look.

"You know," she says, "they'll give him all kinds of trouble at the hospital."

"What sort of trouble?" I say reflexively.

But in truth, I'm in no hurry to know.

"So what should we do?" I hasten to ask.

Attentive, efficient, Ange's two daughters busy themselves by the armchair as Ange sits and watches in silence.

He listens to us, looks at us, not even pretending to be too weak to give his opinion. He has some other reason for keeping it to himself.

I'm standing a few steps away, and although it seems obvious that I have a part to play in the care Gladys and Priscilla are undertaking to give Ange, and essential that I play it, I don't make a move. I clasp my hands over my stomach, fingers knotted. I simply smile at Ange whenever our eyes meet, and he gives me a clenched, tortured smile in return.

I can feel his shame as keenly as my own, like a riptide carrying both of us off together, leaving us to drift for a moment, then sweeping us up again, but never letting us touch, never embrace. Beneath my feet I hear the familiar little sounds of the neighbors.

"It's dinnertime," I say.

"Bring us warm water, compresses, and alcohol," says Gladys.

"Oh God, I think we're out of compresses," I say.

Tears spill from my eyes.

"Run and get some from the pharmacy," says Priscilla.

"I can ask the woman next door," I say.

"The time when you can ask anyone for anything is long gone," says Gladys or Priscilla. "Hurry, go buy some."

I put on my coat and rush out into the cold, now gone dark. I jog toward the pharmacy, stumbling, muttering incoherently. I hear the bells we knew so well, the cheery seven-o'clock carillon that not long ago still announced, simply and affectionately, that it was time to stop preparing our next day's lessons and sip a first glass of good wine (whereupon Ange would say: "Isn't this the sweetest moment of all?" with a playfulness that I felt and understood and loved, because we both knew that our workdays were made of nothing but sweet moments, among which we couldn't possibly choose the best), and now those friendly bells are ringing and I'm tottering on the icy sidewalk, eyes on the ground, unable to hold back a low murmur of "What's happening to us, what's happening to us"; now I feel myself becoming so estranged from my own existence that I couldn't say which faces are real, our faces as Ange and I relish our daily aperitif in the serenity of our blameless conscience or our faces this evening, separated by calamity and incomprehension, so unlikely does it seem that those two situations could be contained in one single reality.

I stop to listen to the bells and catch my breath. The street is empty, swept by the north wind.

The wind roars, it drowns out the bells, and very likely they've stopped ringing when I think I still hear them.

I hurry onward again. I can feel my glasses' cold, sharp frame against my petrified face. I turn onto Cours de l'Intendance, just as deserted as our street, but I keep my eyes down out of habit, a habit so quickly acquired. My glasses slip. At regular intervals, I push them up along my nose with one finger, feeling the cold of the metal frame, the faint touch of the misted lenses against my damp lashes.

6. A changeable pharmacist

"Please, oh please, a box of large compresses," I say, as if there were some question that my money would be acceptable.

I show her the bills, opening my wallet wide and tilting it toward the cash register.

"Don't worry," she says, soothingly.

I glance up at her. I know her. There are no other customers, and in this perfumed warmth, in this scent of honeyed lozenges and milky ointments—the welcoming smell of knowledge and precision—I believe I can let down my guard a little. I look at her straight on, the way I used to. I had her child in my class a few years before—a boy or a girl? *An endless parade of faces, pretty and attentive, a bounty of youthful perfection that in my memory melts into one single face, abstract and sweet, in shades of gray.*

And was she an easygoing mother or a difficult one? She studies me intently with her dark eyes, made darker still by sadness, by pain at my plight.

"I know what happened, and I don't approve," she says.

She stands motionless behind the counter, as if she thought talking to me more helpful just now than filling my order. Outside the wind blows in great gusts, inaudible from where I stand at the counter looking out at the dead leaves and scraps of paper all whipping past in the same direction. Ange and his daughters are waiting for me, and the daughters, whom I've only known as adults, might be struggling in vain to sop up the blood flowing from their father's side, surprised and perhaps concerned that I haven't come home with the compresses.

But she stays where she is, broad, powerful, hieratic. She stands frozen before me by sympathy, by a need to be believed and exonerated, her affliction mingled with relief. She was expecting me, I tell myself apprehensively, but she was also afraid I might not come.

"I heard what they did to him," she says. "Oh, no, really, I don't agree with that. What will we have left, you know, if even teachers, if even good teachers like you and your husband..."

Her tone changes, thick with outrage and compassion. She's stopped looking at me. Faintly anxious, she's eyeing the glass door and the desolate avenue beyond, the brand-new tram now and then sliding by with a brief muffled hiss, brightly lit, almost empty. Doing my best to speak calmly, I say, "My stepdaughters would rather not take him to the hospital, so I really do need a large box of compresses."

"No, no, absolutely, not the hospital," she says, grimacing, horrified. "If he goes to the hospital, oh, who knows what state he'll be in the next time you see him, if you ever do. They'll tell you he expired right there in front of them and they had to incinerate him at once and you'll know perfectly well it's not true, but what can you do, what can you do? No, not the hospital. They won't treat him properly."

"Well, right now I've got to go home and take care of my husband."

Again I feel tears pooling at the rims of my eyes.

"I'll be needing those compresses," I say. "Don't you want to give them to me?"

"Of course I do," she says, "and I will, because I absolutely don't approve of what happened. I shouldn't be helping you, but I am anyway, to show that I don't agree, and to show you that I at least haven't forgotten who you really are."

She reaches under the counter and sets down a box of

compresses before me. Rows of identical boxes are lined up behind her. This one must have been readied specially for me, I tell myself, on the assumption I'd be coming to the pharmacy. But why should they ever have foreseen such a thing, my coming here, pleading for compresses?

I whirl around, eager to get back to Ange and determined not to ask this woman the many questions swelling my cheeks, questions I don't want to hear myself ask, questions that must, I know, be asked all the same. Just a little more uncertainty and confusion, I tell myself, just a little more not understanding and wondering, I tell myself, and then I'll be ready to hear, little by little, what they all have against us, the reasons for a hatred so single-minded, so entire, so sincere. Why should I be in a hurry to hear that, since clearly those reasons aren't rooted in anything about us we can change—why rush toward pointless denials and a forced awareness of your own failings?

But just as I reach for the door handle, the swift, silent tram glides past the pharmacy with our school's principal on board, alone in the first car, her face turned toward the street, a calm, austere, very white face frozen in the bright lights of the tram. And all at once, as her eyes meet mine through the two panes of glass, that very still, very white face erupts in an expression of horrified surprise, of aversion and terror. She goes on staring at me until the tram turns the corner of the avenue, still with that same look of dismay, a look I've never in any circumstance seen on her face before.

The wind howls past the dark shopwindows. All at once a driving rain begins to fall, lashing the pharmacy door, and I let go of the handle, turning back to her, still shaken by my face's effect on the principal's—or was it something other than my face? Was it my being here, in this place and at this moment? Was it a menacing, furious, rebellious look I'd shown her without knowing it?

I blurt out the question I'd been trying to hold in: "What did they do to my husband?"

Slowly she puts her hand to her mouth. For a moment, seeing a shiver come over her face, I'm convinced she's about to be transformed, like the marble-visaged principal, the excessive, grandiloquent, ghostly-faced principal, into an effigy of repulsion. But no, she quietly coughs into her hand and nothing more. Remarkable self-control, I tell myself, because she was just about to let out a cry, or at least a groan, in her surprise at seeing my face again when I'd just turned and started for the door. She never guessed she'd have to keep up the struggle of looking at me face-to-face, and her concentration and vigilance had waned.

"What did they do to my husband?" I say, in agony.

"You don't know?" she said. "Do you want to know?"

"I don't want to, but I believe I should want to," I say.

"Yes," she says, "I understand."

Cloying compassion, here too, as if seeping from the punctured sac of her purulent heart. Her face now set back on course, so to speak, the course of mercy, enveloping me in its warmth, in its gentleness, in its self-satisfied goodwill.

She opens her mouth but says nothing, hesitant, overwhelmed.

I recognize her. She was on the school advisory board a few years ago, an ardent mother, heavy-hipped, quarrelsome, rarely pleased. I recognize her, because a field trip I'd organized had roused her indignation, on the grounds that the museum we visited housed several photographs of mingled fleshes, white, cold thighs, blue-veined feet pressing on white, cold buttocks. *That face now stricken, as if she'd once loved me and were never going to see me again and couldn't do anything about it.* This intimacy puts me off, the exposure of these emotions.

"In that case I must tell you, yes, I have no choice," she says.

"No time," I say, hugging the bag of compresses with all my might.

But, however I wish I could leave, I don't, held back by the exaltation in her damp gaze, her hesitations, her labored playing for time. Now there's nothing more to stop her from telling me what has to be told, what I must make myself want to hear, nothing, not even if the principal's wan, distraught face suddenly appeared at the window, not even if customers came in and saw her talking to me, bent toward a face, mine, that must inspire silence and nothing more. In a flash of panic I think of Gladys and Priscilla struggling to stanch the blood, and I picture Ange, whose concern for me, since I'm taking so long to come home, might at this very moment be sapping the little strength he has left.

But as for her, nothing will stop her from telling her story now.

"It's no one's fault," she says, her breath coming fast, "but it's also everyone's fault. My daughter told me about it. She didn't do anything, she only saw it; she didn't object because those horrible ideas have infected her too, they're infecting even innocent children now, no matter how I try to…to make her understand that she mustn't…that it's not right. My God, how hard it is to make people understand when something's not right…. Don't you agree, Madame?"

"But in this case specifically, what is it that's not right?" I say. "What would be right? I still don't know what you're talking about," I go on after a pause, a little dazed at hearing myself called Madame.

How long has it been since someone last called me that? Terms of respect are forbidden: people simply yell out my last name, that or an offhanded "Hey!"

"Everything you're being made to endure," she says, "as if you were guilty, but people were forbidden to punish you and so everyone's taking their vengeance in their own way."

She's talking as fast as she can, anxious that someone might come walking in, though her fear now is not that she'll be caught talking to me but that she won't be able to finish her story. She's not telling me the truth, I say to myself. She doesn't know what the truth is. That child told her something, but she, the mother, doesn't know anything

"That's not the truth," I tell her in spite of myself, my ears thrumming.

Surprised, slightly indignant, she says, "It most certainly is."

I squeeze the box of compresses so hard that the cardboard buckles beneath my fingers. My chin quivers with a sudden anger, almost hatred.

"When you don't know what you're talking about, you keep your mouth shut," I whisper fiercely. "These things you're telling me don't make any sense. What am I supposed to do with this nonsense? There is no way," I say, "that all this has anything to do with my husband. There is simply, simply no way, and that's all there is to it."

She takes a step back, looking neutrally into my eyes, and asks, "Why?"

"Why?" I repeat, confounded. *Because such atrocities do not happen to a sympathetic, respectful man, a man who is innocent in every way. It's just plain common sense, and isn't that reason enough to refuse to hear one more word of this garbage?*

I say nothing. I shrug, numbed by the continual wail of the wind. Softly, with a sort of gentle impartiality, she says:

"So to you, if such things ever do happen, they have to involve someone other than your husband?"

"That's right," I say.

My voice is weak. She gives me a curious, studying look.

"That's right," I say.

"But," she says (there's a dull-white paste clinging to her moist lips, and I savagely wipe my own, now smelling the sourness of her breath, remembering her belligerent, irate face during the board meetings, horrified to find that woman with her insatiable need to chastise and complain now feeling sorry for me, wanting to help me), "but," she says, "why should any other man than your husband, any other no-longer-young man, unlikely to put up a fight, why should any such man deserve to have done to him what you don't want to believe has been done to your husband? No man in this city deserves it, but your husband doesn't deserve it any less than another!"

Emotion overcomes her. She shakes her head and reaches out for my hand. She changes her mind. She quickly pulls away. She goes on:

"That's what you must understand, oh please won't you understand, that...there's nothing special about you and your husband. It's not you, not exactly you that this ugliness is attacking, and besides, who around here even knows you? Apart from a few people who, like me... But no, it's not you, it's...how can I put it...the untouchability of what you are, your...your stiffness, your purity, your manner, your habits, oh, how can I put it..."

"We're exactly like you," I say.

"So you think," she says, "but, oh God, you don't understand, and I don't know how to... You're so different, so profoundly...excessive, but either you don't know it or, who knows, you refuse to see it, although, once again, this isn't exactly about you as such, and...and the disgust and hostility you inspire in some people, not me, oh not me, is something you can't feel toward yourselves, at least not yet, and... Forgive me, this is so hard.... You have something in your face that people can't stand to see...not on any face... and it's something truly repugnant, not for me, no, not yet, although...that will come, perhaps, how can a person fight off the arguments, the quiet influence of the atmosphere... It's very hard, and my own daughter, a child who so loved her teacher, who so loved you, my own daughter came home spouting such absurdities about you and your husband that I didn't recognize her, such a shy, such a nice little girl, so I turned away without a word, I was shaking, I walked out of the house, I thought some sort of demon had taken hold of her, I went away so I wouldn't hear anything more, but no, it wasn't that, nothing supernatural about it, only the same spiteful revulsion that everyone's begun to feel toward people like you and your husband, which keeps growing and growing, and well yes, it's not easy to resist, it's not easy at all..."

"So it's a sort of fashion, is that what you're trying to say?" I ask.

"No," she answers, "it's a rage!"

She breaks into a laugh, a fierce, nervous laugh that pulls back her lips, reveals her gums, and with a little shiver of distaste I recognize it as the laugh that greeted my protestations of good faith at the board meeting where this woman ripped me apart with her straight, healthy pharmacist teeth.

My God, I tell myself dully, and now, now support and friendship from my enemy! Does she even remember that?

"So you're thinking it will just go away on its own?" she says. "No, seriously, you have no idea what's going on. I think it's time you... I mean, yes, it's time you were aware of it."

A rush of damp air hits me from behind. Imperceptible a moment before, the hiss of the tram can clearly be heard receding down the tracks in the roaring wind.

She sweeps a feverish hand over the counter, as if to erase any trace of a connection between us. The man closes the door behind him, and the sound of the wind suddenly stops.

I hunch my shoulders, slightly ducking my head. The back of my neck is burning hot. *Then he raises his axe, still dripping with the blood of his first victim, the luckless schoolteacher, and with one mighty blow brings it crashing down onto the skull of...*

She says, "Good evening, Monsieur."

She gives me a discreet gesture, three fingers swiftly wiggling my way: Get out! I see trepidation in her gaze, softened by mercantile good cheer.

Slowly I turn away. Then, eyes on the floor, I hurry out, hearing a groan from my throat that surprises and shames me. *Because he didn't have an axe, he was guilty of no bloodshed, had no evil designs on anyone's skull.*

7. We don't need any friends, thanks

Through the door I hear the tinkling rustle of their full Indian skirts.

I can't begin to say how much time has gone by since I left the apartment. I hurried all the way home, once again encountering the number 8 tram as it went by in the other direction, the principal still or again on board, her pallid face deliberately turned, I thought, to the driver's back, forced in a sense by her will or her fear to avoid looking out the window no matter what. But in truth I read nothing particularly disturbing on that face in the few seconds it took the silent tram to graze past me (I was just about to cross the tracks, I jumped back), harshly illuminating me with the white light of its wagons, so sharp and intense that it casts a lunar glow far into the distance on either side.

My heart is almost joyous. *My absurd, gleeful heart! No harm has come to me, no axe has split my brow, no fist has crushed my chest, no insult has spewed from…*

A frigid rain is falling. The avenue is deserted, scattered

with pale patches of light. Nonetheless, my heart is almost joyous. *No stranger has tried to hurt me, so far.*

I push open the door, greeted by their grave, tight-lipped air. One daughter's eyes are red, I notice, a woman I know as detached and remote.

"I have the compresses," I say in a choked voice.

"Oh, what's the use?" says Gladys.

"We don't know what to do," says Priscilla.

They lead me to our bedroom. Everything in me refuses to go in, but I force my legs to move and follow Gladys into the little room where Ange and I sleep every night, where I don't believe anyone but us has ever set foot for as long as we've lived in this apartment. Only one lamp is lit, on my side of the bed.

He croaks, "Here's your wife."

"What's he doing here?" I say, in a surge of repugnance.

Priscilla turns around and sees my disgust. She says, "He came up, he wanted to make himself useful."

"I've brought you bread and ham," says the old man.

"You never should have let him in," I say, exasperated. "Oh God, that…that horrid neighbor!"

He goes on:

"And I've brought you some wine, too, good wine from my *terroir*, to show you that I at least am not afraid to share with you, to share bread, wine, and ham, that's what I'm saying. And I am the only one in this building, and I do mean the only one, who harbors such feelings for you, and not only, as you might think, because your profession is the very one that was my own pride and joy for…"

"Excuse me, excuse me," I say, "I don't want to hear any

more of this; you have to get out of here, right this minute. I cannot accept this man's presence here," I say to Priscilla. "We haven't fallen so low that..."

"Forgive me," he says, "the fact is you've fallen lower than anyone ever has, but that's neither here nor there, because, all things considered, it is not in the dubious pleasure of self-sacrifice that I find my..."

"Really now, he's a fine man, you don't meet many like him anymore," says Priscilla, giving me a pained, shocked look.

"Won't you please go away?" I say. "I'm begging you, Pris, make him go. It's so terribly, terribly humiliating," I say.

"Will you shut your mouth?" cries Gladys. "Look at my father—he's dying!"

I clap my hands over my ears. How can she say such things in front of the neighbor?

"I realized I have to stand by you, come what may," he says, "when a little voice whirling around in my head like a frightened bird told me you were doomed, reminding me that we devoted teachers, solely and entirely consumed by our work, are not, are not at all prepared to face days such as this. Just such a calamity," he says in his plaintive, pompous, droning voice, "could well have blighted my own existence, and I know it's only a matter of luck that I never entered into marriage with a woman like..."

"Oh, things aren't as bad as all that," I say.

"Stop it," Gladys begs. "My poor father, you're torturing him!"

"Then get this man out of here," I say.

He's sitting near the bed, on a low chair, his bony knees

almost level with his quivering chin, at once suspicious and eager to please. I see him discreetly clutch the two edges of the seat and settle in a little further, determined not to be dislodged. He shoots me a venomous, challenging look. *I'll go away when I'm good and ready. It's not up to you. I intend to see my duty through to the end.* His clothes are wretched, dirty, and torn. He has a long gray beard, matted into flat clumps.

He's never been a teacher, I find myself thinking. He's lying, trying to ingratiate himself.

"What school did you teach in?" I ask.

"What could that possibly matter?" says Priscilla.

"The Collège Voltaire, on Avenue Louis-Binot," he says, doing his best to look dignified. "I taught history and geography."

"Who was the principal?" I say, pointlessly, since I have no idea.

"At the time, it was... I'm not sure anymore... Madame Bernard?"

"Ah," I say, losing heart, "that could be."

Pressing my palms together over my chest, I murmur again, "That could be, I suppose."

The two daughters are standing on either side of the bed, stiff and tense, frozen in incomprehension and reproach. *Those two never liked me. Always wished Daddy had stayed with Mommy, even if they themselves blithely go from one man to another with every passing year—what do I care about that now?*

I go to our bed, my ears ringing. What do I care about anything, anything, anything?

A stifling stench of blood floods my nostrils.

Much more alert than his daughters had led me to believe, Ange looks up at me and sees at once, I can tell, that I know what was done to him, and shame falls over us both again, that old shame we've come to know so well, the shame of recognizing that people see us as different from others in the most rudimentary way, even if we can't imagine why.

He quickly looks down again. His face is yellow and glistening. Incongruously, he's drenched in sweat. I gently take his hand on the blood-stained sheet.

"My darling," I say very quietly.

He squeezes my fingers. His breath comes in labored gasps, but I can see that he's trying to keep his feelings to himself, as he always has.

I whisper, "Darling."

Then I turn to the old man bending forward to hear, his filthy beard brushing the sheets.

"Go home," I say. "I'll give you money if you'll just go away now."

"I don't need money," he says, evidently offended.

"Come on, leave him alone," Ange murmurs.

"I've received several inheritances in my life," he says.

"So now we're going to be rude to good-hearted people," says Gladys.

"This is all intolerable," I say.

I fall to my knees by the bed. I bury my burning face in the mattress, pressing Ange's hand to my forehead, my hair.

"You see, you see," I say, as softly as I can, and there's almost a rusted sound to my voice, a withered sound, "we're respectful people, my darling, and it's a fact, yes, that we couldn't help respecting even the wrongs that were done to us, yes, a sort of mute, craven respect, and we felt that respect even for those who set out to hurt us, because whenever there's a rule or a semblance of a rule we respect it, that's right, and if that rule offends us, if it attacks us and makes us unhappy, we tell ourselves that rules aren't made to please absolutely and necessarily everyone, that rules, and even semblances of rules, don't have to make us happy, us specifically, and that on the other hand there are already a great many rules that do suit us, or favor us. And isn't that just what you were thinking, my love, my poor darling, when you were walking behind me, trying to hide your wound with your satchel, isn't that more or less what you were thinking: after all, nobody's expected to want to please me by treating me exactly as I deserve, there are times, unquestionably, when I have to accept being treated in ways I don't deserve, for the sake of a greater good I don't see? Oh yes, it's true, that's more or less what you were thinking, out of pride, and that's not good, that's not good at all..."

"Then you must respect me as you respect everyone around you," that other man says triumphantly.

He loudly blows his nose into a Kleenex, which he then crumples into a ball and drops to the floor, kicking it under the bed.

"May I smoke?" he asks, putting on a humble face again.

"I'll bring you an ashtray," says Priscilla.

"We don't have any ashtrays," I mutter, "we don't smoke. Oh, my God. No, there'll be no smoking here."

I raise my head. I have a scrape on the bridge of my nose, from my glasses, which I didn't think to take off before I pressed my head to the mattress.

"Why are you so indulgent with this person?" I ask Ange's two daughters.

"Forget it, forget it," Ange whispers, desperate for an end to this.

He jerks his hand away and rolls over, turning his back.

"I want to sleep," he moans.

"I have to see the...the wound," I say.

My glasses are askew, I can feel it, my skin red and hot, my hair mussed. Through her fearfulness, Gladys gives me a quick smile. *Such a mean smile, bubbling up from the meanness of her very soul, carefully hidden away until now, such cruelty in that abundant flesh, and yet these are his loving, beloved daughters, two horrid girls he'd give his life for if he had to, every bit of his life.*

Priscilla, who'd discreetly slipped out, comes back into the room and with ceremonious deference bends down between the old man's legs to lay the lid of a jam jar on the floor.

"Your ashtray," she says.

He kisses her hand. His eyes are damp.

And suppose, I suddenly say to myself, suppose it was these two who contrived to bring the neighbor into our apartment, what would that mean, what conclusions should I draw?

No answer comes to me. I feel riddled with bewilderment, cowardice, indecision. I reach out to pull away the sheet covering Ange up to his chest, but he tugs it back with a growl and clutches it in both fists, just under his chin.

"Let me see," I say gently.

"He doesn't want anyone touching it anymore," says Gladys. "He says it's his right to demand that no one touch or even look at his wound."

She shakes her head, impotent and downcast, and nonetheless distant, strangely passive.

"In that case, we've got to get the doctor," I say firmly.

Grimacing, Ange rolls onto his back. His face is unrecognizable, shrunken with pain and a sort of depthless exasperation that I've never seen in all our years together, that I never imagined I'd see, endlessly tolerant man that he was, forbearing, to the point, sometimes, of weakness.

"No!" he rasps. "No, no! You understand?"

He lets out a long moan that makes me tremble all over. I hear more than pain in it, I hear rage and confusion.

"What are we supposed to do?" I ask imploringly. "Please, Ange, what are we supposed to do?"

He rolls onto his side, showing us his back, still clinging to his sheet as if he were afraid I might rip it away. Then he closes his eyes, his eyelids squeezed tight, groaning quietly.

"And you two, standing there watching! Yes, oh yes, what's your suggestion?" I say to Ange's two daughters.

Priscilla kneels down by the old man. She throws back her long hair and he strokes it with one hand, discreet but not exactly furtive. I can't repress a stunned cackle.

"Well, really, now! So many surprises today!" I say.

"It's all right," Gladys answers hurriedly.

My head suddenly spinning, I sit down on the edge of the bed, pressed against Ange. I can feel his shivering warmth in the small of my back. *He has a fever, maybe that's why he's acting so strangely with me.*

I take off my glasses. I cover my eyes with my hands and sit that way for a time, in a reflective pose but in reality powerless to force my thoughts into any kind of logical, useful progression. A torrent of incongruous words is washing through my mind. I feel distracted, in a way that seems wrong to me, even as I feel deeply lost. The harder I try to gather my thoughts, the more they elude me, and when at last I get hold of a few, they seem devoid of all interest or consequence, and so I let them drift on unhindered, and I plunge back into my incomprehensible distraction.

Behind me, Ange has fallen completely silent. This comes as a relief, as a welcome respite. *An ignoble relief, because who here is suffering the most, who here needs a respite from his torment?* I lower my hands and put on my twisted glasses again. My eyes meet the old man's. He looks worried, unless he's pretending. On her knees close beside him, Priscilla hopefully looks up into his repugnant face.

"I don't know," he says, "I don't know, but I think..."

"Yes?" says Gladys, pleadingly.

"My sense is that your father is trying—your very dear father, whom I admire, although he has never honored me with a single hello, I mean a sincere and friendly hello—my sense is that he's trying, you understand, to act as though nothing has happened..."

"Yes, and?"

Why does Gladys seem to be expecting some decisive revelation from this man Ange and I always mutely dismissed as an utter nonentity?

I try to recall if we ever, at any time, overtly showed our disdain for him. *A deft, hurtful, deliberate way of pretending we hadn't seen him at his ground-floor window even as we brushed by him, a way of starting when we heard his greeting and then answering with a show of displeasure and a moment's hesitation, then hurrying on so we wouldn't have to hear anything he might try to add—but is that really so cruel? Is it really so strange? The one person in the building we didn't invite in to toast my granddaughter's birth—but are we really obliged to have fond feelings for everyone?*

No, no, nothing ever happened between us and this man. It's simply that everything about him fills us with boredom and nausea.

He's stopped talking. Priscilla patiently toys with the charms on her skirt. Now and then he extends a finger toward Priscilla's lustrous hair, strokes it without timidity or bravado, and she smiles sweetly—almost, I can't help thinking, as if she were honored by the gesture. Meanwhile, Gladys is stomping around the room, her eyes glued to the old man.

He demurely clears his throat.

"Your father has always thought me a mediocrity," he says, "or more precisely he would have thought me the lowliest creature on earth, had he ever troubled to form an opinion of me. But no, he never granted me so much as one moment of his thoughts, and the plain truth is that to him I simply didn't exist."

"Can that be?" says Gladys.

Apprehension, dismay, and perplexity mottle her face with red patches. She looks at me with something like hatred, as if accusing my influence of transforming her father into such an arrogant man. I shrug. Ange has gone back to sleep. His ignorance of the things being said about him and the innocence of his quiet snores make something petty and contemptible, I tell myself, of that ridiculous person's words.

"What are you trying to prove?" I say, in deep trepidation.

"Don't be so supercilious," Gladys tells me.

She's terrified, her hands pressed to her cheeks. I realize she's afraid this man whose words they so greedily drink in will decide to say nothing more.

"What are you trying to prove?" I say again, hotly.

But he pays me no mind, never glancing my way. He's talking to Ange's two daughters, both of them very fleshy, like their father, endowed with an abundance of hair, and both of them mothers, raising their bountiful broods together, having left various unsatisfactory husbands behind.

"So," he says, "your father would be very surprised to learn that I know him as well as a person can be known."

"No he wouldn't, not at all," says Priscilla.

"He was even happy to see you come into the bedroom just now," says Gladys.

"Yet another surprise," I say, with a venomous cackle. "By the way, how are the children?"

"In any case," he says, smugly conceding the point, "he has no idea how many years I've spent observing him, inspired as much by affection—the most unconditional sort of affection, you understand—as by what I might call an almost passionate admiration for his work..."

"Yes," I say less severely, "his work."

"What work?" says Priscilla.

"Ange has always been interested in..."

"A number of articles," the old man interrupts, "that

your father published in first-rate journals devoted to education and new primary-school methodologies. Those articles, which I have carefully preserved, proved to me that your father was not only an intelligent and cultivated man but a genuine scholar of his profession, and since, in that profession, I myself..."

"Liar," I say. "Imposter."

"You have no right to say such things!" cries Gladys.

"She has a talent for insults, but no idea how to put together an argument," he says, with quiet, priestly self-assurance.

"I know enough to want nothing to do with you," I say. "I'm asking you to get out of my apartment."

He grasps the chair with both hands and holds on tight. My eyes meet his cold, black stare, cunning but not entirely devoid of a certain plaintive longing to make peace, which sends me into a fury. I leap up, jiggling the mattress and disturbing Ange's unquiet sleep. I march over and take the old man by the shoulders, ready to dump him out of the chair if I must, but the disgust we always felt at his body, skinny and doughy at the same time, weirdly fatty here and emaciated there, his slack body, like the very incarnation of his obsequious two-facedness and almost ambiguous gender (because in spite of his beard he has the ways of a strange sort of woman), the disgust that Ange and I took a vague pleasure in feeling together makes my arms fall back to my sides.

I stand in front of him, taut with anger, my only hope that if he saw me backing off he won't take it for fear. *The intolerable idleness of retirement, that long, dreary, official sidelining from what is, for Ange and me, virtually the sole point of existence, our work: that's the other thing that disgusts us and makes us hate him so hungrily. An outcast, that's what he is, and he knows it and he's crying out for our fellowship and sympathy. He could have saved himself the trouble. No work, no life.*

He sniffles. Priscilla hands him a Kleenex. He dabs at his nose and again briskly and casually tosses the crumpled Kleenex under the bed. He wipes his nostrils between his thumb and index finger.

"I had a feeling your father would make the mistake he's now making," he says, "which surely goes to show that I love him and admire him just as I told you, but I also know that he suffers from a flaw, pride, which I will concede must nonetheless be counted among the forces that make your father the remarkable man you know him to be."

"Ange isn't proud. That's asinine," I say. "Oh, I don't want to get into a debate with you."

"In that case," says Gladys in exasperation, "keep your mouth shut and let him talk."

"You people are in my bedroom," I say. "Why should I have to accept that, and why should I keep quiet?"

"Things have changed," says Priscilla.

"We're only trying to help you," he says. "Why is that so humiliating? Nothing's humiliating if it's what you want."

"There's nothing that serious going on. We'll deal with it," I say.

I feel a sudden blush cover my face. I carefully sit down against Ange's back. Above the sheet, his gray hair is sticking up in a way he never lets anyone see, not even me, his wife. He's always the first one up, and every morning he quickly smooths it down with hair oil. And now I can see the brown-speckled skin of his scalp through his tousled locks. I lean over him to straighten his hair, as gently as I can. But the moment I touch him he flinches violently in his sleep and begins to speak a string of muddled words. Afraid he might suddenly break into comprehensible sentences and reveal who knows what that shouldn't be revealed in such company, I pull back. Immediately Ange is at peace again.

With feigned humility, the other man declares:

"And that pride, as I was saying, is not to be condemned in itself, and never have I condemned it, not even, indeed especially not, when that pride signed the veritable death warrant that your beloved father's prejudices had decreed against my pathetic self, since, as I was telling you, I simply did not exist in his eyes. Nonetheless, let me be clear, I never held it against him. Why do all signs now show me that this same overweening pride is forcing your father to deny anything has happened to him? Oh, I can see it, I can feel it. He wants his wound to miraculously close up, just like that, and then he wants to hear no more of his having had a wound at all. He wants to go back to work, and have no one say a word to him about any of this. But you must understand, that is the worst possible attitude at this moment, and I'm here, I came here, in hopes of persuading your father not to forget his wound, as it were, do you see? Not to forget it on any pretext, not even his work or his self-respect or anything else. Because, you understand, if he does fall back into his error, if he insists on pretending that his situation is anything other than seriously compromised, then he will find, yes, that everything is even worse than before, and by far."

I let out a slightly overaggressive little laugh.

"And suppose his situation is compromised—what business is that of yours?"

"Monsieur Noget," he says, with a very subtle bow. "Richard Victor Noget."

"I wasn't asking you anything," I say, "and especially not your name. I've forgotten it already, so there."

"It's a well-known name," Priscilla murmurs.

"If my father was awake and he heard that name, he would never believe it," says Gladys.

"I don't know the name, and I don't want to know anything about it," I say.

He looks at me sorrowfully, although to my deep irritation I see an insulting, sardonic glint in his eye. I try to come up with a stinging counterattack. But even as the most caustic words come to my lips, what bursts from my eyes and mouth is a torrent of sobs.

"I'm so tired," I say. "I've got to... I've got school tomorrow. Please, let me rest."

"I would advise you not to go back to that school," he says in a tone of concern.

"You know, I really don't care what you advise," I say, hiccupping pathetically, desperately trying not to.

"We're leaving, we'll be back tomorrow," says Priscilla.

She stands up slowly, as if against her better judgment. I sense that Ange's two daughters feel an irreparable resentment toward me, now inflamed—because over the years it had faded—by my refusal to acknowledge any decency in our neighbor, any authority, any possible intellectual kinship with us.

A moment later he stands up in turn, equally reluctant. *As if all three of them were convinced that their leaving will set off some sudden decline in Ange's condition, as if they thought it was only their somberness, their melodramatic exaggeration of the events, that was holding him back from the abyss he'll be thrown into by my short-sightedness and my heedlessness the moment they turn their backs, or as if they were afraid I might do something indecent or dangerous, might wrestle Ange, say, into letting me root around in his wound…*

I see them to the apartment door.

He's so short, so stunted and hunched that I have a clear view of the top of his head, striated by a little clutch of sad, greasy locks.

Is he destitute? I ask myself, with a brief jolt of uneasiness, because if he is, then his poverty might move me in spite of myself.

"Don't forget, that school, that's where they did…this thing to him," he says, stopping in the doorway and turning anxiously toward me.

"Don't worry about me," I say sharply.

"This isn't about you. It's a general principle, in a way," he says. "You shouldn't go back."

"I will never abandon my students," I say.

"Your students? So you think your students have nothing to do with all this? You really think they didn't take part, at least in spirit, or intention, or, how should I say, desire? That they didn't overtly or covertly demand just such a display of…oh, I don't know…of power, for example?"

"My students aren't like that," I say, shocked. "They've

changed, yes, probably from hearing too many of the vicious things their parents say, but what they feel is more confusion than hate. I'm sorry to cast aspersions on you," I say, "but if you really were a retired teacher you'd understand my position, you'd find it perfectly clear that I can't do anything but go back to my place in the classroom tomorrow morning. You'd understand that," I say, "if you knew what it is to teach."

"Forgive her," says Gladys. "Oh, you make us ashamed."

She puts her hand to her mouth and bites at the pad of her thumb, her face glowing bright red.

"Our father would never talk to you this way, Monsieur Noget," says Priscilla. "He's far more cultured than Nadia, and he'd recognize your name."

"Your father never deigned..." he begins, slightly bemused.

One hand on the wide-open door, my patience at an end, I wait for them to leave.

Oh, if only I could never see any of them again. If only they'd leave us alone, if only they'd let us die in peace, if that's how it has to be.

Priscilla lets out a loud sigh. I see the faint shadow of a benevolence quivering in her pale, uncertain eyes. I'm so terribly tired, and I feel so dreadfully alone, that I find my will to stand up to them weakening.

"To tell you the truth," says Priscilla, "we came here to help look after my father, but also to urge you to go away as soon as you can, if possible with Papa and if not alone, in hopes that he'll come join you as soon as he's better."

"That would be the wisest course of action," says Noget.

"The fact is, you don't really have a choice," says Gladys, placating.

I let out a sort of little laugh, an acerbic yelp. I say nothing.

"You could go to your son's, for example," Gladys ventures.

I snicker again. Rage is filling my skull with an unendurable heat. Priscilla clasps my hand and presses it to her bosom even as I shrink back.

"For all our sakes, you must," she says fervently.

"If, in spite of these warnings," he says, "you still chose not to leave, which would be a mistake, let me repeat, but if, in the end, you insisted on making that mistake, know that…I would be here, close by, no matter the conditions and circumstances."

"Don't you have a son?" says Gladys.

"If you stay, the tornado will end up sweeping us away too," says Priscilla in a grim, weary voice.

"I'll always be here with you," he says.

I make no reply, my lips pressed tight, consumed by fury and something not far, all this aside, from an aching desire to throw myself on Priscilla's breast and beg her to take everything in hand. But hearing this man use my weakness as a pretext to dare offer his abode as a safe harbor (because isn't he now murmuring that he could even put us up if need be?) is simply more than I can bear. He looks at me, his eyes no longer cold or sarcastic but aglow with a hopefulness I find degrading for Ange and me both.

"The tornado?" I shoot back at Ange's two daughters, through gritted teeth. "For God's sake, you've got nothing to worry about. You're not like us. How could you possibly be hurt," I say, "by anything that concerns us alone? The thing in us that's perhaps being attacked and insulted isn't in you at all, right?"

"And what is that thing?" asks Gladys, challenging me.

I hesitate, then say:

"I can't put a name to it. I don't know what to call it, and I don't know how to describe it. And even if I could," I say, "I wouldn't, because that would be giving in, and that would be beneath me."

"No, you never give in," he says, "even if sometimes you should, just a little..."

"I'm closing my ears," I say. "I'm not going to listen to you anymore, not at all, ever again!"

8. They butchered him but good

When I go back to the bedroom, Ange is still asleep. Darkness fills the apartment—only the little lamp on the bedside table is lit. In the living room, in the kitchen, I can just make out the forms of the familiar furniture, but I feel as if I were entering an unknown domain where some tragic event has occurred, set off by a misstep on my part.

I feel a sort of tension with the apartment I've kept up so lovingly and with such care. A fear stops me just when I'm about to turn on the lights in this room or that. *Suppose all the furniture, all the ornaments turned out to be different from the things I picked out and knew, suppose I discovered the loveless smile of creatures mysteriously endowed with a life in some unknowable way at odds with my own, with our own? How do I know that's not how it will be?*

The wind begins to moan again. The windows are rattling quietly. I go and close the drapes, then pull them open again. *If anything happens, I want the people across the street to at least be able to see, to observe that I did nothing deliberate to provoke it.*

But the street is completely dark, no light shining at any window. Every few yards the pale, silvery gleam of the streetlights illuminates the falling rain, so fine it can only be seen inside that halo.

Does such a silence usually reign in this building at nine o'clock, I ask myself, and is the silence usually so fraught and so breathless, as if, I tell myself, almost outraged, the very silence were plotting some sort of treachery?

And those two girls, really, how underhanded. Oh, that's the only reason they came, to prod us into clearing out.

My voice is low and quiet, but the sound of it makes me start.

I hear a tiny noise, a sort of scratching at the front door. I hurry over, turn the lock (I didn't even do that, I reflect, aghast, shivering), then press myself full length to the door, both palms and one ear against the wood. At first I hear only a muffled, distant beating, the pulsations of my own terrified heart, and then, finally, his voice—cajoling, insistent, friendly, but friendly in a false, smarmy way. Has he been standing there outside the door all this time? Or did he come creeping back up to spy on me?

"Let me in," he says. "I still have so much to tell you."

"You heard what I said. I have to rest."

I do my best to sound neutral and confident.

"You've got to go home," I say. "What's the point of standing there in the cold?"

My hands are wet with fear. Suddenly light-headed, I close my eyes. I'm afraid I'm going to fall, end up slumped against the door, and then, I'm not quite sure how, he'd try to get in.

Little by little pushing the door to shift my insensible body, then finally walking in, triumphant and sinister, straight to the bedroom, lying down beside Ange, and then, perhaps, on the pretense of tending to him, opening the wound and infecting it with his filthy hands, all the while flattering what he believes to be Ange's vanity with florid sentences... Oh, I can't weaken now, no matter what.

"Open the door, just for a moment, and I'll tell you what you need to know, and then I'll leave you in peace and be off. I am," he says (*honeyed, almost loving*), "a former teacher, as you know, and that alone should ease any mistrust you may feel when I assure you I only want to protect you. Come on now, open the door," he says, more firmly.

"No...please..."

"Monsieur Noget," he says.

"Please, Monsieur Noget, we can see about all this tomorrow," I say, faltering in spite of myself at the insinuating gentleness of his voice, now singsong, almost like a lullaby.

"Shall I come back tomorrow? And then you'll be so kind as to open the door?"

"Listen..."

"I'll come back tomorrow," he says. "I'm so glad to

hear you call me by my name. Speak that name in front of your husband and he'll be deeply moved, you'll see, deeply moved."

And then silence again, that dense, heavy silence unbroken by any clinking dish, any mumbling television, not even Monsieur Noget's shambling steps, I note, headed downstairs to his apartment. I feel as if I'd gone deaf all at once.

Unless he's still there behind the door, intent on giving me the most literal illustration of his promise to be there for us always, from this day forward, and nothing and no one will ever drive him away, and we'll simply have to endure that intimacy, as odious as a boil you have no choice but to live with.

I back away into the dark living room, self-conscious, convinced I'm being watched. I tug the curtains closed. I'm sweating. I think I saw the rain coming harder now, pounding the windows—I saw it, but I can't hear it, my mind associates it with a familiar sound, but I can't make out that sound, as if the apartment had suddenly been fitted with some sort of impregnable insulation. And I still don't dare turn on the lamps or spell out the frightening but indistinct thought floating to the surface of my consciousness, pressing me to concede that I have no idea what would happen, what I would see, if I let light fill the living room, where my furniture, my cherished, handsome, expensive furniture, delighted to be deceiving me, might be hiding worrisome strangers, bloodthirsty guardians. That neighbor, I tell myself, might have been sent solely to distract me from what is in fact being fomented right here in my living room, the last place I'd ever suspect.

I stand frozen in place. My ear vigilant despite the feeling I've been wrapped up in cotton, I think I hear breathing. Mine? No, someone else's, it's coming from further away. I firmly cross my arms to keep my hands from clasping my cheeks and heightening my fear. I very slowly back away toward the bedroom. I then distinctly hear Ange's breathing—was that him I was hearing? Was it both of us together?

Inside the bedroom, I close the door and pull the little latch. Then, beleaguered, I sit down on the bed as gently as I can, taking care not to wake Ange. But shouldn't he be stirring anyway? Is it normal, is it healthy to sleep so much? Deep down, I realize, I don't want to wake him just yet, because I'm not sure I'll recognize him, I'm afraid he might say strange things to me, I don't want him seeing me in the near terror the ambiguities of my living room have plunged me into. Little by little I get hold of myself, begin to fight back at my imagination. Stand up, go into the other room, turn on all the lights, I whisper, and see for yourself that nothing has changed.

But I don't. The heavy darkness surrounds me. Even Ange's presence seems charged with danger, with unknowable perils. As long as he's asleep, the menace is quiet. And so, taking pains not to look at him, my own husband, the man I once felt so at one with, I stay perfectly still. I stare at the little latch on the door. I would certainly feel a heartfelt horror if I were to see that little latch move and burst open, succumbing to a mighty force applied from the living room, but I've so thoroughly convinced myself it's going to happen that I'm almost exasperated to see it not happening. At least, I say to myself, at least let me know what or who

I'm facing. But even if the door did suddenly burst open, would I know? Would I be capable of understanding what I saw before me? And would I see anything before me at all? Those questions torment me.

The wind is howling in the back courtyard, outside the bedroom's only window. I bend over the bed to peer through the glass. Below me I see Noget, bareheaded in the rain, emptying his trash into the dumpster. Suddenly he looks up and our gazes meet. He gives me a faint smile, licking his lips back and forth. Nothing is left of his humility, his repellent desire for conciliation at all costs—nothing is left of all that, only the brazenly unveiled expression of a precise, confident intention. *I'll get you. Just you wait. I'll get you, and we'll be...friends?*

I quickly turn away from the window, my heart full of hatred and spite. What's the next step in his plans for Ange and me? And what, I ask myself, is Ange's two daughters' role in it? And even Ange's, in his possibly simulated sleep? No, wounded as he is, Ange couldn't possibly be feigning anything at all, and besides it's not in his nature. But what exactly is his nature now? In such an aberrant situation, so deeply contrary in its brutality to the man he is? I have no idea, I tell myself, disheartened. I have no idea.

A desire then comes over me, a desire I would immediately struggle to choke back had I not spotted Noget's voracious gaze a moment before, a desire I'd do all I could to choke back had I not half decided that Ange is only pretending to sleep—oh no, I say to myself, he's asleep, like a poor tortured animal slipping into semi-unconsciousness between two beatings. I do nothing to quell that desire, and neither does it disturb me, at least not enough to keep my fingers still and my body stiff and slumped on the mattress.

I kneel on the bed. With one hand I grasp the little bedside lamp, and with the other I turn back the sheet that covers Ange up to his chin. What I then see rips a moan of horror from my throat.

Ange hasn't woken. The lamp wobbles in my hand. The little chain of the switch tinkles against the base. *Oh God oh God oh God.* I try to hold it more firmly, but in vain, and the little chain tinkles in time with my trembling. *Oh God, oh almighty God.* I want to put the sheet back, but my fingers are clutching the blood-stained fabric, creasing and crumpling it, powerless to lift it.

Ange begins to shake his head this way and that on the pillow, as if gravely tormented by the little pings of the chain against the lamp base. See, then, see then if you love me, and don't ever forget what you see.

I murmur, "Oh, my poor, poor darling."

And I wish Ange would open his eyes to give me a serene, nonchalant gaze, and so show me he's not troubled in the least by his wound, that it is indeed his body the wound has punctured, but only temporarily, and only because it pleased him to give it a home. But Ange's eyes remain closed, his lids squeezed tight. He merely shakes his head on the pink-sweat-drenched pillow (is there blood in his hair?), and I think I detect, in his suffering, in his obstinate sleep, a stubborn resentment toward me.

Ange has never shown any trace of rancor at anything I do. Our marriage has always been marked not by passion or exaltation but by concord, and our harmony is sometimes of the sort that defines indestructible friendship, the kind we read about in books, since neither Ange nor I have ever had friends we didn't end up parting ways with. And so I cannot understand the silent, outraged animosity seeping from Ange's clenched body. I immediately blame it on his two daughters. What they might have done, what they may have said, I have no idea. I remember the oddly fixed gaze of their children, the few times I met them, something very cold, cynical, and sardonic in their pale little faces—that's how those two women's children are. But doesn't Ange feel only the deepest affection for those children? What his daughters might have transformed while I was away, might have transformed in this apartment, around Ange, inside him, I don't know.

Ange's loyalty has been corrupted. *They weren't trying to treat him; they were aggravating the injury, poking at the wound, opening it beyond repair, and then injecting it with the poison of mistrust aimed against me—but why?*

Situated just over his appendix, the wound has stopped bleeding. All the same, no one seems to have cleaned it. There's a brown crust of dried blood all around the gaping crater dug by some tool I don't dare imagine, something both broad and sharp, something, I tell myself, like a stout wood chisel or a gouge, which someone took the time to wiggle back and forth in Ange's flesh after thrusting it deep inside.

Ange is still wearing his checked shirt. I'm angry to see that his daughters didn't even cut or tear it away where the weapon ripped through it, and now the fabric has fused with the congealed blood. Ange's two daughters did nothing, they didn't stanch the blood, they didn't disinfect the wound, they didn't even try to close it.

So in what vile way did the daughters their father so cherished fill all that time?

A thick, dull-yellow liquid is oozing from the tattered tissue deep inside the wound. I think I smell a foul odor coming from that discharge, but surely the wound isn't rotting already.

Suddenly Ange raises one arm. His gesture is so abrupt and unexpected that his hand collides with the lamp, dashing it to the floor. The bulb goes out.

"I said no one could look at that," Ange shouts hoarsely.

He rips the sheet from my fingers and furiously covers himself up again.

"How many times do I have to say it?" Ange says, in that same dull, hollow voice, now tinged with a desperate sadness.

And I'm horrified by that new voice in the dark.

"Ange, it's me," I say.

"I want to be left in peace. I want," says Ange, "to be left alone."

"Ange, are you in pain?"

"Let me be, all of you."

I awkwardly stand up again, shivering in grief and anxiety. I feel around for the lamp and set it back on the bedside table. I go to the door, clap my ear to the wood to hear anything that might be going on in the living room. Then I come back and sit down on the bed, as far from Ange as I can, not wanting to upset him but unwilling to abandon him, even though that's exactly what he demanded, in that furious, plaintive way so unlike him, that amnesic and, I tell myself, selfish, ungrateful way, as if deliberately forgetting any bond that unites us.

But shouldn't I be making him undress (because under the sheets he's still wearing his pants, belt, and socks), shouldn't I be cleaning the wound, putting on a bandage, forcing him to swallow two pain pills? How to imagine struggling with your own weakened husband, and then, once that battle's behind you, setting out to rebuild your honor to whatever degree you can? How to conceive of such a sad, ugly situation?

And most of all, how to imagine walking through the darkness of the living room to the bathroom, where we keep our medicine, and then walking through it again in the other direction, the living room alive with rustlings and pantings whose source I can't locate and whose meaning I can't find, though the first image that comes to my mind is Monsieur Noget vigorously fornicating and taking pains to be heard by both Ange and me, but particularly by Ange, who's lying there petrified in his misery, motionless on his bed of sorrow and pain, and what does he want from us, what do we still have that he wants, what is he trying to make us understand?

I get up again, again I listen at the bedroom door and check that the latch is closed—and again those rubbing sounds, those moans from the living room. My neck and forehead are dripping with a sweat that stinks powerfully of fear. So what is it? Is it the storm, the wild wind? But just now, I remember, in that very living room, I couldn't hear a sound from outside.

"Monsieur Noget?" I whisper, my lips pressed to the door. Then, louder: "Monsieur Noget, is that you?"

Oh, I immediately tell myself, he couldn't possibly

have come in, since I chained the door. It's impossible—so? And with that, knowing Noget couldn't have come into the apartment, knowing that and at the same time having to accept that these rumbles and hisses can only fall within the domain of the impossible, I feel I no longer have to think about them or torment myself over them, I have only to maintain a safe distance between them and me.

Crushed by exhaustion, I lie down on the bed, keeping well away from Ange. I can see his eyes in the darkness, wide open now, staring at the ceiling, as still and watchful as his whole body seems, silent, stiff, and suffering. I don't dare say a word. And how sad, I say to myself, how sad is my fear, and my silence. Because I'm used to telling Ange my every thought, because he's the one person in this world whose judgment I've never feared, the one person who never, at any moment of our life together, wore me down with recriminations or questions about my attachment to my work, the one person, finally, who was never ignobly tempted to hold up my son to me, for example, and my school, and accuse me of caring more for the latter than the former. And this evening I avoid even reaching out to lightly stroke Ange's forehead—why am I suddenly his enemy?

9. We find comfort in food, and it's a terrible mistake

I leap out of bed almost as soon as the gray dawn's gloomy light begins to filter into the room. I give Ange a cautious glance. He's not asleep (has he slept at all?), and he's staring blankly at the wall. A rush of love and sympathy throws me against him. I take his head between my hands, ignoring his attempts to pull free, I kiss his lips, smelling a strange odor of blood and putrefaction. He gently pushes me away and wraps himself up in the sheet in such a way, I tell myself, that if he does fall asleep again I'll never be able to pull it away and tend to his wound without waking him.

What exactly am I not supposed to see? And why does he imagine I'm hoping to see it, whatever it is? Doesn't he know me, doesn't he know I always want to know as little as possible of things that fill me with horror?

I force myself to say, "Ange, you know as well as I do, you must see a doctor."

"There's no need for that now," he says listlessly.

"What does that mean?" I say, deeply unsettled.

"Just that there's no need. There's nothing more to say," says Ange.

I can feel the mounting annoyance in his voice, the irascibility I find so startling. I hurry to answer:

"You think you've understood something I still haven't grasped, and what I think is that you're trying to protect me, and that's why you've turned so hard and mysterious. But you must know, there's nothing I can't bear to learn, and I might even know everything already, my darling Ange. You don't have to protect me."

Am I sure of that?

"Those are just words," says Ange, in a tone of infinite sadness.

He goes on: "Be careful, you talk too much."

Then he closes his eyes, rudely, to cut all this short.

That last sentence sounded less like a piece of advice than a threat.

I'm speechless. I can't help shaking Ange by his shoulder, even though his brow immediately furrows in pain. For the first time a sort of rage now comes over me too, and when I see him wince I simply think: Am I not suffering too, at being treated so unfairly?

I spit back:

"And what do I say when I'm talking too much? Because I feel like the only one around here who hasn't figured out what it is that's so terribly momentous! Oh, but I'm not going to spend all my time begging forgiveness for everything I'm evidently somehow doing wrong," I say, but my anger is already subsiding, and as I look at Ange's haggard face and gray eyelids I wonder, tormented, how to go about saving him when he doesn't want to be saved.

I hear a series of resounding knocks on the front door.

"The neighbor," Ange murmurs.

"This time," I say, "he's staying outside."

Troubled, Ange begins to stir.

"No, no, come on now, obviously you have to let him in."

His whisper is fretful, with that edge of irritation again. Between his half-open eyelids, his gaze is veiled and exasperated, devoid of all affection.

Now the door is rattling from the blows. I leave the bedroom, undo the chain, and throw the door wide open.

"I don't suppose," he says amiably, "that you've eaten the ham I brought yesterday?"

"No," I say.

"No matter, I have some more here, freshly sliced. And

also, look," he says, cheerful and eager, "I've got bread, nice warm bread that I kneaded and baked myself, and then some plum marmalade I made in my own kitchen—forgive me for belaboring the point—and I've got some butter for you too, since I wasn't sure you would have any, and all this is for you and your husband, and in all sincerity, you'd make me so happy if you deigned...if you would be so good... Besides, we already agreed..."

"My husband asked me not to kick you out," I say.

I try to put on the weary, sullen look that I think is the only thing capable of repelling the detestable intimacy he's trying to slip into every tiny intonation. And all the while the warm scent of the bread is making me weak, almost grateful. I'm so hungry my lips are trembling. I step aside so he can come in. On his way past he looks up and gives me a quick glance, equal parts triumph and submission.

He's wearing filthy old corduroy overalls and a Columbia University sweatshirt. He goes straight to the kitchen. *He feels perfectly at home, he thinks he knows he's not going to be thrown out again, he thinks he's earned his place here.* He sets his provisions down on the table, invites me to sit with a broad gesture untouched by irony, then turns toward the coffee machine, opens the cabinet where the cups are kept, and takes the coffee from its drawer, all very precisely, with the brisk self-assurance of someone who knows exactly what he has to do and adapts his every movement to that goal.

"I have to leave for school soon," I say.

"Yes, yes," he says, "that's fine."

But how can this be, how can he be here making the coffee

just like Ange used to do, how can he be here so at ease, victorious and subservient at the same time, this man we could scarcely bear to glimpse for a few seconds a day?

"We have no need of a servant, you know," I say.

"And a friend? You don't need a friend?" he says, his tone light but serious, his back still turned.

Appalled by his impudence, I say, "Ange and I have always gotten along very nicely without friends. You can take my word for it. And to be perfectly frank, the fact is we find friends a nuisance, since you ask."

I pull off a handful of bread. A wisp of steam floats up from the torn loaf. I stuff the piece into my mouth, and the taste is so delicious and comforting that a painful tingle drills into my jaw, my cheeks, the corners of my eyes. And yet, I tell myself, and yet he made this bread with his hands. He sits down facing me, cuts a slice of bread, spreads it with a thick layer of the butter he's brought, a deep yellow block freckled with tiny droplets of water, and smears it with plum marmalade.

"Here, if I may, eat this," he says, holding it out with exaggerated courtliness.

He gets up to pour me a big cup of coffee. I distastefully note his fat, flabby hands, his dirty nails. Gray whiskers pepper his face. And, when he forgets himself, his eyes are so cold that they make me afraid.

And yet he made this bread.

He jumps up and says, "Now, let's have a look at our patient."

"He doesn't want anyone coming near him," I say.

He gives me a confident little smile. He spreads another

slice of bread with butter and jam, sets it on a tray beside the cup of coffee he's poured for Ange. He walks out of the kitchen with the tray, and I hear him whispering, "I did warn you not to go back to that school, didn't I?"

I eat a thin slice of delicate, aromatic Bayonne ham, another of his offerings. And all that food is good and endlessly consoling, but, coming from him, it leaves a bitter taste in my mouth.

Then I get ready to set off for work, like any other morning. I walk through the living room again and again, humming, refusing to pay any mind to the feeling, still strong as ever, that the room is full of something that wasn't there before, something fundamentally unfriendly. That suffocating feeling isn't entirely unfounded, I know, but I refuse to dwell on it. We'll deal with that later, I tell myself, not wanting to be late. I can't help turning one ear to the bedroom, where I hear a whispered conversation.

He doesn't want me to hear. But what treachery are those two plotting against me?

I take a shower, pull on a sweater and pants, both black (because I'm not as trim as I might be), I do my hair, which I wear short and dyed red, I try to bend my crushed glasses back into shape.

I gently push open the door to our room. Ange is still lying on the bed, wrapped up in his sheet, but Noget has slipped the two pillows under his shoulders, and his head is drooping back, his neck slightly twisted. Sitting on the bed, Noget holds up his head with one hand and with the other puts the bread and jam to Ange's lips. Ange looks at me. His gaze darkens in terror, discomfort, and uncertainty.

I see that, and I immediately put it out of my mind.

"Oh, I'm going to be late for school," I say. "So you're eating, my love?"

"All this good food is just the thing for what's ailing him," says Noget. "I've always made my own bread, even back when I was teaching; I used to get up an hour early just to make my dough, because I loved my work just as you love yours, but even more than that I loved and respected bread, that most sacred of all foods."

He's trying to provoke me; he wants to see if I'll question his past as a teacher again. Oh, who cares, in the end, what he really did and what he only wishes he had.

I ask, "Have you looked at…the wound?"

Oh, I can't wait to be away from here! This airless, slightly nauseating room (still that faint smell of decay, I tell myself) suddenly oppresses me more than I can bear.

"All in good time," he says. "Don't worry. I'm not going to let your husband pretend everything's fine."

"Everything *is* fine," I haughtily retort.

"I strongly disapprove of your going back to that school," he scolds.

"Not only is the school my place," I answer, "but I have to tell the principal that Ange will be away for some time so she can see to finding a substitute, and so no one, especially the children, will be inconvenienced by…"

"Don't go!" Ange pleads hoarsely.

But I shake my head, dizzy at the idea of staying in the apartment, spending the day going back and forth from the dark, malodorous bedroom to the living room crammed with unknown, malevolent souls.

I throw out a cheery "See you this evening!"

And again I see and willfully ignore the fear and shame darkening Ange's gaze as Noget brings the cup of coffee to his lips. I hear the porcelain clink against his teeth, as if he were clenching them tight as Noget tries to force him to drink. That was very good coffee he made, I tell myself. Shouldn't it be me, shouldn't it be his wife helping Ange eat, helping him drink, helping him, yes, go to the bathroom? Why should he accept that help from the neighbor and not me? For that matter, I ask myself, squirming, is he really accepting it? Because everything I see tells me Ange is enduring that solicitude only because he thinks he has no choice.

He never suspected this man would go to such lengths, would push his advantage so far as to play mommy with him.

10. Maybe it's over?

For the first time in months, my students are awaiting me in a neat line rather than scattered all over the schoolyard, as they'd taken to doing when Ange and I fell out of favor, such that we'd grown used to spending fifteen minutes each morning rounding them up while our colleagues, unwilling to get involved, had already made their way to their classrooms and started the day.

This morning, beneath the low clouds, all the children are lined up, attentive, almost silent. I walk toward the principal. She's watching over the schoolyard from the front step of her office, and not the tiniest nerve twitches in her hard, white face when she sees me coming. Something is easing her mind, I tell myself in relief, something about me. I keep my arms crossed over my buttoned-up overcoat, because it's still so cold.

It's so cold!

"My husband's going to be out for a while," I say.

"Yes. For what reason?" asks the principal.

"You don't know?" I say.

"No, I don't," says the principal.

And from the story the pharmacist told me I know that she's lying, but I find her answer oddly comforting, as if the principal were trying to make it clear, by a lie if need be, that she's not my enemy.

"I can't talk about it," I say, shaking my head. "But everything's going to be fine, and for that matter I volunteer to take my husband's students in my own class, if that's possible."

"Oh, I don't know," says the principal.

Her gaze turns distant and thoughtful. Her chin tenses, suddenly covered with little wrinkles.

"I'm not sure what the children would think," she says, hesitating over each word.

"But since when," I say, "really, since when do we ask the children's opinion in these things?"

Her very white cheeks pinken a little. She fans the air in front of her, wriggling her hand, and her fingertips graze my face. Then she puts on a surprised look and asks, "You've left your husband all alone? Doesn't he need you?"

"My place is here," I say.

So was she thinking, was she secretly hoping we'd both

disappear? Us, the best teachers in the school?

"Don't take your work too much to heart," she says curtly.

"I like my work, and I'm very conscientious about it," I say.

"Yes, but with you it's almost virtuousness," says the principal. "And, surely you agree, virtuousness must be..."

She barks out a sharp, menacing laugh.

The bell rings, and the principal remakes her expression, replacing the aggression and mockery with a neutral benevolence. That benevolence is all I want to remember of this exchange.

I go off to collect my little students, my heart light in a way it hasn't been for ages.

It's cold and gray, and the air is opaque, thick with a heavy fog risen up from the river, but at long last I have a feeling Ange and I might hope to find our way, little by little, toward better times.

Should we, I ask myself, see what Ange suffered yesterday as the low point in our torments, and the beginning of a change for the better? Yes we should, there's no question, no question.

This morning I find the children's gaze limpid and straightforward when they look at me, and when I dare to look back at them they don't turn away, don't show any displeasure, any sense that I deserve to be punished or destroyed. Their behavior seems almost what it used to be—a touch more timid, I must admit, more skittish, as if I were a new and perhaps unpredictable teacher, as if in short they'd forgotten the woman I was, the woman I believe they loved in perfect confidence. This muted apprehension I feel weighing on my classroom makes me sad. So here we are, I tell myself, now I have to work at becoming the person I used to be for them. Ange's students have been sent home. *He'll be glad to hear that, he can't stand being replaced.*

When recess comes, I head toward a little group of colleagues gathered in the schoolyard. I stop ten feet away, eyes on the ground, pretending to be preoccupied by the cleanliness of my shoes, and then, sensing a favorable vibration, friendly waves emanating from the circle, now opening up ever so slightly to make room for me, I wordlessly slip in between two of my colleagues.

Their conversation stops short. After an awkward moment, one of them woodenly mumbles, "How's Ange doing?"

"He's fine," I say, with a lighthearted little laugh.

"What a dreadful accident," he says.

"What accident?" I say. "There was no accident."

"It's best to think of it as an accident," he says, in a discouraging voice.

I feel the vaguely sympathetic waves emitted by the little group as I drew near now beginning to fade. I even think I can feel the circle tightening again, trying to expel me. And then I speak again, softly: "Accident or no, Ange will be back very soon."

But Ange is dying at this very moment. Isn't he? My darling Ange? What is that neighbor doing to Ange's body at this moment?

"I left him in the care of a certain Monsieur Noget," I say, unable to repress a dismissive laugh.

"Noget?"

"Noget the writer?"

Their stunned disbelief troubles me. *Who is this, this Noget person? Have I ever heard that name before?*

"Yes, I suppose so," I say, hesitating.

"You suppose or you know? You mean *the* Noget?" one of the women snaps impatiently.

My colleagues have all turned their eyes on me. Their fervid expectancy seems to fill the foggy air with a menacing hum, a strident buzz whose silencing depends on my answer. I grimace a smile, push my glasses to the very top of my nose.

"Yes, I mean him," I say, masking my perplexity.

Because how is it that they've all heard of him and I haven't, that the merest mention of his name dazzles them and means nothing to me?

A pensive, moderately respectful silence follows. I stop worrying about shielding my eyes, and see no sign of anger or weariness when our gazes meet.

"Well, that's strange," someone says slowly.

"In any case," says someone else, "your husband's in good hands, he's in admirable hands."

He sounds almost sorry he's not in Ange's place. Oh, when was it that someone last envied us, we who so long luxuriated in the warm, beneficent water of other people's longing for our life, our serenity? Again I feel buoyed by an extravagant joy and confidence. Now I can't wait to go home, to tell Ange what I've discovered today: that implacable will to harm us is no more. Gone, too, is the revulsion we inspired, the innocent, primitive fury that came over some people at the mere sight of us. In my optimism, I go so far as to wonder if we weren't overestimating the gravity of what happened to us, I even wonder if we might have overestimated its reality. *Were people really trying to lay us low? How ridiculous, possibly! What a sinister joke we were playing on ourselves, perhaps!*

I happily puff out little clouds of steam as I hurry back to my classroom.

"How good you're all being today, children," I say several times over the course of the afternoon.

And then, just when I'm speaking those words for the third time, a little girl bursts into tears. I wonder if I chose the right word. Are they being good, or are they simply paralyzed by nausea? They seem unusually apathetic, as if they've been forced to swallow a heavy dose of tranquilizers.

I go to the crying girl and see her hunching her shoulders, defending herself from my patting hand but at the same time resigned, not daring to beg me not to touch her. For a moment that depresses me.

Is it starting up again already?

I run my hand over her narrow back, her quivering shoulder blades, feeling her little frightened-bird heart pounding wildly.

"There now," I murmur, "no one's going to hurt you."

"You'll see," she says, "you'll see."

She sniffs, delicately pulls away. The moment she looks up, what seems to me an affection filled with pity and despair fills her eyes with tears. But I resolve not to let any grimness get in the way of the new sense of our situation I've found today.

With a brisk clap of my hands, I brightly announce that everyone can now go out and play in the schoolyard for the rest of the day.

I can't stop myself from adding, "Since you've all been so good today!"

None of them squeals in pleasure, excitement, surprised gratitude, as they would have a few months before. They hesitate for a few moments before they stand up, as if not entirely convinced this is a good idea, or one they necessarily have to obey, and then a few of them leave the classroom with a sort of tentative stiffness, and the others awkwardly follow.

I see one boy steal a glance at my desk and chair. I try to see what he's looking at—what can it be? He blushes, then suddenly turns deathly pale. *Oh God, what was he looking at? What are they all seeing that I'm not, what is it that they know and I don't? Where was I all this time, when I should have been seeing and knowing?*

And I notice they all keep their distance from the platform my desk sits on, and since some of them have no choice but to walk past it to get to the door, I suddenly wonder if that might be why they seemed so uneager to go out and play. *There's something there, in the corner with my things, something that scares them to death.* How strange these children are! It's going to be a long, involved process, teaching them to be normal with me again, making them forget I was ever shunned, even reviled, or maybe that I thought we were (being shunned and reviled) powerful enough to transform our students' idea of us. Yes, so everything is our fault—the responsibility for this monstrous misunderstanding lands squarely on the two of us, my beloved Ange and me.

We were prideful, we were too pleased with the quality of our work, we were certainly haughty and disdainful, and we vastly overrated the significance and menace of the signs people were sending to tell us we were being disagreeable, and that too we did out of pride.

But why, I ask myself, why this wound inflicted on Ange? Isn't that real? *Ange knowingly provoked the attack, then deliberately aggravated the wound? Or maybe there was no attack, maybe it was Ange himself who… Or could it be that nothing happened at all? Only an accident that left Ange completely undone, used as he was to having his life so well in hand?*

I spend some time straightening my classroom (*as carefully as if I knew I would never be back*).

The bell rings. I put on my coat (*and I feel something strange, something indefinable, but immediately banish it from my perception*); I pick up my fat accordion-fold satchel and go out into the schoolyard, my coat buttoned all the way up because it's so cold out, an unflappable smile on my lips.

My misted-up lenses force me to look at my surroundings with a certain insulated distance. Is that why I don't immediately see how alone I am, how vast the circle of empty space all around me, as if, I tell myself much later, I had in my hand not a satchel but a live grenade? But I notice nothing, or almost, and I'm so determined not to let my good mood slip away, so resolved to radically rethink my attitude (*because our wrong-headed interpretation of the world around us did us so much harm, caused so much needless grief!*), that this evening it would take an oddity far more unambiguous than this to divert me from my happy course.

I feel very slightly breathless, as I always do when the city is draped in thick fog, when I become painfully aware of the weight of my flesh, overabundant though carefully contained by dark elastic clothing, when I feel the surprising heft of my body, which took shape over the years as I looked on, vaguely amused, taken aback, dismissive. That's not exactly me, it's a neighbor I'm not unfond of but for whom I have to feel a burdensome, tedious, faintly degrading responsibility—oh, who cares about my body, I think, quietly pleased with myself.

But this evening I'm breathless. I turn onto Cours du Chapeau-Rouge. Here again, is it the fog that's distancing me from everyone else on the street? Is it that I can't see, or are people actually steering clear of my panting self?

The tram passes by, very close, silent and almost invisible in the dull-white mist. The tinkle of its bell sounds as if the now almost palpable air had snatched it up and clutched it tight, leaving only a little choked rattle. *And I don't glance inside, for fear I might see petrified faces, poor creatures with terror and panic in their eyes at the mere sight of me.*

Suddenly I wonder: Could it be my coat? I think back to my students, the way they all sidestepped my satchel and coat on the platform. An unfocused apprehension grips my heart. Just keep walking, I tell myself, just go on as if nothing were amiss. My coat feels heavy on my shoulders. *Just keep walking, with a smile on your lips.*

Finally I reach the deserted Rue Esprit-des-Lois. I put down my satchel on the sidewalk, and then, slowly and calmly, never shedding the polite smile that will assure any neighbors spying on me through their windows that everything's just fine now, I take off my coat. I hold it out before me and spread it wide.

I stagger from the shock. I feel the corners of my mouth turning down. My jaw begins to tremble. Yes, yes, yes, I whisper, get hold of yourself.

I carefully fold my coat with my shivering hands. I still have the composure to wrap the cloth around the bits of flesh stuck to it. I bundle it up, take my satchel, and walk on to the building's front door. I keep my coat squeezed tight under one arm, even though it's so cold out, far colder than before.

11. Everybody likes meat

Here he is, with his thin face, his bright, prying eyes, letting me into our own apartment. He spreads his arms. I throw my coat at him.

"There are pieces of my husband on there," I say.

My knees buckle. I collapse in the doorway. I must lie prostrate like that for some time, half conscious (because I can hear all sorts of sounds from the kitchen or bedroom, the scuff of slippered feet, the whistle of the tea kettle, the clink of silverware), unable to move or speak but somehow resigned, blithely or indifferently accepting my powerlessness, as in a dream. How tedious, I think calmly, unsure what my mind means by this complaint. My weight is resting on my right hip, and it's very painful. I desperately want to stand up, but my will seems to have parted ways with my mind, which is serenely registering the various sounds coming to it from the building or the apartment as my soul bleeds and moans.

Three safety pins (or were they hairpins?) thrust through shreds of flesh, bits of some meat like pinkish, fibrous pork (because that's what it was, wasn't it?), and their size and look made me think of human flesh and so bits of Ange's flesh, since this morning I saw—yes, you saw it, admit it—that they'd thoroughly carved up his side, sliced into it, but of course it could just as well be any sort of animal meat, and it could also be nothing more than a cruel prank, so why let it spoil your mood...

"I warned you, you shouldn't have gone back," he chides me.

A tangled, dirty gray beard, hollow cheeks pocked with fifty-year-old acne scars, a sharp, heated gaze without a single trace of sympathy.

"Try to get up," he says. "I'm not strong enough to lift you."

I'm so bulky, so ponderous. You're just like a pillow, my son used to say as he burrowed his forehead into my wobbling bicep. Oh, my son, why aren't you here, resilient and decisive, here with us, we who are well past the age when we can grasp what we've never known!

"How's Ange doing?" I murmur.

He hesitates.

"As well as can bc cxpcctcd," he says.

"I want to see him."

My voice is defiant and willful, as if he'd made some move to stop me from going into the bedroom.

"You'll have to get up first," he says.

I carefully roll over, hoist myself up on all fours, puffing, little caring that Monsieur Noget is right there.

The illustrious Noget! What a joke!

I struggle to my feet, leaning against the wall.

"Where's my coat?"

"I took it down to the trash," says Noget. "I showed it to Ange, and then I threw it away."

"You shouldn't have shown it to him. He doesn't need to face that sort of idiocy on top of everything else. It's just kids playing a filthy trick."

He doesn't answer. I can hear his very slightly labored breathing. His gaze softens, and I can see that for him everything is already settled.

"It's every bit as serious," he says, "as what they did to Ange yesterday."

"How do you know they did something to Ange? How do you know he didn't do it himself? I mean," (my voice turns combative, insistent) "how do you know he didn't aggravate an injury somebody caused without meaning to, because he wanted to be shattered completely, because he wanted a valid reason for disappearing?"

And no, that's nothing like what the pharmacist told me, but why place more faith in her words than in any other equally plausible scenario? The pharmacist wasn't a witness, and no one has told me they saw anything firsthand.

"You're barking up the wrong tree completely," he says, infuriated. "You refuse to see the source of the trouble."

"No one will explain what it is," I say tartly.

But I don't want to know. I don't want to know exactly what it is.

He runs his fingers through his beard, his shaggy hair. With a sort of cautious reticence, as if anxious not to offend me, he says:

"You two, it must be said, have...an inappropriate attitude toward life—unacceptable, from certain points of view, and I would even add, forgive me, obscene—and of course that in no way justifies people tormenting you, and indeed no one would be tormenting you if it were only that, but since there's also, as you know, as you suspect...your face, and the look on your face..."

"What's wrong with my face?" I say, feeling myself blush.

He briefly looks away. This is the first time I've seen him sincerely uncomfortable.

"Oh, I know," I hurry to answer.

And for the first time, too, his discomfort spreads to me, and I want it to go away. I brush off my clothes, straighten my glasses. My bra has come unhooked. My breasts joggle under my sweater with every move I make.

"I still haven't seen my husband," I say.

"He was...he was gravely shocked by your coat," he says, feigning concern.

He can hardly hide his delight, his unwholesome excitement. He's the source of the trouble. And I've left the man who means more to me than any other in his hands. What weakness could have made me do that?

Emboldened by a very cold anger, I slip my hands under my sweater and rehook my bra, staring fiercely into his slightly veiled, fascinated gaze.

"Incidentally, my colleagues seem to have heard of you," I say with a scoff.

"Oh, really?" he says.

I get the feeling he's pleased and flattered to hear it, but not surprised. *Like someone long used to being recognized, being noticed.* Head high, I walk past him toward the bedroom. I go in and close the door behind me, turning the latch. One bedside lamp dimly lights the room.

"Don't lock the door," Ange whispers.

Wincing, he props himself up on one elbow. I nearly gag from the stench.

"He'll think you don't trust him."

"So what?" I say. "Of course I don't trust that stranger. Remember how we hated him?"

"I never hated him," says Ange, with a kind of pained fury.

He drops back onto the pillow, gasping, exhausted. I'm finding it hard to breathe myself. The smell of decay is unbearable. I open the window, and the frigid air pours into the room.

"Oh, please," Ange says wearily. "It's so cold. I can't…I can't stand it."

He begins to weep quietly. I close the window and kneel beside him. I'm making such an enormous, torturous effort not to sob along with him that it almost distracts me, almost takes my mind off all this.

Ange's cheeks are sunken and glistening. I gently pull at the sheet to uncover him down to his hips, gazing perfidiously into his eyes, aware that I'm taking advantage of his weakness. The wound is black. The dried blood has become a lumpy, ragged crust. A green-gray liquid is pooled around the rim. That purulence, that's where the awful smell is coming from.

"What they did to you," Ange murmurs. "Your coat…"

He casts a terrified glance at the door.

"I'm begging you, don't antagonize him," he says.

"Ange, my darling, don't torment yourself over that coat."

I whisper those words in his ear, fervently, stroking his damp forehead, realizing he's oblivious to it all, both my caress and my study of the wound. All he can think of is the grave problem the locked door clearly poses in his mind.

Beneath his mild demeanor, Ange was never afraid of anyone or anything. And here he is, shaking like a beaten child. My God, are our students afraid of us?

"Someone played a horrible prank on me," I say, "and I'm angry about it; I'm going to try to find the culprit, and believe me, they haven't heard the last of it."

"It's not a prank," Ange whispers, "and you know it. It's a crime. We're done for. It's all our fault, we can't forget that."

"That's not how you saw it before," I say. "He put all that in your head."

"They tore off pieces of my flesh!"

Ange's voice is so soft that at times I can't hear him. His eyes dart this way and that, stricken with panic.

"He explained how mistaken we were," he says. "He's right, but it's too late now to become someone else. I can never go out again. Even right here, anything can happen. Well, no doubt that's only right. I only wish it didn't hurt so much."

"Let me get Doctor Charre to see you," I beg, desperation rising inside me.

"Absolutely not."

Ange grows more agitated. In a sudden burst of fury, he explodes at me.

"You still don't seem to get it, you're talking like you would have six months ago. Doctor Charre...especially not him. No one we've ever known...can be allowed in this room. Are you trying to speed up my death? I'd like not to be in pain, but I'm not ready to die yet."

"What about Gladys? Priscilla?"

"They can never come here again!" cries Ange, gripped by an unnameable terror.

Am I secretly happy to hear it? Dismayed all the same, because I know Ange used to dote on his two daughters, I push back: "Your own children?"

"They think they're doing the right thing, they think they're helping, but...what they do to me...it's even more horrible. No, no, they can never come near me again. They hurt me too much. They don't listen to me, they've lost faith in me.... How I've suffered. They'd kill me, thinking they love me and...that they're going to save me...but they don't listen to what I say, it's lost all...value in their eyes. They know it's our fault.... They don't want to be contaminated."

"But by what?" I say.

"But by what?" he repeats, cruelly mimicking my voice, ridiculing my ignorance.

And it strikes me that I've never seen Ange aim any such humiliation my way, even if he might have unleashed just that kind of sullen mockery on others when I wasn't around.

"By everything we are," he says wearily. "We're bad people, we're unworthy. We were blind. You still are. My daughters are afraid they might become like me, and I can understand that, but for old Ange Lacordeyre it's too late."

"Will you let me treat your wound now?"

Ange shrugs. I stand up, furtively open the latch, and slip into the hallway.

He emerges from the dark living room. With one bound he's beside me, astonishingly nimble, quick, light. *He's spying on us at every moment, and he has been all along.*

"I've made dinner. It's time to eat."

"Yes," I say.

"You must not be afraid of me," he says in an authoritarian voice, "and you must not convince your husband to be."

"Are you a spy?" I say brazenly. *And I laugh to myself, daring to use such a word with no fear of seeming ridiculous.*

By the dim light of the hallway, I see his brow furrow.

"A spy? In whose service?"

"I don't know. No one knows less about all this than me."

"That's no reason to talk nonsense."

I go into the bathroom for compresses and disinfectant. He follows on my heels.

"Is that for your husband? No, don't you see, you mustn't try to treat him," he says, agitated. "He can't be allowed to forget what they did to him!"

I lower my head, pretending to think, then walk around him, scurry to the bedroom, and quickly lock the door behind me.

Absolute silence invades the apartment. I put my ear to the door. From the other side, just against the wood, comes his calm, confident voice: "You're not going to heal him. It's no use. There's nothing more we can do. That smell—do you understand?—that's the smell of death."

"Who are you?" I whisper.

"The illustrious Noget," he answers sarcastically. "Isn't that what you've heard people call me? You alone, in your purity, have never heard of me."

My fingers clench against the door.

"Yes, but," I say, very softly, not wanting Ange to overhear, "is that a crime?"

I feel so discouraged, so exhausted that I lay my face against the door as I used to on my son's chest, or on Ange's. I'm afraid I'll find Ange's furious, desperate eyes staring at me if I turn around.

Letting out a sob, lips against the door, I say, "So it's a crime never to have heard of you?"

"Yes." (*His gentle, assured, soft, seductive voice, a voice without warmth.*) "Everything you don't know speaks against you. There are some things you really can't not know, isn't that so? Things you must endeavor to know and understand. Oh, you're so…so presumptuous."

"Nadia!" Ange calls.

My whole body jumps, as if a corpse had awakened and spoken behind me. I unstick myself from the door and slowly walk toward the bed. Have I somehow wronged Ange?

"Now I have what I need to take care of you," I say.

A sardonic glow lights his gaunt face.

"You smell that stench coming out of me?"

"Yes, we'll have to get you cleaned up," I say. "Your daughters should have seen to that yesterday."

"Come here, come here, closer," says Ange.

He extracts one hand from under the sheet and brutally pulls me to him by my neck. I hold my breath. The smell is coming from his glistening skin as well, and his hair, and his mouth.

"Listen, I'm starving," Ange says in my ear, "but I want it to be you who gives me the food he's made, not him. OK? Today at lunchtime, while you were at work..." (He breaks into tears, moaning.) "He fed me at lunchtime. I never want that to happen again. But whatever you do, whatever you do, you can't tell him, OK? Never complain to him about anything."

"Who is he?"

"Who is he?" Ange repeats, parodying me in that hurtful new way of his.

He gives an irritable shrug. Please God, I reflexively say to myself, don't let me come to hate this new Ange.

"Who is he?" I say stubbornly.

"The great Noget," Ange mumbles.

I fold back the sheet, down to his legs. I manage to stifle a shudder at the sight of his wound, but the smell is so strong that I have to get away. I open the armoire, grab a big handkerchief, and tie it over my nose.

Ange looks at me, dull, morose, but with a tight little smile that so hideously expresses a sort of grim pleasure, a sneering delight rooted in the very vileness of the situation, that I can't help crying out:

"How you've changed, Ange!"

"Yes, maybe a hole in the stomach does a little something to a man," says Ange, "and maybe seeing pieces of his own flesh stuck to his wife's coat with safety pins, maybe that does something to a man too, you're absolutely right."

"That was pork or rabbit meat," I say firmly. "Everything

around us is fine. We just have to convince ourselves of that."

He throws a nervous, untrusting glance at the door, then whispers, "Noget doesn't want me to forget what happened, he says I have to meditate on my wound and the multiple meanings of my suffering."

"But there's nothing to understand," I say, loud and clear. "We got all worked up over nothing, out of vanity. It was nothing but vanity, Ange, that was making us think people despised us."

I crouch down beside the bed. I start to cut away Ange's shirt around the wound. I can hear my own breath, quick and heavy. Even with the handkerchief, the nauseating smell makes me light-headed. I dip a compress into the disinfectant, then try to sop up the pus that's overflowed onto Ange's stomach, under his pants, soaking the mattress and sheets. No matter how much I wipe away, more seems to gush up from deep in the wound to replace it.

"Where can it all be coming from?" I cry, demoralized.

"It's his poor soul seeping out! Dinnertime!"

And Noget gives two loud raps on the door. Ange groans in fear and surprise. For many minutes we stay silent, listening intently for any sound from outside the room.

"He's right, isn't he?" Ange whispers, his jaw tense, his whole wasted, sallow face even more drawn than before. "It's...it's everything I am, it's the very essence of...of my being oozing out of me, isn't it?"

I try hard to laugh, but a succession of squawks is all that comes out. And yet, I tell myself, troubled, it's true, this Ange seems less like himself all the time.

I use up the entire box of compresses. And still the pus

comes, ever darker, reeking. I'm gagging behind my handkerchief. The whole room is permeated with the stench. I stand up to open the window.

"No," shouts Ange. "I'm cold, I'm cold."

In the unusual silence of the courtyard, the neighborhood, his whine resounds like the voice of the last man alive. It echoes so lugubriously that I gladly close the window. Now I feel an almost desperate longing to sleep. Let everyone fend for themselves, I dully say to myself, utterly drained. But my habit of thinking myself responsible for everyone around me and everything that happens to us, good or disastrous, has been with me too long to be cast off just because I want to.

I leave the room, not looking at Ange. An exquisite aroma of tomatoes and garlic slow-cooked in olive oil streams from the kitchen.

I find him patiently waiting by the table, set for two. I can't help exclaiming, "That smells so good!"

"I made ossobuco," he says modestly.

Can he really be our enemy when he makes dishes that so ease our pain? Is that just another medium for the spell he's trying to cast on us?

"I avoid ossobuco," I say, trying to put on a severe, even slightly disgusted air.

But how hungry I am, and how enticing it all is!

"I have a cousin in the Périgord who raises calves and pigs," says Noget. "It's the only meat I'll eat, and the only meat I bring you. It's a top-grade farm. There's nothing to worry about, it won't make you sick."

His gentle, considerate voice makes me ashamed. I'm so

hungry that a bitter liquid fills my mouth. I can't help thinking he's secretly studying me. But I'm so tired, so confused.

Does it really matter that much, in the end, just who this man is?

"No, I'm not afraid of that," I say.

I take a step toward the steaming pot (which he would have rummaged through the cabinets to find) and stiffly bend over till my face is almost touching the rounds of veal simmering in their orange sauce.

"Isn't it a little fatty?" I murmur.

"That's the marrow," he says. "Your husband's very fond of marrow, isn't he?"

"Yes," I say, "Ange loves marrow."

I immediately chide myself for adding, "He liked to spread it all over a piece of bread and put it under the broiler."

"Well," he says with a condescending little smile, "when there's marrow in the sauce, you can hardly expect it to be light."

"What do you want from us?" I ask. "I'm begging you, tell me straight."

I drop onto a chair, close to him, and look straight into his unpleasant face, feeling the tremor in my chin.

"As you see," I say, "I've lost all my pride."

"All I want is to help you," says Noget, categorically. "I have no other mission."

"But did someone send you?"

"I work for no one," he says.

Suddenly he looks away, and I suspect that he might well be lying, that he's definitely lying.

Hopeless, I stand up. A sort of exhausted indifference

is settling over me. I pick up one of the two plates from the table, fill it with meat and sauce. Noget carefully spoons a helping of noodles on one side, and then I leave the kitchen to go and feed Ange.

He's moaning in his sleep. He wakes when I enter the room. Drool is flowing from the corners of his mouth.

"I'm hungry, that smells good," he says.

For the first time in ages, he smiles.

He's used to the stench now, I tell myself, feeling faint. I sit down on the edge of the bed. I observe that the pus is still coming. Then I put a spoonful of meat and noodles to Ange's lips and he greedily swallows it down, and as I watch his sauce-smeared mouth open and close, and as an image drifts through my mind of Noget's fat hands making the dish, clutching the meat, slicing the onions and tomatoes, Noget's will endeavoring to arouse our appetite, focused solely on us and our desire to eat, I know I'll never be able to choke down our neighbor's homemade ossobuco, not only because I find Noget repellent but because there's some hidden intention in his cooking, because in his unclean hands food acts as a tool for what must be, I tell myself stonily, something like our enslavement.

12. Did we offend the bad fairy?

Two days later I grudgingly call Gladys.

One of her children answers. When I'm done introducing myself, he lets out a cry and drops the phone. Several minutes of silence go by. I wait, the receiver pressed to my ear, having come to accept that my most ordinary acts will now arouse the most incongruous reactions.

I'm standing at the big living-room window, and I see the rain falling in Rue Esprit-des-Lois, and the dark façades across the way, the balconies no neighbor ever steps out onto anymore, at least not when I'm here. In our building too, people seem to have moved away—because whatever happened to the Foulques, the Dumezes, the Bertauxs, all those fine, quiet couples who just eight months ago packed this very living room, glasses of champagne all around, toasting my granddaughter's birth?

We'd invited everyone in the building, apart from Noget. Now I never see them around anymore, I don't hear them, their cars even seem to be gone from the street. Was that a mistake, then, spurning Noget and showering everyone else with various expressions of our cordial feelings, our faintly condescending esteem? Yes, it's true, Ange and I have always felt vaguely superior to our neighbors and colleagues. As for Noget, the queasy aversion he inspired in us was almost hatred, unquestionably.

"Is that you, Nadia?" says Gladys's voice at last, slightly distant and veiled, as if she'd taken the precaution of laying a piece of cloth between her mouth and the telephone.

"Yes, it's me," I say. "I gave your son quite a scare, didn't I? The one who answered the phone?"

Gladys ignores my chirpy tone. She doesn't make a sound. A shiver runs down the back of my neck. I quickly turn toward the living room doorway, but I see no sign of anyone. Which of course doesn't mean I'm alone.

"You and Priscilla haven't come to see your papa," I say.

"No," says Gladys after a long pause.

Her voice is even fainter than before. I force myself to go on:

"He's not well at all."

"I didn't think so," says Gladys.

Her answer comes after a few seconds of silence, as if it took that long for my voice to reach her, or as if she had to weigh every word, every intonation, before she could even think of speaking to me. But, I ask myself, what cruel misuse could I possibly make of Gladys's words?

"You promised you'd be back," I say, slightly lost. "It's just a little strange..."

"We're learning to separate from him," says Gladys.

Her voice has become almost inaudible. Suddenly frantic, sensing that this conversation will be our last, that Gladys will never again answer my calls, I shout into the receiver, "Hey, Gladys!"

"Well," says Gladys, "I think I'll be hanging up now."

"Wait! I have to tell you, both of you, that...I'm going away."

Stinging tears fill my eyes. All the same, I stand firmly on my two feet, looking out at the lashing rain, to deprive the being clearly hidden in my living room of the pleasure of seeing me collapse.

"Yes?" says Gladys, further away all the time. "You're going away, you say?"

"To my son's. But, oh, Gladys, I'll have to leave Ange behind, he's in no shape to travel."

I speak very quickly to keep Gladys with me a little longer, that woman I've so often wished I could never see again, exasperated by her hostility, pragmatism, and ostentatious saintliness when she came for a visit, for instance.

"Ange will stay here, in the care of our neighbor," I say, feeling an unbearable shame, "but you two must come and see him, keep an eye on him, or…oh God… Please, Gladys…"

"I'm going to hang up now. I do have children, you know. Oh, Papa never should have had anything to do with you… I'm hanging up…"

"You will come, won't you, Gladys?"

I press the receiver to my ear so hard it burns.

I then see one corner of a curtain being lifted up in an apartment across the street. The Chinese student who lives there—yet another I haven't seen on the sidewalk for months, for so long that I thought she'd gone away too—is standing with her forehead against the glass. Our eyes meet. She gives me a quick smile. I find that comforting beyond all reason. I remember she used to walk around stark naked behind her sheer curtains, and when Ange saw her he looked away in anger and said, "That little whore, who does she think she is? I'm going to call the cops on her if she keeps that up."

Ange took a certain pleasure in saying those words, but, I ask myself, who could ever have heard them but me? Only lately have I sensed a spiteful presence lurking in our living room. Before, it was just the two of us, Ange and me, and no one would ever suspect me of repeating anything Ange said, because I'm a discreet and even taciturn woman, when I'm with adults.

I then hear Gladys's voice fading away, dying out, as if blown off on a wind too strong to resist.

"I'm learning to forget my father, and so is Priscilla," says Gladys. "We don't have a choice, you know. There's no choice… It's better for him this way too."

"Why is it better for him?" I shriek.

Just as I feared, it's too late: nothing more comes from the receiver but the slow beep of the signal telling me to hang up.

I go to the window and peer out at the rain, hoping I might see the Chinese student again. My entire being is still basking in the consolation of her smile, short-lived though it was, almost imperceptible. *Wasn't Ange, wasn't my beloved Ange going too far, hating that girl just because she liked to show off her pretty unclothed body? Once he pretended to slap her, broadly miming that slap in front of the window, a savage look on his face, to make it clear to her once and for all that he found her nudity so offensive that he couldn't control his rage. And did that have any effect on her? She looked at him in surprise, then lowered her eyes to her breasts, her legs, as if she herself were just realizing she had nothing on, or as if she were trying to find anything in her appearance that might so upset Ange that he might want to destroy her from afar, and then she gave an innocent laugh, with an elegant shake of her head.*

I also remember the evening we had our friends in to toast the birth of Souhar (why on earth did you call her that? I asked my son on the phone, troubled and unhappy), when Ange pointed the student's window out to everyone, braying, "You know how that girl behaves?"

Whereupon he described and then imitated her way of parading around, and he managed to create such an impression of obscenity simply by walking with little mincing steps, his belly thrust out, his bottom held high, that it made the Dumezes and the Foulques deeply uncomfortable, I sensed, because they're such good people, so innocent in a way. I wanted to tell Ange, "No, no, that's not what she looks like at all," but I only smiled in amusement, afraid Ange might order me to imitate the girl myself if I criticized him. And I'm not chaste enough to properly reproduce her natural, carefree display, I told myself, and my impersonation would be nearly as untrue and indecent as Ange's. We don't have anything like that girl's wonderful weightlessness, I thought, no more than her slightly simple, slightly unpolished good-heartedness, and that's why we can only be a hideous sight when we try to mock her.

Finally night falls, swallowing up the dark day, the ceaseless rain. All at once I feel a cold breath on the back of my neck, and I hold my own breath, as I always do when he comes too close.

"I've made dinner," he purrs, his dry, icy lips grazing my neck. "*Paupiettes* with mushrooms and cream, and a little artichoke risotto you're going to love. I have the crème fraîche delivered from a dairy in Normandy that guarantees all the wholesomeness and flavor I demand, just as you and your husband do, isn't that so? You love good things as much as I do, don't you? Come and eat, I have a plate all ready for you. Meanwhile, I'll go feed our poor Ange."

"I'll deal with that," I say quickly.

Only then does it occur to me that the time for such precautions might have passed, since I've resigned myself to leaving Ange behind, handing him over to Noget.

Standing in the kitchen, I eat the food he's made for us, hurried and vaguely disgusted, then tiptoe to our bedroom. Through the half-open door I see Noget's back as he bends over Ange, and it comes to me that I bend over my students in exactly the same way when I'm scolding them, trying to intimidate them with the full weight of my furious, looming flesh. Ange is holding the fork himself, spearing pieces of meat on the plate Noget is offering him, and eating very quickly.

He's not letting him take his time, I tell myself.

His cheeks are puffed out, still full of food, and already he's stuffing in another piece, then a huge forkful of rice. Noget hurries him along.

"Come on, come on," he grumbles, "I've got things to do."

But after all, who am I to find fault? Aren't I relieved that Noget has taken my place in the stinking bedroom?

I've taken to sleeping in the room we use as a study. The smell of Ange's wound makes me woozy. I can't stand to be by his side for more than a few minutes, vainly mopping up the pus, running a washcloth dipped in eau de cologne over his forehead and cheeks, which turn yellower and more hollow with each passing day. Ange now looks at Noget and me with the same gaze, at once evasive and pleading, frightened and slightly lethargic. But when, just in case, I venture to murmur, "Do you want me to send for Doctor Charre?" his wasted face flushes, and he furiously shakes his head.

"I've told you a hundred times, I don't want to see anyone," he grumbles. "Don't you understand? He'd give me a shot...a lethal injection... I'm sure he's got a syringe all ready…with my name on it. He's just waiting for his cue… waiting for you to call."

"But why should that be, Ange?" I ask patiently.

And he laughs meanly, trying to mimic me, but he doesn't have the strength and soon has to give up, making do with an almost loathing glance that fills me with horror. What has my husband turned into? The man I loved, the man who was one with me, where has he gone?

13. If only he were my son

I haven't been in to school for three days, and I must face the fact that the principal has never tried to get ahold of me, that no colleague has shown any concern. Nor has any parent written me, or passed on a little note or a sweet drawing from my students, as they did the few times I fell ill over the years.

I seem to have been erased from the life of the school, just as completely as Ange.

Not wanting to meet up with Noget, I never leave the study where I sleep except to race to the bathroom or look in on Ange. Nonetheless, even when Noget is away, I can feel his prying spirit around us, his watchful shadow. Just when I think he's home for the night, I suddenly hear the creak of the hallway floorboards, the squeak of our bedroom door, and when, sitting up on the cot in the study, I cry, "Is that you, Monsieur Noget?" no one answers, and all at once everything in the apartment goes quiet.

What is he here for? I knead my hands, too frightened

to move but rebuking myself for not protecting Ange in his vulnerable state. I don't believe he's hurting him, exactly. And Ange never complains about him—yes, that's true, but would he dare? He's simply exerting some sort of force on or around Ange, and the nature or intention of that force I don't know. *As if he wanted to make sure that Ange never recovers.*

The morning of the fourth day, I drink the coffee Noget brings me before I'm even up (he must wait there behind the door, listening for the little sounds that tell him I'm awake), and that coffee truly is the smoothest and richest I've ever tasted. Then I get dressed, carefully choosing my clothes, and make up my eyes and mouth. My face in the mirror seems different, a little wider than usual, even fuller, my chin heavier.

It's all that rich food he's forcing on us, I tell myself, and I feel at the same time apprehensive and vaguely as if I'd been tricked.

"You use too much butter and oil in your dishes," I tell him as I walk into the kitchen.

He's busy buttering the generous slices of warm bread he brings every morning. There are croissants as well, I see, and buns studded with lumps of sugar.

"The butter is just pouring off that bread," I say, irritated. "Why are you trying to fatten us up like a couple of pigs for the slaughter?"

He looks up at me, a gaze without warmth that he does his best to instill with a sort of polite amiability.

"Because I like you, nothing more," he says. "You've always had a taste for good food, haven't you? I've seen you two coming home from the market with fine Italian charcuterie that perfumed the whole staircase, or little vegetables you sometimes braised all afternoon long, so I realized that like me you have a fondness for…"

"And what about our neighbors," I interrupt, my annoyance overflowing, "the Bertauxs, the delightful Foulques, those nice Dumezes, I suppose they're all away on vacation?"

"Oh, those people," he says scornfully.

He falls silent, pretending to be too polite to fully speak his mind.

"What do you have against them?" I ask, minding my tone.

"Who's here at your side? It's me, isn't it? You haven't seen hide nor hair of them, and you're not going to. They wouldn't even want to admit they'd ever met you."

He purses his lips, breaks into a sullen pout, pretends to be concentrating on the bread and butter. There's a decency in his offended reserve, his sort of long-suffering forbearance, that shakes my confidence.

"I'm sure you're mistaken," I say softly. "I'm sure our neighbors aren't ashamed of us. As soon as they get a moment to give us a sign of their sympathy…"

"Oh, oh, oh," he says, disgusted.

"You don't know the first thing about it," I say.

I feel oppressed and disheartened, just as I always do when I talk with Noget. He muddles my thoughts, trying to drag me into the mire where he feels so repellently at home, where every event is judged from the single, unchanging viewpoint of suspicion.

"There must be some reason you've decided to leave," he says coolly.

Burning hot blood rushes to my face. My cheeks feel monstrously swollen. Don't even think of mentioning that to him, I tell myself.

Suddenly I feel such pity for myself that my eyes fill with tears. I've devoted my life to my work, to the children, and now everyone's shoving me aside like a piece of trash so vile you don't even want the sight of it lingering in your memory.

"I'm just going to visit my son," I say. "I haven't even seen my granddaughter yet." I can't help adding, in a bitter yelp: "They named her Souhar!"

Noget doesn't answer. An odd tension settles in between us, like when I rehooked my bra in front of him.

"Souhar. Weird idea, don't you think?" I murmur.

With ostentatious care he arranges Ange's breakfast things on a tray, and I dully observe that I've grown used to his tangled beard, his dubious clothes, his ambivalent form, slight and pudgy at the same time, and it no longer offends me.

In hopes of dispelling the awkwardness I've created by bringing up Souhar (but how painful I find the mere thought of that name!), I go on: "Surely there'll be a school to take me in where my son lives."

"Oh, you think so?" says Noget, courtly and cold.

I leave the apartment without stopping in to say hello to Ange, for fear he might ask where I'm going.

Rue Esprit-des-Lois is gray and damp this morning, yet again. Every day now for weeks, the fog rising up from the river has hung over the city until nightfall, filling the streets with the smell of silt.

I look up and can't see the sky. The topmost floor of our building, home to the very decent, very sweet Foulque couple, has vanished into the mist.

I don't have my coat to wear anymore. I shiver in my bulging old cardigan. This cardigan shouldn't be so tight on me, I tell myself, angry at Noget, and angry at myself too, for blindly succumbing to the seductions of his cooking. It's hard to believe. I don't eat that much of it, because even though I've grown used to his appearance, I can't shake my mistrust of any food chosen and cooked by his hand. And still I've ballooned, and I'm plump enough to begin with, and all this from just barely touching Noget's dishes. Ange must be terribly sick, I suddenly tell myself in a flash of painful lucidity, to be getting thinner day after day even with Noget working so hard to stuff him—as if, I tell myself, shivering, that abundance of food were running out through Ange's wound in the form of pus.

I walk through the clinging fog to the Saint-Michel neighborhood. I'm glad the few passersby can't see me clearly. I might run into parents from school, who wouldn't even treat me with the contempt they've shown over these past several months, them and everyone else, which I'm now used to, in a way—no, they'd pretend they hadn't even recognized me, now that I've been expelled from the school.

I take several wrong turns before I finally reach La Rousselle police station.

I haven't been here for years, not since my son left Bordeaux and so deprived me of any pretext for calling on Inspector Lanton, a young man I was very fond of, my son's lover at the time, and even what one might call his partner, though they never actually lived together. I hope he still works at La Rousselle—and how distant and enviable seem those days, not so long ago (three years? four?), when I and sometimes Ange used to stop by the station after school for a cup of coffee with Lanton, whose face always lit up with a sort of filial gratitude when he saw me, who always found time to chat and joke, even when he was busy, and to tell us all the latest sordid goings-on in the city, knowing that Ange and I took a fervent interest in such things.

Ange is particularly fascinated by murders. He would blush with repressed exaltation as he listened to Lanton, his thigh jerking nervously. As soon as we were out of the station, he would work himself into a lather, brandishing his satchel and trying to demonstrate that it was the excessive liberty of contemporary society that led to these pointless, small-time murders Lanton had told us about. These speeches wearied me. And so I eventually found ways to visit Lanton without Ange's knowing, and those tête-à-têtes sealed the bond that subtly united us. I was deeply unhappy when I learned that my son was breaking up with Lanton. Oh, I should have gone on visiting the station, I later reflected, rebuking myself for stupidly relinquishing my free will out of respect for the unspoken law that orders us to have nothing to do with our children's former lovers, especially when the separation was painful—because Lanton, a finer young man than my son in many ways, suffered terribly at being left.

The waiting room is full even at this early hour. Troubled, I stare vacantly into space, and then, once I find the courage to look at the crowd straight on, I realize we're alike, they and I.

How can I put it into words?

It shakes me to the core. I don't know any of these people, all of them perfectly ordinary men and women. And yet I realize it could just as well be Ange and me waiting here, with our faces so like theirs, our expressions rigorously identical to theirs, even if they vary slightly from one to the next—that makes no difference, it's a multiple echo originating in our similar souls, a oneness I've just seen for the first time.

Poor Ange, was it I who contaminated him?

I'm almost unsurprised to see my ex-husband, my son's father, slumped in a corner chair. Of course, I tell myself, of course, him too.

He hasn't spotted me yet. In fact, no one is paying me any mind, and it can only be because everyone here finds all the others' faces so familiar. For my part, that resemblance disgusts me. How I despise them all of a sudden, every last one of them, with their anxious brows, their hunted look—all those frustrations, all those fears oozing from their glistening skin. Do I have that same shining skin, greasy with fright and fatigue?

I approach the counter with a slightly hesitant step. The policeman on duty gives me an irritable glance.

"I'm here to see Inspector Lanton," I say, in my firm schoolteacher voice.

"He expecting you?" the man asks, seeming to think it unlikely.

"He's expecting me," I say, deeply relieved to hear that Lanton still works here.

"OK, I'll let him know."

I turn around toward the room. My ex-husband is

watching me with the dubious, aggrieved eyes our son inherited. I reluctantly walk toward him. I'm starting to sweat in the oddly tight cardigan, but I don't want to take it off or unbutton it. I want everyone here to have only the vaguest idea of me, to have no notion what sort of top I'm wearing under my cardigan, and so on. In short, I don't want to reveal anything that might confirm how entirely I belong to this family of people.

"Nadia?"

"Well yes," I whisper, "it's me."

His lips slowly tighten into a sarcastic little smile that immediately takes me back to the life we once lived together. I frown, telling myself: Never once did my poor Ange take up the cruel weapon of sarcasm.

"You're looking prosperous," he says, inspecting me from head to toe.

He smiles again, joylessly. He's become a little man with long hair and a restless face racked by nervous tics. So, I say to myself, shocked, this is my first love, and perhaps even, yes, the one true love of my life.

"You're here to see Lanton too?" he asks.

"Yes," I say, deeply surprised. "Why do you want to see him?"

"To get my ID card renewed," he murmurs, scarcely opening his mouth.

He's seems terribly tired and anxious. I give him a steely look, not telling him I've come for the same thing. I feel stronger than my ex-husband, and more confident.

"You hated him, you hated Lanton," I say, very quietly. "You couldn't stand it that he was our son's lover."

"That's true," he says, "and it still makes me sick just to think of it."

I can see that he's close to shouting in rage at the mere mention of their relationship.

"You're so infuriating!" I explode, because his offended, irascible air takes me back to the time when our son abruptly broke up with Lanton and I suspected my ex-husband of driving him to it.

"And yet here you are coming to see Lanton," I say, viciously.

"Not by choice, I assure you," he says.

I look at him more closely. He seems to have fallen on very hard times. He's wearing a gray corduroy suit I remember from long ago. A dull-white residue coats his lips.

"I don't understand what's happening to me," he sighs. "You wouldn't believe it if I told you. Every day, you hear me, every single day brings a fresh load of inexplicable torments. I'm sick of it."

Pointless though it is, and pathetic though he now seems to me, I can't help lashing out at him, whispering furiously, "You were so mean, so unfair to Lanton! Do you really think their relationship was any of your business?"

"Well, I at least happen to think that everything to do with my only son is my business," he retorts, showing his yellowed teeth.

This veiled reference—which he's still sharp enough to work into the conversation, I see—to my supposed lack of interest in our son (meaning that I preferred my students to my child) sets me off.

"Oh, yes, you, the perfect father," I say, "meddling in

his son's love life so he can ruin it!"

"Aren't you glad to have a granddaughter? That Lanton would never have made you a grandmother, I can tell you that," says my ex-husband, cruelly triumphant.

I open my mouth to answer, then close it again, ashamed. I was just about to bemoan the choice of that name "Souhar," which I can't think about without feeling a pain like a kick in the stomach, which is to say a humiliated, undeserved pain, as well as a violent one. But it feels wrong to complain about that to him, so I say nothing, even as I seethe at his self-indulgent distress and arrogant insinuations.

"Why do we have to go on being enemies?" I say plaintively.

He shakes his head, denying the indisputable truth just as he did back when we loved each other, pinching his lips with the look I still know so well, the look of a man who has right firmly on his side.

"Well, I'm certainly not anyone's enemy," he says. "And I must tell you, I couldn't be happier to be a grandfather, and besides, she's a wonderful baby."

"You've seen her?" I say, hurt.

He's surprised.

"Souhar? Of course I've seen her."

"Don't say her name!" I bark.

"They came to visit me six or seven months ago," he says with cruel relish, having obviously understood that I'd seen no sign of them.

"She's such a smart baby. They let me feed her, and by the end of the stay she had a special smile just for me. I love babies," my ex-husband intones.

"All the same," I murmur, "Souhar..." And I add, my eyes stinging, "I so wish we could be friends, you, me, and Ange. Ange is terribly sick at the moment..."

But he's stopped paying attention, suddenly reminded of his immediate difficulties by Lanton's appearance in the waiting room. He stands up, waves, cries out, putting on an act of joyous surprise:

"Over here! I'm Ralph's papa!"

Lanton's fine, limpid gaze drifts over him so scornfully that even I feel indignant and hurt for my ex-husband. How I loved him back then! I find myself drifting into the strange distraction that's been coming over me lately, just when I should be most focused and vigilant. I shake my head.

"I was looking for *you*, Nadia," says Lanton, giving me the same tender smile he always did when I came calling.

All around us, the hopeful silence that greeted his entrance dissolves into crestfallen murmurs.

"I think all these people were here before me," I say, a little flustered.

He casts a vague glance behind him.

"Well, they'll just have to wait," he says. "It's not like they've got anything better to do, right?"

An ignoble relief courses through me. Lanton shows such disdain for those people that, if I was really as like them as I thought, he'd have to treat me more or less the same way, I tell myself, which means I'm not really like them after all.

He graciously takes my arm, and I follow him back behind the counter and into his office, the same as before.

"Nadia, I'm so happy to see you again," says Lanton.

He clasps my two hands and lifts them to his lips. My face flushes deep red with emotion. It's been such a long time since someone spoke kindly to me.

He takes a step back and examines me. His brow furrows.

"You've put on a great deal of weight," he says reproachfully. "You're not watching yourself at all, are you? That's not good, Nadia. You were such a nice-looking woman, weren't you?"

Ridiculously, I stammer out something like an apology. My head is spinning. I sit down on a chair facing his desk. He lets out an affectionate little laugh and hurries over to take me in his arms.

"Forgive me, forgive me. Forget all that, it doesn't matter. I know it's you, and I'm so happy you're here."

"Who else would it be?" I murmur.

"When you haven't seen someone for years, you're not always sure you'll recognize them," says Lanton.

He's dressed in light-colored jeans, a thick white sweater, elegant boots. He's tall, tanned, and muscular. There's a distinctive gleam in the two green slits of his eyes, a gleam, I tell myself, of power and fulfillment. Still today, Lanton is a far more handsome man than my son.

"Well, I recognize you," I say. "You look wonderful."

"Why did you stop coming to see me?" Lanton asks.

Agitated, he begins to blink very quickly. Looking for something to do with his hands, which I suddenly see trembling, he hooks his thumbs over his belt and lifts one buttock onto a corner of his desk.

"Was it really that hard on you that I stopped coming?" I say, disconcerted.

"Yes," says Lanton. "I thought we were friends, quite apart from anything I had with..."

"Forgive me," I say, "oh, I swear, I didn't know..."

I don't dare say how terribly I missed him, how many times I almost went to see him, little caring, in the end, what my son thought of me, whether I was making him unhappy. But I never did, because that other young man is my son, not Lanton, and I believed it was my son I had to implicitly obey, and yes, now I regret it, I regret it so deeply that I feel an unjust anger at my son well up inside me.

We sit in silence. I'm not sure I trust Lanton now, because the brutality I saw him display in the waiting room seems new to me.

I look toward the window. There's nothing to see but the fog, dense and still.

"Why does this fog never lift anymore?" I ask gloomily.

Then, in a sudden burst of vigor, I appeal to him:

"You noticed how I fat I've become, well it's true, that happened after my son left you; I put on some of this weight over a couple of months, but it's especially been in the past several days, because we have a stranger cooking for us and more or less forcing us to eat all the fatty, delicious things he makes; it's true, they're exquisite, but he's secretly loading them with fat, I don't know how he does it, because I can't tell it's there, it never bothers me while I'm eating... Anyway, that's what's going on, and... Oh God, Lanton, Ange is so sick, and I can't do anything about it..."

"Don't do anything at all, no matter what," says Lanton. "Don't call the doctor, don't take him to the hospital."

"Why do you say that?"

Lanton crosses his arms, buying time. An uncomfortable expression flits over his face.

"You know perfectly well, my dear Nadia," he slowly begins, "that people like you aren't exactly in favor…"

"What on earth does that mean, people like us? Besides, Ange isn't like me," I say.

He puts his index finger to his lips.

"Not so loud, Nadia. The walls aren't that thick here."

Leaning toward him, I whisper, enraged, "I assure you, I have no idea what I am, and I can't think of any sort of people I belong to."

"That may not last," says Lanton, hesitant, profoundly ill at ease. "You might change, Nadia. What's the name of this stranger who's forcing his food on you?"

"Richard Victor Noget," I say glumly.

He whistles, admiring and surprised.

"If I had the great Noget looking after me, I wouldn't turn up my nose. And even if he's taken it into his head to fatten you up, just let him; a lot of people would give their eyeteeth to find themselves under Noget's glorious wing!"

"Well, I've never heard of this Noget person," I say.

"You see?" says Lanton.

I look at him, not understanding. But Lanton's beautiful, tan face seems to have turned slightly hard and annoyed, as if from an irritation he's struggling not to show, and so I hold back my question (what is it I'm supposed to "see"?), and I remember I came here this morning to ask for his help. I shiver at the thought that he could easily send me away empty-handed. And with that I think: If we hadn't grown so close when he was my son's lover, might he not treat me just like the others, might he not hate me and scorn me as casually and straightforwardly as he did them?

"I'm going away, my friend," I say quietly.

"You're doing the right thing," says Lanton.

"But I'll be leaving Ange here...until he gets better."

My voice begins to shake. A rush of shame burns my cheeks.

"This Noget will be looking after him."

"Really? Looking after him?" says Lanton, skeptical. "And where are you going, Nadia?"

"To my son's."

Lanton's jaw clenches violently. He crosses his arms and tucks his hands into his armpits, as if to give himself a hug or to shield himself. He stares at me.

"It's been so long since I last saw him," I say. "He has a child now, a girl, and, can you imagine..."

I let out an overwrought little laugh.

"No, you'll never guess what he named that baby."

I break off, my throat tightening. Lanton's eyes are half closed. Saliva shooting from my lips, I half shout, "Souhar! He named her...Souhar!"

Then I slump back in the chair, genuinely exhausted, drained.

"But maybe none of this means that much to you," I say after a moment, "my son's new life and these impossible ideas he has, like calling his daughter..."

"Enough, Nadia, enough!" says Lanton with an exasperated groan. "You're right, what do I care? What do I care if he named his kid that? What do I care that this kid exists?"

"I just wanted you to understand how much he's changed," I say. "He's clearly not the guy you knew anymore. Can you imagine him as the head of a family? All the same, it's a real joy for me, a pure joy, even if I haven't met the baby yet."

Suddenly Lanton seems dispirited. He slides off the desk, slowly walks to the window, peers out at the fog. Keeping his back to me, he asks, "Why did you come here, Nadia?"

"I need to get my ID card renewed," I say.

"And him…he's expecting you?"

"Oh no. He has no idea yet."

I don't add that I'd rather not tell my son I'm coming before it's too late to stop me, but Lanton must have guessed, because he murmurs, "You're planning to tell him once you're on the boat, right?"

"Yes," I say with a sheepish little laugh. "But he can always toss me into the harbor if he doesn't want me there. Incidentally, my son's father is here, out in the next room, you saw him, he needs a new ID card too…"

Lanton pivots on his luxurious boots. He's livid, but I notice his eyes are damp.

"I will never lift one finger for that guy," he cries. "He can go die, for all I care."

"He is his father, after all, Lanton," I say.

"Not one more word."

He would never have snapped at me like this in the old days. I say nothing more, afraid it might turn him against me. I feel desperately sad for my ex-husband; I feel like I'm failing in some very basic duty I owe him.

Suddenly Lanton sits down at his desk and begins to write a letter, as quick as he can. It still takes him a full ten minutes. Then he folds the sheet in four and slips it into an envelope, which he seals.

"I'll take care of your ID card," he says, slightly breathless from an emotion I can't deduce, "and in return you'll do me the favor of giving this letter to your son."

"Of course."

The atmosphere between us is heavy with tension. *How tenderly we once loved each other, words flitted back and forth between us with a butterfly's delicate grace. He loved me more than his own mother, he trusted me, and I was as proud of him as if I'd raised him myself and made him so handsome and accomplished.*

There then comes to me a thought that must tint my cheeks and forehead with a distinctive shade of pink. Lanton notices. He lets out a little laugh, his lips curling in a heartless sneer, and says, "Something I should tell you about my letter to your son, Nadia: I'll know if you don't give it to him, because then he won't do a very specific thing I'm asking him to."

"Suppose he doesn't do it anyway," I say, "just because he doesn't want to?"

"Impossible," says Lanton firmly.

I see a threat in his eyes. A tingle runs down my legs, right to my toes.

"I know where to find your husband," says Lanton.

Aghast, I begin to shout, "Ange isn't that sick, I can still take him with me!"

"Ange is very, very sick," says Lanton coldly.

I stand up, quivering with anger.

"Of course I'll give your letter to my son," I say. "Why would you think I won't?"

And my anger is sincere and intense, but at the same time faintly unreal, as if Lanton and I were masterfully playing characters very different from what we are in real life, even the exact opposite, and I realize there's no way I can possibly stop loving him or hold anything against him.

Evidently Lanton's feelings are in tune with my own. He comes to me and clasps my cheeks in his hands. *How horribly awkward!*

"I don't want you to go away mad," he says urgently. "In the name of all the good times we've had together, Nadia… Do you remember? I want you to have only happy memories of me, happy memories…"

I murmur, "Dear Lanton, do something for my son's father."

I gently push away his hands and give him a hug of my own. His hair still has the teddy-bear smell that used to make me smile, and it moves me deeply.

My ex-husband is still slouched in his chair when I cross back through the waiting room on my way out. They're all there, in fact—all those people, *our comrades in sorrow*, who, like him, place their faith in Lanton's unlikely goodwill. I wink at my ex-husband (how I loved that man! I tell myself again), because now I'm sure Lanton will see to his ID card, however deeply he hates him. And what about me, for that matter, don't I hate him every bit as much?

In the course of just a few years, my son's father has turned into one of those aging, disheveled, disgruntled wrecks who trudge along the sidewalk, cackling or cursing in time with the sour tide sloshing back and forth in their skulls. Just because that man cares nothing for what people might think of him, does that mean he speaks deeper truths than the rest of us, I ask myself, we who have learned to fear giving offense or seeming ridiculous above all other things? No, it most certainly does not, it might even be that this dark indifference strips him of any useful understanding of the world around him, I tell myself, profoundly sad for him.

He doesn't react to my wink. He seems defeated, ground down by worry. But as I walk past him he leaps to his feet.

"Nadia, you're huge," he says.

"Yes, so what?" I say, nettled.

He bristles, he scowls, he breathes his hot, noisome breath into my face (how I once kissed that mouth, I tell myself again, how I sucked at that tongue!).

"You don't understand, my dear, that your fat is offensive," he whispers. "I certainly can't afford to be overweight, I'll tell you that."

"Oh, I don't eat that much," I say.

Uncomfortable, not looking at him, I add, "I can help you, you know. Here."

I dig into my bag, take out a fifty-euro bill, slip it into his raincoat pocket. He pats the pocket with a snide, almost furious little laugh.

"And I can help you again," I say.

"Yes, and where will you be?"

Caught short, I hesitate. I murmur, "At our son's."

"That's impossible," he says, aghast. "He'll never allow

it. Oh, what do I know? He's going to be shocked, deeply shocked to find you so fat."

"I'm still his mother, aren't I?"

"I don't know if he'll see it that way," my son's father answers, after a moment's thought.

For the first time his gaze is sincere, troubled by something other than his own sad fate. He lays his hand on my arm, parts his lips, and in the end says nothing.

I slip away and hurry toward the front door. Words from such a man's mouth aren't necessarily any nearer the truth than any others. Why, then, am I afraid of what my ex-husband might want to tell me?

You're afraid of everything, I tell myself once I'm out on the sidewalk. I must look worried and lost. My breath is heavy. And then there's another thing I must face: long accustomed to educating children, my students as well as my son, I don't like being taught lessons. Often—and yes, I regret it, I feel terrible about it—I've cut short conversations in which I foresaw a lesson coming, or sensed some such intention. And I would laugh or throw out a joke or walk out of the room, and I could feel my skin prickling and shuddering at the threat constituted in my mind by the possibility that some wisdom was about to be imparted. Ange is the same.

What sort of lesson is being forced on me by that intolerable name "Souhar"? What is my own granddaughter meant to be telling me, a girl just a few months old? Yes, Ange is the same. The moment someone sets out to enlighten him on any subject at all, he cries out: Oh, I can't stand pontificators!

I slowly walk away from the police station, my throat tight, short of breath—it must be the fog, permeating the city with a metallic smell. All at once a man comes striding energetically past me, jostling me, and by his baseball cap with its long transparent visor I recognize him from Lanton's waiting room. "Betrayer!" he whispers in my ear.

At least that's what I think he says.

"What's the problem?" I say, my voice turning slightly shrill, then breaking.

He stalks off. The fog whisks him out of sight before I can even get an idea of his age or his build, any sense of a connection he might have with Ange or me. I must have misunderstood, I tell myself. That was just some generic obscenity he tossed out at me, as timid men sometimes do in this city, then scuttle off with their hands in their pockets, their heads hunched between their shoulders.

It's still early. Cours Alsace-Lorraine is deserted. Just when I'm about to cross the street, I see the tram emerge from the milky dimness. As if it were far, far away, slowed by the fog, I hear the little bell's pointless tinkle, which now seems to be desperately chasing after the tram rather than running along before it. I wonder whether I should step back or run across the tracks. I bound forward. The tram speeds by just behind me with a furious hiss.

The tram is looking for me, trying to catch me; it deliberately comes racing along to run me down.

Gasping, I turn around. My son's father is sitting in the last car, his face olive in the fluorescent light, and when he sees me he smiles, with that same kindly, gentle smile he had when we were first married.

He couldn't be driving it, could he? He couldn't have anything to do with the way the tram is behaving, him, my son's father?

I recognize the guilt I can never shake when I think of my ex-husband, a guilt now made sharper by that innocent, friendly smile. Yes, my son's father is a bit self-absorbed, but he's also innocent, and he doesn't hold a grudge. Unlike him, I rarely forget my own long-term interests. Oh, what a loser, I sometimes think, moved and ashamed. But also: After all, what did I do that was wrong? There's no law I defied, no obligation I didn't scrupulously respect. What did I do? I negotiated my divorce with that man so that every possible wrong was imputed to him, and he never suspected things could have been otherwise. He owes me money to this day. More precisely, this is what troubles my conscience: I can now confess that I began my love affair with Ange long before I asked for a divorce, and, knowing my husband had no idea of my liaison with Ange, I demanded, very unjustly in moral terms, that my husband take full responsibility for the failure of our marriage, oh yes, most unjustly, because he was a stubborn man but naïve, gruff but easily manipulated, and I had only to complain of this or that (perfectly unobjectionable, in truth) aspect of his behavior to make him lose all his self-assurance, his judgment, almost his memory, and agree that he'd never been much of a husband.

"Isn't it his fault if your son prefers men to women? Clearly it is," Ange had told me in his wise, placid voice, when I was wondering how to go about getting a divorce.

And so I repeated to my husband, "After all, it's your

fault that our son prefers men to women, although that doesn't bother me in the least."

I repeated those words to my husband, knowing this side of our son's life bothered and even tormented him. I repeated them to my husband, knowing he'd find it hard to come up with a good counterargument. But why dredge up these old stories again? Yes, my ex-husband still owes me money, but the fact that I've stopped asking him for it absolves me of any symbolic debt I might owe him—that's how it seems to me.

He was an electrician when we were married, and he made a good living. I believe he gradually stopped working after the divorce—is that my fault? Was it my job to keep him on track? Really, what can you do for a man driven to self-sabotage by sadness and spite, by baseless remorse and low self-esteem? Ange and I wanted the three of us to come together in a sort of polite friendship, but he refused all our dinner invitations. Nor did he come to our little party on the birth of that baby, the ridiculously named Souhar (please God, I sometimes say to myself, appalled, may that name bring her no misery, may it not be the death of her, even!).

14. My inconstant city

I start back toward Rue Esprit-des-Lois, guiding myself by the occasional distinctive shopwindow. I can't make out the street names in the fog. I see only a handful of people, all in a hurry. They materialize at narrow intersections, as if they've been waiting there, hidden behind the corner of an apartment building, listening for my footsteps so they can burst out, wordlessly startle me, then vanish into the thick white murk.

This is a figment of my overwrought mind, and I know it. I'm perfectly sane, perfectly capable, even in my mistrust and trepidation, of grasping its outlandishness. But knowing that doesn't stop my heart, *my poor fat-encased heart*, from racing each time someone pops up before me, looking slightly haunted (is that real or feigned?), and fixing me with the wide-eyed stare of someone who doesn't see the person he was expecting.

No, I'm not out of my mind. Why should I be so convinced that everything I see has some direct connection to me? I can't rid myself of the feeling the whole city is spying on me. *And my heart is cornered, surrounded by the baying pack, and it's hammering on the wall of my chest, wishing it could break out of its cramped cage, my poor aging heart, my poor trembling heart.* I was born right here in Bordeaux, in Les Aubiers neighborhood; I've spent my whole life in this city, and I love it with a fraternal tenderness, like a human soul mate. But now I find Bordeaux slipping away from me, enigmatically shunning my friendship, its streets seeming to change their look and direction (is it only the fog? I ask myself), its citizens grown hostile over the past few months (and I'd gotten used to that, and it had, over time, become bearable), seeming no longer to hate me, exactly, but to be stalking me.

I break into a labored little trot. More than once, unable to distinguish the sidewalk from the street in the bands of floating mist, I unwittingly step into traffic. Still I see no sign of Rue Esprit-des-Lois.

I stop running and hide in a doorway to think. I went past the Place de la Cathédrale, then turned right toward Rue des Trois-Conils and then Rue Sainte-Catherine, so I should have come onto Rue Esprit-des-Lois, just past the Grand-Théâtre. And yet I seem to be somewhere near Cours Victor-Hugo, which should be far behind me. How can that be? Is it only the fog? I can't possibly have gotten lost; I've been walking the heart of this city, *its black old heart, its cold old heart*, for the past half century.

I can't have gotten lost, I tell myself, concentrating on the need for objectivity. So it must be the city itself trying to throw me off, my beloved city, whose fidelity I thought beyond question. And what about me? Whom or what have I betrayed, assuming I understood what that guy in the cap was saying? I've never knowingly let anyone down, I've always felt outrageously responsible for my thoughts and deeds, and even other people's. So? If my city has turned unfaithful to me, *in its old, dark, ungrateful heart*, I will never trust anyone again, not even my husband.

Feeling calmer now all the same, I step out of the doorway and try to get my bearings. The Musée d'Aquitaine is in front of me, I can half see its vast outline through the fog. So all I have to do is go back the way I came till I reach Tour Pey-Berland, then immediately turn right, toward Cours Alsace-Lorraine.

I retrace my steps for a hundred-some yards. There should be an intersection here, but the street goes on, very straight, a street I'm sure used to curve. I walk faster and faster. Nothing looks familiar. I'm out of the neighborhood of tall apartment buildings; now there's nothing but little low shops, barren trees towering starkly over their roofs. This isn't the way I'm supposed to be going at all; I don't live in one of these suburbs.

I stop again, terrified. For a moment I turn this way and that, vainly searching for a clue. I come back to where I started. The city seems to be contorting before my eyes—here a street elongates and narrows, there the boulevard widens and winds. It's the fog, I tell myself, it's these long, drifting white bands distorting the sight lines. Is it really just the fog?

Oh God, who will come to my rescue? Am I being punished because I've so long prided myself on never seeking anyone's help?

I tentatively walk toward a newsstand, the one open business on the street. I glance at the woman behind the counter. An anxiety submerges me, deeper than mere confusion, and I hurry off as fast as I can. Like at the police station, I clearly saw that this woman and I were alike, or at least the same sort of person, the same type, different from the passers-by or Lanton, different from my colleagues or Noget, who aren't the same as us, now I secretly know it. But where is the difference? That I don't know yet. It's something to do with the look on our faces, our souls' reflection on our faces.

This faintly disgusts me, though there's nothing ugly, exactly, in what I've just glimpsed. Still, it's uncomfortable, like the accidental unveiling of some mystery usually kept covered up. That's why I avoid asking anything of this woman.

I don't want anyone seeing us face-to-face, no third-party gaze—another customer's, say—confirming our oneness by enfolding us both in a single sour wariness.

I hurry along the sidewalk, not knowing where my feet are taking me. I make a sharp turn into an alleyway I assume will be the Passage de l'Épée. But no, it leads to a little square I've never seen in my life—three benches, a statue of Montesquieu, old black paving stones—*dark and perversely changeable, the heart of my city?*

I thought I knew Bordeaux intimately, and now strange new pieces of that big, familiar body are in a sense daring to come to the fore. I try to read the name of this square. But I'm not a tall woman, oh, little more than five feet three, and the fog blinds me to the plaque that must surely name this place. How can I never have come this way before? Have my walks through Bordeaux become so routine over the years that I blindly overlooked whole neighborhoods of my beloved city, right in its very center, which I thought I knew as well as the thoughts in my head?

There's a brand-new post office, some clothing stores, still closed. Relieved, I make for the post office. A man is leaning on the counter before the one window. I recognize him as Richard Victor Noget. Well, how about that? I say to myself, amazed. So I can't be that far from Rue Esprit-des-Lois!

"Monsieur Noget!"

Never before has the sight of him brought me more comfort than fear, more pleasure than distaste.

"Oh, there you are at last—we were worried," he says severely.

"Yes, well, I got lost," I say.

With my panic suddenly subsiding, I have an urge to pour out my sorrows, to arouse someone's pity.

"It's this horrible fog," I blurt out. "Nothing looks like itself, Bordeaux isn't Bordeaux anymore, it's completely changed..."

I raise one arm to wipe my forehead. In spite of the cold, I'm drenched in sweat, so terrified was I at the idea of walking in circles forever through an anonymous city, *its heart gone dark.*

The look on Noget's face is closed, distant, uncomfortable. As I approach, he hurriedly slips something under the glass, toward the clerk: the letter he was just sealing. I can vaguely feel him trying to hold my gaze, staring into my eyes so I'll keep looking back, and I sense that he's trying to distract me from his hands. I automatically glance down at the letter the clerk has just taken. I read my son's name upside down on the envelope. My lips begin to tremble. I look at Noget, and I see that he knows I've seen.

"You're writing my son?" I say in a tiny, faltering voice. "You know my son?"

And the odious thought of my granddaughter's name once again floods my thoughts—yes, it's an obsession, and it makes me grit my teeth till it hurts, and for a few seconds it so consumes me that I lose all awareness of the world around me.

My mouth filling with saliva, I murmur:

"Really, of all the names in the world, why that one?"

I swallow audibly.

"How do you know my son?" I bark.

"I don't," says Noget.

"You're writing to someone you don't know?"

I let out a cynical little laugh, but my legs are weak and wobbly. I'm a woman with thick, sturdy legs, and yet suddenly they feel too weedy to support me, suddenly I'm like an enormous poppy waving back and forth on its stem.

Casually combing his beard with his fingers, Noget gives me a sharp, scrutinizing look. The sheepskin jacket he's wearing is too big for him, and I recognize it as one of Ange's. Well, at least someone's getting some use out of those old things, I tell myself, all the more unconcerned in that Ange got that jacket long ago as a gift from his daughters.

"Don't be alarmed," Noget says soothingly. "Ange and I simply thought we'd best let your son know you'll be coming; we knew you wouldn't want to, but, don't you agree, it would be indelicate to give him such a, how shall I put it, such an emotional shock..."

Has Noget ever spoken to me so gently? I burst into sobs.

"I don't know...if that was a good idea," I say.

Nevertheless, I feel my agitation and doubts, my confusion and hatred, flowing away with my tears, draining my *fat, heavy old heart* of the questions that had been choking it.

I take a deep breath and lay my hand on Noget's arm.

"I'd like us to be friends now," I say fervently.

He gives me a quick, slightly stiff smile.

"I don't know if you consider your son a friend too," (he says with the slow, serious, sententious voice I so loathe, which inevitably reminds me of his imposture, as if he were still trying to convince me he'd once been a teacher by adopting all the stereotypical ways of a pedant) "but I'm surprised you were even thinking of playing such a trick on him."

"And I'm tired of people condemning me as a vindictive mother, or a mother who can't even love her own son," I say sharply.

"I've learned that your son is a doctor, married, with a family..."

"He has one child, a daughter," I say, in an agonized murmur. "Her name is Souhar."

"That doesn't matter, it doesn't matter."

I cry out, "Yes it does, it's so ridiculous!"

"If you'd just let me finish," he says, raising his voice. "So your son is settled, he's chosen to place the obstacle of distance between his new life and Bordeaux, because although he's always had a harmonious relationship with his stepfather, with Ange, he quite clearly found it intolerable to live in the same city as his mother."

I can't believe what I'm hearing. I gasp in shock.

"Ange would never have told you any such thing! If my son ran away from anyone, and let's say he did, though nothing could be less certain, it can only have been his father, my ex-husband!"

"Really?" Noget exclaims.

I see a gleam of cruel joy in his eyes, a vicious delight. I take a step back.

Any attempt at friendship or peace with an enemy is seen as a sign of weakness.

I put my arm over my face to fend off a blow. But Noget doesn't move.

"In that case," he gleefully goes on, "how do you explain that when he recently came through Bordeaux it was his father your son went to see and to show his child, and even to stay with, I believe, and how in that case do you explain that he chose to keep you in the dark, that he didn't even come show you his little Souhar, or introduce his wife? Strange, isn't it, for a son who's not afraid of his mother?"

"But how do you know all this?" I say.

I feel slightly light-headed. I taste bile in my throat, my breath is bitter. Inappropriately, I can't help thinking it's been a long time since breakfast.

I moan, "I'm so hungry I could eat a whole roast!"

"I've made croque-monsieurs," Noget says cheerily. "Not the kind they give you in cafés, with the dry edges and the cut-rate ham, because, you see, I make my own sandwich bread, I cut it into thick slices that I brown in butter, then I lay on the best Comté cheese I know and a fine piece of old-fashioned ham, and then on the top slice, just under the cheese, do you know what I put on to keep everything tender and moist? A thin layer of béchamel sauce, that's what. But to answer your question: Ange told me, of course; how would I ever have guessed on my own?"

"Ange doesn't know all the details," I say weakly.

My stolid heart, my weakening, stolid heart, keep on bravely beating in your prison of fat!

Trying to assert myself a little, I add, "I can't eat croque-monsieurs, I need something light."

"Actually, I believe," says Noget, "no, I'm certain that Ange himself met your son and his wife and child at some point during their short stay in Bordeaux. That's what your son wanted, and I imagine he advised Ange not to mention it to you so you wouldn't be needlessly hurt, unless it was Ange who decided not to tell you. Evidently Ange and your son were very happy, very moved to see each other. Ange also told me how thrilled he was to see little Souhar's face at last."

"No, no, you're making that up," I say.

I smile, very consciously feigning a superior, disdainful expression.

"I most certainly am not," says Noget, vexed.

"I've heard quite enough about this," I say a little too loudly. "The things that go on in families, you know..."

I whisk the air with both hands. An oddly acidic, pungent sweat runs down my forehead, despite the cool air in the post office, and I note that Noget and the clerk are giving me a cautious, uncertain stare.

Am I such a perfidious woman, then? I thought I was exemplary, respectful, and kind—could I have been that wrong?

I step outside. For a few seconds I'd hoped that the fog might have lifted, that I'd see the square differently, recognize it as a place not among my usual haunts, to be sure, but which I could at least remember passing through sometime long ago. But even if the fog's thinned a little, nothing seems familiar. The statue of Montesquieu is made of green-tinged, mossy stone, the benches are old. A half-dozen streets set off from the square. I have no idea which I should follow to go home, no idea where in Bordeaux I may be. I even find myself doubting that I'm in Bordeaux at all. *But if not, where would I be, I who never travel?*

15. He's not like he used to be

Noget takes my arm and leads me down a little street I know well. It's Rue Lafayette, which runs straight into ours, just a few minutes away from that strange square I'd never seen in my life. Humiliated, I say nothing of my surprise to Noget.

Once we're in the apartment, he cries out excitedly, "Just let me put my croque-monsieurs in the oven for ten minutes!"

My mouth suddenly fills with saliva, and I so yearn to eat that I feel a flood of gratitude toward Noget, even though I'm convinced now that his kindness is poisoned, and his cooking somehow infected.

He's only feeding us to enslave us, I tell myself; he knows his treats keep us quiet, and every mouthful numbs us and binds us. How thrilled he must be to have the two teachers surrendering to his authority, to the force of his virtuosity with butter and fat, those same two teachers who once heaped such scorn on him!

I now think Ange and I misused our superior status, but in our defense might I swear that, if we were sometimes cruel, there was no real malice behind it (*oh, we thought far too little of him to feel anything about him at all*), no intention of hurting this person, that everything we did we did, I believe, innocently? But in fact, I then ask myself, isn't that worse?

I look into our bedroom, expecting to find Ange asleep. But his feverish, dilated eyes cling to mine.

I go in, trying to take only cautious little breaths. The stench is beginning to seep into the apartment.

"You want to see my wound?" Ange asks, his tone pathetically hopeful, as if desperate for some way to keep me close by him.

I reflexively jump back as I lift up the sheet. The awful cavity in Ange's side seems even deeper than before. It must be nearing his liver now, I tell myself, horrified. Mingled with bloody little fibers, the pus is still running into a shallow dish Noget has nestled against Ange's side. All around the wound, the roll of curled flesh and dried blood looks like an old piece of leather, a bone gnawed by a dog. My lips quiver in anguish and pity. Choking, I murmur, "Does it hurt, my poor love?"

"Terribly," says Ange.

He nods toward the door.

"He's going to get hold of some morphine for me," he softly goes on.

"And how, may I ask, is he going to do that? Get a prescription from Doctor Charre?"

In spite of me, in spite of my resolution to show Ange the most perfect tenderness and indulgence, a cold fury corrodes my words, because I can't forget what I learned from Noget, and I look at the suffering face of the man I so loved, who was a part of me (but evidently the most secretive part, the most deceitful, the least honest?), and I picture that same face looking down at my granddaughter, the child they named Souhar, and then smiling at my son, smiling at that woman I've never met, and then, at bedtime, settling onto the pillow so near my own face, displaying the same utter transparency I still see in him now, even as I know he's been telling me lies.

Can I really trust Noget? He couldn't have made up anything that precise, I tell myself.

My only hope is that Ange had reasons both innocent and legitimate for lying to me, the same purity of soul that we had even as we treated our neighbor with such disregard. That's my only hope, I tell myself, if I want to go on trusting in Ange—that he betrayed me out of an excess of compassion, an excess of sincerity.

"He doesn't need a prescription to get what he wants," Ange answers crossly. "Do you realize he knows all about my ideas on education?"

"I think I remember his claiming to, yes," I say.

"Almost word for word, he recited my latest article, on the importance of self-denial," says Ange, perking up a little. "He agrees with me.... A good teacher must have...a vocation for sacrifice; as he teaches he must continually remind himself that he could have...done something else, and what that something else is varies from person to person, but it must seem to him preferable in every way.... And yet he casts it aside so he can teach... He's stifled his other ambitions, his true desire, for that task...a task far finer than any other. He's given himself entirely...to the school. Noget... Noget shares my opinions, you know."

I don't answer, I look away, my lips slightly pursed, because I've always found Ange's ideas on education faintly distasteful, vaguely repellent.

I force my voice to sound lively and bright.

"I saw Lanton this morning, he said to tell you hello."

"I very much doubt that," Ange scoffs. "He called just now. Noget gave me the phone, and...let me tell you...your dear Lanton seemed none too friendly to me."

I almost shriek, "What did he want?"

"Something about a letter you're supposed to give your son."

"Yes?"

"Oh, I…I don't know much about it."

Ange closes his eyes, looking drained.

"If you don't give him that letter, I'll be the one Lanton takes it out on."

"But how?" I say, desperate. "What will he do? He doesn't have the right."

"Of course not, he has no right to threaten an upstanding citizen just because he wants something or other from that citizen's wife and stepson. Oh, of course…he has no right to do such a thing."

Ange has fallen back into that mocking tone I can't get used to. He's wishing I'd let him go on about the school and those who serve it, wishing I'd sincerely delight in the knowledge that Noget admires and shares his ideas, wishing I was less flagrantly dubious of his crackpot theories.

But soon I'll be going away, very likely for a long time, so I give Ange's cheek a caress, and this gesture reminds me of a thousand others, fervidly loving, that Ange and I gave each other over those many years, effusions untouched by any trace of calculation.

Our youth was already behind us when we first met, but we loved each other, I tell myself, with an adolescent freshness of sentiment. There were no secret misgivings in the life we lived together; our enchantment was never sullied by memories and grievances, by recent hurts and past humiliations. I overlooked Ange's tedious doctrines on the subject of our profession, and he never asked my opinion, so it was just as if he'd never proclaimed any such thing.

But now that this man has discussed those ideas with him, flattered him, Ange has turned vain and touchy, I tell myself; he wants me to approve and rejoice. Ange has lost the ingenuous spirit I loved more than anything else. Desperately sad, I murmur, "You remember I'm leaving next week?"

"Yes," says Ange, gently squeezing my hand.

"I'll send for you as soon as I can. I'll get settled in, I'll see where things stand, and then, even if you're not quite recovered, I'll arrange to have you transported."

"Yes," says Ange, almost indifferent.

"Isn't that what you want?"

"Yes."

"And Noget, do you think we can trust him?"

"Absolutely."

I bend down over Ange, I press my mouth to his ear, even though the smell (*deeply in love, I liked to lick his ear, smell his skin, not one nook of that poor body repulsed me*) makes me gag. Urgently, I whisper, "Are you afraid of Noget?"

Ange jerks his head to one side, as far from me as he can. A grimace of pain contorts his mouth.

"Don't say such idiotic things! It's intolerable," he spits out, exasperated.

Tears come to his eyes.

"You don't get it, you don't get it at all, you're still convinced all you have to do is whisper if you don't want to be heard, you still think there's such a thing as privacy and secrecy! Nothing is…private between us anymore."

Just then the door opens and Noget appears, cradling a platter of huge, steaming croque-monsieurs.

"At least *you'll* be here with me when I die," says Ange, in the teary tone he uses with Noget. "You'll look after me, won't you, you'll look after my soul?"

"I made some of these croque-monsieurs with Emmental and the others with Comté," Noget says amiably. "As you know, Comté has more flavor, but there's something to be said for Emmental, which lets the ham come through more."

"I'm not very hungry," says Ange.

"Oh," says Noget, very severely, "you're going to eat anyway. You must."

16. So many things changing and vanishing

I haven't had my period for several months now.

I know I could blame it on stress, but I have a feeling it will never come back, that my fertile days are behind me. Given my age, it seems a safe bet. Doctor Charre could tell me for sure, but I don't dare go see him, fearing that some of Ange's suspicions might turn out to be founded, or at least that the atmosphere I'd find in his office, assuming he consented to see me, might force me to concede that Ange has good reason to be wary of him, even if he's been our doctor for years.

I've stopped going out. I keep to the apartment,

half-heartedly packing my bags. The fact is, I'm afraid I'll lose my way again out in Bordeaux, where every day the shape of things is erased by a fog as thick as the day before. *I'm afraid Bordeaux wants me lost, and next time Noget won't be there to find me.*

Not knowing how to fill the time, I stare at myself in the mirror, trying to make out who that woman might be, that woman who seems to be me, but whose image I can't quite reconcile with my sense of myself. Not that I think I'm more alluring than my reflection. It's not a question of beauty or charm or youth. It's just that my lazy mind never adjusted to the changes taking place in my body, never registered the thick veins slowly rising up from deep inside my fat or muscle to just beneath my skin's surface, never took note of the humble dull-brown excrescences, like tiny petals of flesh, sprouting under my arms and between my breasts, whose nipples are now more rumpled and grainy than they used to be; my lofty mind never deigned to acknowledge that the jiggling flesh on my arms and thighs will now jiggle like that for all time, just as I've now been excused for all time from the modest chore of containing my menstrual blood. Oh, none of these metamorphoses matter that much to me. I look at my naked body as it little by little takes on the thousand attributes of decline; I order my mind to see and remember the details of that dereliction, but I feel myself dismissing that sad, insignificant body, I feel a secret admiration for my mind's arrogant unwillingness to dwell on my body's banal changes.

I feel as if those two, my body and my mind, are two children of mine, and one bores and disappoints me, and the other makes me proud. *Isn't that just what I used to feel about the two very different young men who were my son and his lover Lanton? Didn't I discreetly prefer Lanton's company to my son's, and of those two, wasn't it Lanton I couldn't imagine never seeing again?*

A call to my bank confirms that Ange and I are still being paid, even though we haven't gone back to the school. Either the principal never reported our unexcused absence to the ministry, I tell myself, or they're trying to say that this is exactly what they want from us: they want us to stay well away, because our isolation or disappearance is worth far more to them than the money we're costing them.

Then, two days before I'm scheduled to leave, Noget comes up from the lobby with a letter. He says: "Your son's written you."

"How indiscreet you are, and how rude!"

I brusquely stand up from the table where I was eating what Noget calls "breakfast," in English: a bounteous array of goose rillettes, ham, thick slices of buttered bread, and little sugared brioches, all washed down with milky coffee. I snatch the letter from his hand and scurry to the shelter of the study, feeling myself waddle, feeling the blubbery jiggle of my hips beneath my nightgown.

I sit down on the bed. I stare at the envelope for some time before I can even think of opening it. It's been so long since he wrote me!

The stamp shows a chalk cliff plunging into the Mediterranean. My son's handwriting is still careful and clear, with pretty curls on the capitals, just as I taught him twenty-five years ago. This immediately fills me with pride. *What if he asks me or orders me not to come?*

I stand up and pace around the room, clutching the envelope to my breast, begging the letter to be kind. My emotion is so deep that my breakfast of charcuterie surges up in my throat. I stand still. The apartment is perfectly silent, as is the whole building. Outside the window, as always now, the thick fog with its sweet scent of silt.

> Dear Mama, my dear little mama, what will you think of that beginning? I imagine you reading those first words and feeling a sort of shock at that unexpected pleasure, your son Ralph addressing you with every sign of affection when there's no reason you should feel any affection at all from poor Ralph, as you well know, and so I imagine you on the verge of tears and pleased deep inside to find that the love of a son always wins out in the end, that duty always wins out, that the mother always wins out! You know how to cry, even if your real eye stays dry, by which I mean the eye you never show. All the same, you know how to cry like any normal person. My dear mama, let me get to the point. First of all, I forbid you to rebuke or criticize me in any way. You're raising an eyebrow, pretending not to understand what I mean. You understand perfectly well. Even when you're not saying a word, you're questioning, judging, accusing. That I will no longer accept. I will accept it no longer because I am a man. But are you capable of grasping

that incontrovertible fact? Second, you must accept that changes can take place independent of your will or knowledge. In a general sense, I can't live in this world. You never knew that, did you? People like you can imagine only what they themselves feel, nothing else exists. I look around me and I see two houses and a tree and a sheet-metal hut and one single cloud against the blue sky. That's all I see. I tell myself that my dog, here beside me, might see other elements of this reality, or elements of a different reality, parallel to this one, that I can't even imagine. That's how you are: nothing can be real except what you see. But I'm still stuck in argumentation and recrimination, and that's not what I wanted. All I have to do is say things to you and I find myself dragged into the realm of combat and conflict, which I've come to hate more than anything. That I will no longer accept. I can't live in this world, as I told you. But I've grown used to it. I find a certain pleasure in my new existence. I like my work. I'm a new man. Just this morning I delivered a woman, and the baby was stillborn, which isn't a bad thing, since in that woman's arms the child's life would quickly and inevitably have become a living hell: she's an alcoholic, half numb to the world, unreachable. I looked after her well. I comforted her. I filled out all sorts of papers on her behalf. As you see,

I am a determined man. So you were driven out of your school? Now you understand that, even for you, school was not a safe haven. Do you understand that? Your beloved school! How you must have suffered! For a long time I was jealous of your school and your students, but won't you be jealous of my patients? I believe I've forgiven you everything, because I am a new man. For that I owe a great debt to Wilma. It matters little to me or to her if you like Wilma or not, it's not at all certain you'll be taken with Wilma as you were with Lanton, so taken it made me jealous and angry. Wilma will be less your type. Who knows? Maybe you'll even fall in love with my dear Wilma, and I won't be able to compete, and I'll have to pack my bags! I'm joking, you understand. I am a NEW MAN. I have a whole long list of grievances against you. I've decided to keep them to myself, I don't want my grievances dragging me down. Nonetheless, when I think you were planning to show up here unannounced, I feel rage gnawing away at me little by little. For goodness' sake, why can't you be sincere and straightforward with me? My father is sincere and straightforward, and I think I'm a man who inspires people to treat him in that same way, a NEW MAN. But you? I'm stating my case, I'm doing my best to convince you, and all the while I know there's no point. Among all the other aspects of my new—and, I hope, I hope, definitive—personality, there is kindness. I've become kind. And so I will be happy to welcome you, dear Mama, like the KIND NEW MAN I am. As a doctor, I see abominations every day. As a man, as the man I am now, I transfigure that ugliness, and so come almost to love it, and then I forget it. That's my process. The woman this morning, the one I helped bring the dead child into the world, deserves to be called a Madonna every bit as much as the one true Madonna, of whom we actually know nothing, isn't that so? Can you guarantee that the Virgin Mary wasn't a drunk? You can't! I love everyone around me, I love the poor human race. It wouldn't be right to envelop the whole world in my love and compassion and not include you, Mama, and so I envelop you in my love and my pity. I'll see you soon, then. I can't yet pull the thorn of resentment from my heart—my heart isn't perfect, and that thorn has been there for so long—but we'll see. Incidentally, you absolutely must repay my father the money you took from him. He needs it more than you do, the poor man. You probably don't know it, but he's in deep financial trouble, if not outright broke. You robbed him blind. You have to repay him. They drove you out of school, fine. But for what? I can't get a clear picture from here. Was it undeserved?

> Isn't there anything you did wrong? It seems a little much to claim that they fired you for no reason. I'm counting on you to explain all this. Think of my father, try to be ashamed: he's destitute!
>
> Your son, Ralph

Anger submerges me in a cold numbness.

I reread the letter, that dishonest, underhanded letter written to me by my own son, my only child—how did he ever come to this? To these heights of mendacity, of grotesque lyricism? Oh, I say to myself, my son's become a mystic, how could it be that in the very prime of his life he turned into exactly the kind of person I, his own mother, most loathe, by what subtle intuition, what mysterious perceptiveness did he understand me so well that he could remake himself as a mystic, knowing my deep loathing for that turn of mind, that posturing, self-important approach to life? And then there's this Wilma—who is he talking about?

I hurry out of the study and into the bedroom. I shake Ange from his open-mouthed slumber. He wakes with a start, reflexively covering his wasted face with his forearm as if to fend off a blow. *This is just how Ange's students used to defend themselves, much to Ange's irritation, when on occasion he tried to give them a smack in the face—no, not a smack, just a swat, nothing more—but the students in question were hard kids, long used to being hit and practiced in the art of warding off blows with their skinny arms, their bony elbows, and so it was on those arms or those elbows that Ange's hand landed, sometimes painfully, which only fueled his rage and led him to strike all the harder, to avenge himself on that insolent limb. Afterward, he was always sorry he'd lost his temper, he thought he'd let himself down. He strove to incarnate pedagogical perfection, and he saw any trace of violence as a personal failing.*

All trace of fleshiness is gone from Ange's face. I can distinctly see the outline of his bones beneath the skin on his cheeks, his jaw.

Is someone here mistreating Ange?

In urgent agitation, I ask, "What's my son's wife's name again?"

"Your son's wife?"

His gaze darts nervously around the room, and it's true that I've just wrenched him awake, but he still gives me the troubling sense that he's stalling for time.

I give him a severe stare.

"What's Ralph's wife's name, Ange? My granddaughter's mother?"

"You don't remember?" he mumbles.

Then, after a few minutes' silence, pretending, I'm sure, to search through his memories: "Yasmine."

"Yes, that's right," I say, troubled, "her name is Yasmine."

"So why ask, if you already know?"

Ange's eyes seem slightly shifty. This daily accumulation of suspicions, silences, and irksome questions, when it's always been not our rule but our way to hide nothing, to tell each other everything about everything, this mounting pile of hard, hurtful secrets makes me deeply sad. Never, I tell myself, whatever happens, never will we be able to claw our way out of such a deep pit of mistrust and ignoble suppositions.

Noget knees open the door and comes in. Along with the jar of rillettes (his mother raises poultry in the Landes, he says; she makes these superb rillettes herself, he says, jam-packed with long, melting fibers of goose flesh) and the inevitable Bayonne ham, I see a steaming little bowl filled with something gelatinous and orange-tinged, whose powerful odor nonetheless makes me immediately secrete the yearning saliva I'm now slightly ashamed of. Ange turns his head away in apparent disgust. *He can't smell the stench of his own infection, but he's repelled by the aroma of fine food!*

Noget quickly explains that he's brought us a bowl of *tripoux*, a typical dish of the Auvergne, made with tripe, sheep's feet, and calf's ruffle.

"Not from my own kitchen," he says, apologetically.

All of a sudden I remember my period has stopped. Lost in that thought, I distractedly lay my hand on my stomach.

"You're not pregnant, are you?" Noget asks.

"No! Far from it."

My forehead is hot and damp with a sort of radiant happiness, an intense relief. I realize that the end of my period is the first normal thing that's happened in months, the only one I can explain rationally, without having to weigh a whole range of hypotheses.

As Noget goes on looking at me, scrutinizing me, the tray still in his hands, I tell him, "I'm the right age for menopause, you know."

"You must be mistaken," Noget says quietly, after a pause.

He adds, "Your son is a doctor, he'll tell you what's going on."

And once again rage washes over me.

I storm out, leaving Noget to feed Ange (*are you sure you're not making this fuss simply to spare yourself that sight, Ange mutely begging to be left in peace and Noget filling his dry-lipped mouth with that heavy, questionable food?*), quickly get dressed, and leave the apartment with my son's letter crumpled in my cardigan pocket. My sweater is so tight around my waist and breasts that I can't fasten the buttons.

I rush out the front door, unthinking, gravely oppressed by indignation and the sense of a terrible injustice.

17. In the clutches of Rue Fondaudège

I scurry along to Rue Fondaudège. I can't help muttering to myself, half aloud. My fury won't stay bottled up in my skull.

The fog is still there, as it is every day, and I've come to think it will never lift again, that it's become a part of Bordeaux's character, its very essence, that this fog is the city's breath, in a sense, as if, I tell myself, some deep-seated, stubborn, perhaps incurable illness were rotting my beloved city's entrails, and that's why its breath has become so unwholesome.

There's no danger if I follow Fondaudège, I tell myself through my gritted teeth, I can always turn around and go on till I cross Place de Tourny, and then I'll be back on

Rue Esprit-des-Lois.... But, oh, how dare he, how can he be so...so brazen, he who was always so...timid, so polite. How can he...imply I'm a thief, his own mother...and a thief who can't be reasoned with, who refuses to talk things through...to understand, when I've spent my entire adult life trying to understand others...my son most of all... And then this talk of that stranger, that Wilma, and the insinuation that I was in love with Lanton... What a despicable joke, how idiotic! Like saying I'd fallen in love with my own son, yes, that would be every bit as stupid and offensive. And yet he's willing to let me come see him, out of the goodness of his heart; he's on his way to full-fledged sainthood, apparently... What a joke! So my son is a pure soul, but not a word about the baby, about...Souhar; what does it mean, this silence about my granddaughter, as if there'd never been a baby at all, or she can't be spoken of anymore—but to protect whom? to protect what? Or maybe I'm not worthy of being told about my own granddaughter? Is there some danger of befouling the baby, or of bringing misery down on her fragile newborn head, that would come with simply writing her name in a letter to Grandmamma Nadia?

I stalk down the street, furiously stretching my cardigan over my stomach. Soon I'm gasping for breath, unused as I am to exercise, but I keep walking down the interminable, unchanging Rue Fondaudège, not wanting to go home until I've walked off my agitation. Eventually I look at my watch and find I've been walking for almost an hour. A fear comes over me. Fondaudège is a very long street, but not so long that I can briskly follow it for an hour without it making a turn and taking on a new name. As I recall, Fondaudège becomes Rue Croix-de-Seguey; it stops being Fondaudège after maybe a little less than a mile. And yet here I am still walking down Rue Fondaudège, not as fast as before, wondering if I've already come too far from home.

The cafés and shops have all disappeared. There's nothing but modest houses, soot-stained apartment buildings. I'm not going to turn around, I resolutely tell myself, until I reach the end of the street. Bordeaux is my town, and haven't I walked this Rue Fondaudège hundreds of times since I was a child?

I can feel my rage at my son (*"my little heart," I so long called him, and now here he is forsaking his mother's old heart*) waning as my anxiety swells, because this street is very visibly not coming to an end. I feel I've gone too far to simply turn back, because that would be showing an ominous acceptance of this aberration, granting that Rue Fondaudège is no longer the Fondaudège I've always known, which is impossible, which simply cannot be possible.

Once I've carefully studied her face, I ask a woman coming toward me, "Excuse me, what's the name of this street, please?"

"Fondaudège," she shrugs, pointing to the sign above our heads on the wall. "Rue Fondaudège."

"And how long before I reach the end of it?"

"It's a very long street, you know," the woman says as she walks away.

With tiny, cautious steps, I keep going.

The street has begun to feel familiar—tiny storefronts with graying plaster, long-closed repair shops, doctors' and dentists' offices with dusty windows and dingy curtains—

though I don't recognize anything in particular, as is so often the case in my city nowadays, now that the fog has settled in, but all at once I stop short, or rather I realize my feet have stopped short, at an apartment building half masked by scaffolding, in mid-renovation. My throat tightens in foreboding.

Oh, yes, I reluctantly tell myself, that's right, it was here.

And although I don't want to, I push open the door, which puts up the same resistance it always did, and I automatically brace myself and lean forward to force it open wider, just as I've done hundreds and hundreds of times, because I lived here for many years with my ex-husband, before I met Ange. What mystifies me is that we lived at the very start of Rue Fondaudège, not an hour's walk down the street. Or, I ask myself, does it merely seem farther because I've grown older? No, that's no explanation, I've been walking at a very good clip.

Why has my period stopped?

My mood has turned sullen and sour. I can't help feeling that, for bad reasons and in an act of covert blackmail, my son is forcing me to do something I don't want to do, something there is in fact no reason why I should do. And I have no obligation to obey my son in this or in anything else.

And yet here I am on the stairs I've climbed so many times, clutching the sticky banister—here I am slightly breathless at the door to what was once my apartment, and if I say "was once," it's because I don't live here anymore, but for the sake of the truth and my own sense of dignity I must make it clear that I still own this apartment on Rue Fondaudège. In the divorce settlement, my lawyer (*he came to the little party I threw to welcome Souhar's birth, and then, as if by some deliberate choice, we never spoke again, even though we'd become almost friends, and come to think of it haven't all that evening's guests inexplicably disappeared from our life, from the building, the street?*) managed to have me awarded full ownership of the apartment my ex-husband and I bought together, yes, it's true, it's true. I've been renting it to my son's father, for a modest sum, ever since.

What you don't know, I'd like to shriek at my son, is that your father hasn't paid his rent in months, and I haven't asked him and I never will, over Ange's objections, Ange who thinks your father is taking advantage of me, but I don't care that that man might be cheating me, I don't care, precisely because he's your father and my ex-husband and I once loved him boundlessly.

The little brass plate that announced that my ex-husband was an electrician is now gone from beneath the buzzer, I see.

He had a good reputation, he had to turn away customers, he worked for people with big houses in the Bourse and Grand-Théâtre neighborhoods. Is it my fault if that smart, capable, highly sought-after man couldn't endure the sorrow of our separation or get over the upheaval of the divorce? That was the problem, I wish I could tell my son; it was his weakness of character, his excessive attachment to the status quo, that was what set off his decline, that and nothing else. Not, as you insinuate, because I'd reduced him to poverty, and it's true that I did well by the settlement, but there was plenty of money left over for him to lead a perfectly fine life, if only he hadn't chosen the path of self-pity, defeat, and disinterest.

There's no reason why I should be here, I tell myself, deeply angry.

He'll help me escape from Fondaudège before it saps my last ounce of strength or suddenly coils around me and chokes the life out of me; I'll never get away on my own, now it's Fondaudège's turn to wreak its vengeance for whatever it is I've done!

I summon my courage and press the buzzer, just as I used to do when I came home late from school, for the pleasure of hearing my little heart's feet slapping the floor. He would undo the latch, leap into my arms, and nestle against me, even though he was already a big boy by then. My son must have tried hard to forget that, and yet, I tell myself, almost triumphant, his soul today is built on the unbridled love he felt for me back then, which kept him clasped to my breast for so long that I had to detach him, gently push him aside so I could come in—the soul he has today, so cold to me, is made of that too!

That was what I loved about Lanton, my son's lover. He wasn't ashamed to hold me in his arms for many long minutes when I went to see him in his office at the police station, he felt no need to hide his deep fondness—that was what I so loved about Lanton, the innocence of his displays of affection.

Was that childish of him, was it sappy? Was it ridiculous? How stiff my son seemed next to him, how preposterously sarcastic and distant.

A second press of the buzzer, and, just when I'm about

to be off, at once relieved to have been spared a meeting with my ex-husband and dreading the thought of going back to my struggles with Rue Fondaudège, the door cracks open.

"What is it?" he anxiously whispers.

"Don't be afraid, it's only me," I say, showing my face through the opening to reassure him.

He recoils, as if he's seen some terrifying apparition.

"What do you want from me now?"

His voice is hoarse and unsteady, but even now, even ravaged by anxiety and disillusion, it vibrates in my ear in an intimate, familiar way, immediately calling to mind all the many times it spoke to me sweetly and freely. Although I have no wish to revisit the site of the life we lived together, us and our son, I hear myself asking, "Can I come in for a minute?"

Weren't those the best years of my life? All three of us together on Rue Fondaudège? My ex-husband grudgingly opens the door all the way and lets me into what is in reality my own apartment.

18. What we did to him

He guides me down the street, holding my wrist, not to keep me from fleeing, I think, nor for a chance to be close to me, but perhaps simply to protect me on this street that's gone to such lengths to lead me astray, even if, I tell myself, on a street with no tram line I'm already at far less risk of an intentional accident.

I'm thinking of asking him if, as someone who rides it, he's noticed the dark designs the tram has on certain people's lives. I don't. Why should I be confiding in him, why should I trust my ex-husband, a trust he would soon betray? *Because I long for just that with all my being, because I so wish I could go back to those Fondaudège days, when neither of us could even imagine being wronged by the other, so much so that when I started lying to my ex-husband about Ange, I didn't even realize I was lying, unconsciously convinced that I was incapable of duplicity, every bit as incapable as he was.*

We walk through the cold, damp air, the persistent smell of silt that fills the city. My ex-husband lets out a surprised little laugh.

"Really," he says, "I don't see how you could have gotten lost. Look, here we are at the Place de Tourny, nothing's changed."

"That's because you're here with me," I tell him, not backing down. "The geography only changes when I'm alone. It's perfectly logical, don't you see, if the point is to give me a sign. But it's a sign I don't know how to decipher."

He coughs quietly, faintly uncomfortable. He's not in good health, and I feel bad for him.

"Are you just going to keep getting fatter and fatter?" he suddenly asks.

"Really, now, that's none of your business," I say, offended. "I imagine the food will be healthier at our son's."

Eager to put a stop to any further discussion of my weight, I quickly add, "I've stopped getting my period; it's menopause coming on."

"Are you sure?"

"Of course I am," I shoot back.

"It could be something else," my ex-husband says with a frown.

Just then, as we stood stopped by the fountain on the Place de Tourny, under the mist-shrouded bare branches of the linden trees, I spy Noget walking toward us. My ex-husband has seen him too.

"That's Richard Victor Noget!" he says, amazed.

"You know him?"

He gives me an incredulous look.

"Don't you?"

"I do now, now that he comes to our apartment every day," I say softly, "now that he makes all our meals and looks after Ange like some sweet-talking jailer hovering over his prisoner. I'd never heard of him until he wormed his way into our life."

I don't dare confess to my ex-husband that when things were going fine for Ange and me we looked on our neighbor Noget with horror and contempt. I don't dare reveal such a thing, foreseeing his skepticism, and then his dismay, because the timid stare he's giving Noget overflows with respect.

Irritated, I ask him, "And how have you heard of this Noget?"

"Well, I don't know! Hasn't everyone? I think he's written some books."

"Then how is it I've never heard his name in my life, and why didn't I know the first thing about him until he essentially moved in with us?"

My ex-husband turns to look at me. His gaze seems to

turn away inside of him, to veil itself with a cloud of caution, uncertainty, or reticence, which brings a pang to my heart, because I know that look well. This man I so loved, now older and frailer, often hid behind a gaze grown suddenly opaque to tell me without having to say it that some question I'd asked was misplaced, or ridiculous, or foolish, and was in any case outside his sphere, and he didn't even want to try to answer.

Nonetheless, he whispers, "The trouble with you is you only know what you want to know."

"But it's not as if I somehow went out of my way not to hear about this Noget," I said. "I mean, really, it's not my fault if my eye never happened to land on his name. Has he been on television?"

"Of course he has," says my ex-husband, with a tinge of impatience.

"We don't have a television," I say.

"There's your problem," says my ex-husband.

"Well, too bad," I say.

I trail off, perfectly aware that I'm being unreasonable. We fall silent, standing motionless, side-by-side (two separate, isolated halves of a single heart that was once enough for the two of us, now we've atrophied, both of us lost and alone, resentment and guilt the only feeble bonds we have left) until Noget saunters over to join us.

With a servility that sets my teeth on edge, my ex-husband gives a little bow.

"I'm so proud...so happy...to meet you," he mumbles. "I'm Nadia's ex-husband."

"A pleasure," says Noget, very warmly. "I was coming to

look for you," he says to me, "in case you were having trouble finding your way. But I see you have a guide already."

The two of them chuckle, my ex-husband obsequiously, Noget derisively. I give the former a quick nod, then walk away without awaiting the latter.

Rue Esprit-des-Lois is in front of me, at the end of the Allées de Tourny, I can clearly see the sign of the hair salon that marks its beginning. Why, then, do I have the feeling, as impossible to ignore as a siren, that in a moment the street is going to slip away in front of me? That if I start down it alone, on my own authority, with no one leading me, then the street will know it and take steps to escape the grip of my certainty, perhaps fade away or contort or, like the infernal Fondaudège, grow endlessly longer and longer until I've been literally erased?

I race toward the street, hoping to catch it off guard. I hurry along, head high, eyes fixed on a distant point as if to limit the risk of exposure to my incomprehensibly (because I so love my city) fickle surroundings. And even as I trot along, falsely confident, feigning innocence, doing my best to go unnoticed by the street itself, I can feel the weight of the flesh squeezed into my cardigan, I can hear the clomp of my heavy footfalls. I smile a little, thinking: Look at you, butterball, trying to cleave the air like a well-honed blade!

And I think of my ex-husband still living in the apartment that used to be ours, that's now legally mine alone, though it gives me no pleasure or sincere sense of triumph, because a thing can be legal and still be unjust, and in this one case I can't blind myself so entirely as to enjoy being right. I genuinely can't, I tell myself, ever so slightly proud of my integrity.

To tell the truth, until my legs took me to that building I used to live in, I'd forgotten I still owned my ex-husband's apartment, unless I'd deliberately banished that thought to some unvisited little corner of my memory. And whenever the pragmatic Ange tried to remind me the rent checks weren't coming, I always hurried to answer, "Don't even get me started!"—pretending to be so outraged at my ex-husband that I feared I might lose all control if Ange forced me to deal with it, when in fact all I wanted was not to think about it, out of remorse, or pity, or who knows.

And I think of my ex-husband still living in the apartment where, I like to believe, we spent the most harmonious years of our lives—him, our son Ralph, and me—and I murmur to Ralph, whose letter I'm fingering deep in my pocket: Would you ever dare say you weren't happy on Rue Fondaudège, and happy in the most uncomplicated way? Must you really now play the aggrieved, ungrateful son, drunk on recriminations? I was an ordinary mother, reasonably conscientious, respectably affectionate, so why do you insist on forcing me into the role of an implacable enemy, and you the valiant foe battling with her year after year, aiming not to annihilate me or expel me from your life, but simply, oh, this is how it feels, simply to flaunt your struggles, to hold up your heroism for all to see? I suppose it makes you happy to imply that your mother is such a terrible person. But what did I do that was so awful? Or that can't at least, after so many years, be forgotten? The possibility that my son still resents my leaving his father for Ange makes my blood boil.

And I think of my ex-husband still living in the

apartment where, less than an hour ago, I found myself for the first time since I left him, sitting across from him in that living room now drenched in the atmosphere—his atmosphere—I so strove to eliminate or minimize when we lived together, which cannot be more clearly defined than by the words "provincial" and "proletarian." Yes, I come from Bordeaux, I've never lived in Paris. Why should I look down on the provinces? That's all I know, and it's everything I love. But more than anything on earth I despise a certain kind of stodgy inertia, a staleness in the air, an obliviousness to new trends in interior design, and even ten-year-old trends, a clutter of pretentious gewgaws, idiotic furniture, a sickly mishmash of styles from all over the world, and those were my ex-husband's tastes and habits exactly, which not untactfully I'd managed to banish from our married existence, and now I find them again in this apartment that used to be ours, as if when I left I'd unwittingly taken with me all the subtle transformations my influence had worked on my ex-husband's personality, his upbringing, his ways.

I find that dreariness reigning over the place once again (thick drapes pulled tight over the windows, wooden chairs with flat cushions that tie to the uprights, a smoked-glass coffee table on a Chinese-style rug, Berber poufs, etc.), where it never dared show its face, intimidated by my intransigence, back when I lived there with my ex-husband.

How well I know those ways, those aspirations! No matter how I hate them, they still have the power to move me when they catch me off guard, which is why, just now in my ex-husband's charmless living room, I was left mute by depression no less than by the irksome realization that his upbringing had ended up winning out over everything I'd taught him.

You know, I had the same upbringing you did, I often told my ex-husband back then, in hopes of persuading him that it's never too late to clamber out of the abyss of ignorance and bad taste, as, to my mind, I had.

I never let him meet my brothers and sisters, or anyone else from my family. You wouldn't like them, I said. But what I actually feared was the opposite: that he'd find them entirely likable, because they are, I believe. I feared that their pleasantly soothing company might reinforce my ex-husband's commonplace tendencies, I feared that any time spent with those unrefined people might undo all the work I'd expended to elevate my ex-husband's heart, *his devoted but unformed heart, his rudimentary heart*, and that deep in his childlike self he might see my connection to that family as a good reason to align his tastes with theirs.

My ex-husband was a simple, open-hearted soul. He never did quite grasp the cold hatred I felt for the environment I'd pulled myself out of, he never could clearly imagine such a thing, because he knew full well that in any case I'd grown up surrounded by thoughtfulness and benevolence.

Resenting parents who treated you perfectly well but whose lifestyle you hate: that he could not understand. My refusal to go anywhere near Les Aubiers, where I lived as a child, to go anywhere near those streets lined with crumbling sidewalks and public housing developments: that too he could not understand. Yes, for all my efforts, my ex-husband remained a simple soul.

And what can I do about that? I say to myself, half

aloud, still fulminating at my son. Was I supposed to not mind his dismissiveness toward my work, like someone who sees teaching as nothing more than an agreeable pastime to fill up the long, empty days? Was I supposed to not mind that he spent every Sunday watching television, insisting that I sit beside him so he wouldn't be alone, so he wouldn't be laughing all alone at the comedies he so loved that he pouted and sulked when he saw that my lips never broke into a smile, that they remained tightly closed, pinched with disdain for those endless inanities?

Ange and I never watch television, I mentally tell my son. Are we supposed to be ashamed of that, are we supposed to be ashamed that we're even a little proud of it? Really, my darling, really, my little heart, I don't see why we should.

Now I'm walking more confidently, I recognize every house I see from the corner of my eye, every shop I pass by.

Most importantly, I see them more or less when and where I know I should. Nothing has changed.

My fingers feel the corners of my checkbook in my other cardigan pocket. Yes, I half say for my son's ears, as you see, I wrote your father a check, but I wasn't happy to be doing it, I was put out, because I'm appalled by your emotional blackmail, and I have no reason to be giving money to that man, who owes me more with every month that goes by.

What I don't admit to my son, not even in my thoughts, is that I'm finding it harder and harder to part with my money, even though I'm no longer young, even now that I'm richer than ever before. It's got nothing to do with my ex-husband specifically. Besides, didn't I take him for everything he had? I did, I did, I tell myself, with a tense little giggle, what's the use of denying it now? That divorce settlement was a swindle, for my benefit alone. I'm slowly turning into a miser, I tell myself. *Is it Ange's influence? Can every change of character be explained by someone else's influence?* Oh, it's such a hard thing to quell deep inside, *in a petty old heart*, that abhorrence of any dent made in the glittering treasure, however short-lived and miniscule, that ridiculous disheartenment at the thought that every fresh influx of money serves not to pile the gold ever higher but only to counteract the expenditures, that anxious little breathlessness I've begun to feel, and to recognize, when I have to decide for or against a purchase, and then the flood of warm pleasure radiating all through my body when I find some pretext to dodge or defer it.

In that way too, Ange and I are alike. *Or did you think you had to become just like him?* Ange only buys what he can't avoid buying, and only after labyrinthine mental calculations, the need for that purchase vying with the deep joy he'd feel at forgoing it.

It's the same thing with me. Ange and I understand each other so well. Because, although we never say so out loud, we both feel the same bliss at sacrificing a superficial, ephemeral pleasure for the kind of deep, lasting satisfaction that comes over us when we imagine our pile of riches. There's real happiness to be found in doing without, I tell myself as I finally reach the front door of our building, when nothing is forcing you into it, when you do it purely by choice. I remember the two of us sometimes gripped by a sort of euphoria when, after we'd gone back and forth over something pretty to wear, a book for Gladys or Priscilla, a belt for my son—or, more often Lanton—we walked out of a shop with empty hands and full pockets, and of course how could I ever confess without blushing that at such moments we felt like the masters of the city, so perfectly in control of our longings, our reflexes, our whims that we could find in their very frustration a delight more meaningful than we ever could from their fulfillment?

All that is the absolute truth. And so, I say to myself, my angry mind still on my son, it was painful, writing that check for my ex-husband, more painful than someone who's never known avarice could possibly imagine. He didn't want to take it at first.

"It's all right, I don't need your money," he mumbled, unconvincingly.

The apartment reeked of privation, of joyless renunciation. He himself, my ex-husband, had lost a great deal of weight. He told me he was thinking of trying to make a fresh start in Spain. His hand lunged for the check, as if he'd suddenly changed his mind. He took it without thanking me, and defensively muttered, "Still, this will help me get back on my feet."

Finding my check snatched away just as, with some relief, I was about to stuff it back into my pocket, I felt like I'd been robbed. I furiously looked around at the yellow walls, the cheap blond-wood furniture.

My ex-husband hadn't lost his lush hair, now gray, but still curly and silky. I pictured myself back then combing his hair with my fingers, tugging at the tangles to hear him complain, laughing—that was this very same head, these same curls, light chestnut at the time, it was this same broad, full-lipped mouth, which, I must concede, never spoke a word untouched by a kindness without affectation or self-awareness. Yes, yes, my ex-husband was the best person I'd ever come across back then. I loved to give him things, all sorts of things, all kinds of presents meant to make up for the vast difference between my kindly husband and myself, because even before I met Ange, when I still had a mind without secrets, a heart without guilt, I felt innately less honorable, less transparent than my ex-husband, as if I knew I'd betray him before I had any reason to consider doing so, as if my more knowing heart had foreseen that it was the fate of that kindly, simple soul to be mistreated, to be plunged into despair and disgust, as if, yes, there were nothing more burdensome and infuriating about someone we love than obliviousness to our fickle, sometimes wicked thoughts, our ambivalent feelings.

Standing there with him in his wretched living room, I said to myself: It made you so happy to buy him all the things he loved, and now here you are put out that he ended up taking the minuscule sum you're so grudgingly offering him.

I was almost faint with shame. However disillusioned, untrusting, and hardened he'd grown, my ex-husband hadn't seen my reluctance, hadn't guessed the ugliness of my offering.

Because isn't it a ridiculously small amount, chosen precisely so I won't feel the loss, so it will be just like I'd never given him anything at all?

I pictured myself as I used to be, here in this same living

room, which was cheery and elegant at the time; I pictured myself dazed as I am now, not by shame or remorse but by joy, by a fascinated disbelief at my tremendous luck at having this man I so loved as my husband, and as my son that charming little boy whose eyes, raised to mine, fluttered with terror at the mere thought that I might leave the room without his knowing it.

And that man was kindly and good and that child desperately in love with his mother, and my ex-husband's handsomeness, like in the fairy tales I read our son, seemed to have been bestowed on him as an illustration of that kindness, a visible translation of the exceptional goodness he had in him and didn't even know it. A little shard of unhappiness sometimes lodged in my young, slightly oppressed, questioning, timid heart when after an absence I rediscovered my ex-husband's beauty. It literally shocked me, and I went to him in a fog of pain that must have made me seem cold and stiff.

My ex-husband had no interest in his own physical splendor, and no idea of it. He's so unsophisticated he doesn't even see it, I sometimes said to myself, shaken. But I knew that wasn't true. Along with the gifts that had been granted my ex-husband, he'd been given an inability to judge them, as if to make them more wonderful still.

What's left of all that now? I asked myself, sitting with him in his tacky living room. What's left of that love, that long, loving alliance, all the things we said to each other, which could only mean, if they ever meant anything at all, that we're still bound together to this day?

And the passionate love my son felt for me, what's left of that?

I didn't realize it at the time, I told myself, but Ange's shadow was already very discreetly darkening this room where the three of us used to sit, happy and serene, it was already there, lurking in a corner, remaking our future, because, though I surely didn't realize it at the time, my heart was beating at a slight remove from the two others, imperceptibly less innocent, less constant, less convinced.

Today my ex-husband is a hard, scruffy man. His good looks were taken away from him, it seems, when his kindness turned into sneering mistrust and blind belligerence. Meanwhile, I… Oh, I tell myself, I've turned out just fine. Unlike him, I've lost nothing, since I'm now married to the one man who's like me in every way. *I'm happy, I'm happy, I'm happy.*

As a sour silence began to fall over us, I asked my ex-husband, "Did you stop working by choice, or…"

"Or what?"

"Or was it the customers who stopped calling?" I went on, squirming.

"And why would that be?" he said, with his gruff, stubborn air.

He doesn't know, I thought, shocked. He has no idea how things are—or is he pretending?

"Strange things have been happening lately," I said. "You must have noticed. I can't see why you'd be spared. Ange and I had to leave the school."

With those words, a gush of tears swamped my eyelids.

"Your problems at school are none of my concern," said my ex-husband. "I don't understand what you're talking about. You know perfectly well why I stopped working after the divorce."

My lawyer, with whom I'd become friends (he even came to the party in Souhar's honor), had told me there was something desperately sad about my ex-husband's attempts to move me or influence me by feigning depression and burgeoning alcoholism.

"You've got to let his tantrum run its course, just like you would with a child," Ange had told me.

And I'd come to think exactly the same thing, buttressed by Ange and my lawyer, both of them thoughtful and perceptive men.

"Really, you can't have been as devastated as all that," I said, forcing an arch smile. "Just because I left you?"

My ex-husband didn't answer. His eye absentmindedly landed on my (ravaged? bloated?) face, on my bust, which my slightly slumped posture must have made even broader and fatter, and I could guess at the thought, the astonishment running through his mind: Could this woman, this unrecognizable woman, really have made me suffer as I did?

Unable to hold back, I cried out, "You've changed a lot yourself!"

But he hadn't said a word, so I seemed to be lashing out for no reason. He wearily rubbed his forehead with one hand.

"No," he murmured, "I still don't understand why you left. We were happy, weren't we? But I don't care anymore. That's all over and done with, right?"

I briefly pictured the two of us sitting as we were at that moment, but in a life we'd gone on living together, simply chatting at the end of a workday, out of reach of Ange's menacing shadow, in all the clarity of our identical, melded souls. *Would misery have come down on our heads, would hatred have surrounded us on all sides, if I hadn't gone off with Ange? But how would my ex-husband have protected us? With the impregnable halo of his goodness?*

"Ange and I have the same tastes, the same opinions, and you know it," I say softly. "Didn't we invite you over more than once? We did all we could to build a friendship with you. We reached out to you, and you pushed our hands away."

I didn't add how deeply I admired Ange, at the time, for his open-mindedness in trying to welcome and console my ex-husband, who from what I could see had fallen into hatred and despair all the same. Did Ange fruitlessly strive to befriend my ex-husband in hopes of proving his depression was feigned, or at least wildly exaggerated? That was the question I suddenly asked myself, all these years later, sitting on a floral-print futon in the vulgar, dingy place our charming living room had become thanks to my ex-husband's unelevated mind and atavistic ways. Ange would have found it unbearable to sit all day in a living room furnished and decorated like this, I wished I could tell him, be irritated at him, at the overtness of his sorrow, and then add: life is more complicated than you think, oh, innocence is too easy a way out.

And yet, I said to myself, and yet... I felt a resurgence of the stifled remorse that had tainted my new life of love at the time, the vague awareness that Ange and I had, in a way, debased my ex-husband, not really meaning to—or did we? I'd dimly felt that by deceiving and hurting my ex-husband, and then trying to draw him to us, into our discreetly luxurious apartment, we had—not without a certain pleasure—defiled something that was beyond us, something that irritated us.

Which was what? A kind of saintliness? But Ange and I looked on such words with horror, and not just the words but everything they stood for.

Nonetheless, I tell myself—standing at the front door on Rue Esprit-des-Lois, unable to bring myself to push it open and go back to our apartment—nonetheless, we turned my ex-husband into a bitter, mean person, capable, for example, of quietly working to alienate our son from Lanton out of pure self-interest, out of stupidity and intolerance, because he didn't feel one way or another about Lanton. All that, I say to myself, as if the perfect kindness of someone you haven't yet wronged can only turn into mindless cruelty, spurred by resentment and disillusionment, as soon as things change. Maybe, then, my ex-husband wouldn't have turned so cruel if he hadn't been so kind, I tell myself. Doesn't that alone prove he was no saint? Because if he were, hurt or not, he would have stayed just as he was. His hurt and dishonor would in fact have made him even finer than before.

"The only reason he wanted me in his apartment was to make fun of me," said my ex-husband, speaking of Ange.

"Certainly not," I said, indignantly.

"He wanted to show you I was an idiot, with the living proof right there in front of you. He must have thought you weren't quite convinced. He would have asked me questions about all sorts of things that I wouldn't have known how to answer, and so by his standards I would have been humiliated," my ex-husband calmly went on, his voice steady, almost detached.

He said this without accusation or blame, simply as an

observation, almost unsurprised, and beneath his mask of sadness and premature age I caught a startling glimpse of the man he once was, his quietly radiant way. *And that's how he would have stayed, unchanging, if Ange and I hadn't...*

As if in a last, desperate effort, even with nothing left to win or defend, I leaned toward my ex-husband on that hideous couch, sinking my nails into my palms, and whispered, almost pleading, "But you know perfectly well that... I mean, the whole thing was that...I stopped loving you!"

He looked at his palms with a little smile, raised his head, and again I saw the man he would have been, should have been, if only we'd let him.

"So?" said my ex-husband, smiling sweetly.

Then his face suddenly jerked back to the present, closed up, shrank. He let out a sharp, manic, mindless little laugh.

"So they kicked you out of your school, huh? What on earth were you two getting up to, that it came to that? Even the worst teacher in the world usually can't get fired."

He clearly has no idea what's going on, I thought, weary and surprised at the same time. I felt just as I do when I'm faced with a hopelessly backward student: I didn't know where to start.

"Now I understand: you don't see what's happening," I said hesitantly. "You yourself, my poor friend... Who would ever want to hire you now? None of your tony downtown customers from the old days, I can tell you that. You're marked, just like Ange and me. You think you chose to banish yourself because you didn't want to be where you are, and you think you quit working because somehow that's what you wanted or because you were supposedly so depressed you didn't feel up to it anymore—you're convinced you have your own reasons, in other words, but that's not how it is at all. You're one of those people no one can stand to see in the city anymore. So are Ange and I. Oh, ask Lanton if you don't believe me. And I'll tell you another thing."

I leaned in so close that my breath grazed his face. He backed away primly, repelled and offended. *So now I disgust him? And who is he to be disgusted by me?*

"Even the city," I went on, "you'll see, try it for yourself, even the city's had enough of us. Either, I don't know how to say this, either it contracts like it's trying to expel us, or it dilates monstrously to make us lose our way, or else, and I've seen this with my own eyes, it reshapes itself so you don't even recognize it."

My ex-husband stared at me in silence, dubious and uncomfortable. I could feel myself blushing.

"Please," I said, "don't look at me like I'm crazy. Don't tell me I must be tired, don't tell me I might want to see a psychiatrist. Ask Lanton, ask Ange, you'll see."

"Hmm," he grunted.

He tried to force his face into a neutral, vaguely indifferent expression.

Thoroughly disheartened, I stood up and made for the door, very aware of my heavy, hobbled gait (my thighs slapping, my fat knees colliding, my belly compressed by the cardigan), but cold, uninterested in his opinion. My ex-husband caught up with me as I was reaching for the doorknob.

"Come see," he said, in a hungry, husky voice.

After an awkward pause, he took my arm and led me to what was once our son's bedroom. He threw open the door and stepped back, beaming with pride. Really, I say to myself as I finally open the door on Rue Esprit-des-Lois to go back to Ange, really, what a ridiculous man, how pathetic. My cheeks are hot again, in mingled shame, spite, and disbelief, and there in the entryway to our building I find I have to stop and rest until my heart, *my scandalized, insulted heart*, starts to beat a little slower.

"It's the perfect child's room, isn't it?" my ex-husband said.

He seemed eager to hear my cries of wonderment, and he gently pushed on my back to herd me further into the room, our son's bedroom for almost twenty years, which he'd decorated with all the many images of his successive idolatries, from Winnie the Pooh to Kurt Cobain, his beloved bedroom that he wanted left untouched even long after he'd moved out, where he didn't hesitate to make love with Lanton, now and then, after they'd had dinner with my ex-husband, such that in the end he stopped inviting them, much to the relief of all three, I imagine.

Really, though, I'd said to Lanton, amused in spite of myself, that's just not done, you're not supposed to screw within earshot of your father-in-law, and in a teenager's bedroom, what's more.

Lanton had burst into that lighthearted, innocent laugh I so loved, blushing adorably. And as if to defend my son, he'd confessed, a little embarrassed but also vaguely boastful, that it was all his own idea, those trysts in the virginal bedroom after they'd choked down the food inexpertly prepared by the papa (as he called my ex-husband), that on his own my son would never have drawn anyone at all into that old sleigh bed of his, which in any case was too short for Lanton's lanky frame.

Now the walls were covered in pink wallpaper with fine tone-on-tone stripes, the floor carpeted in dark pink, the room filled with a multitude of stuffed animals, evidently chosen for their pinkness, which ranged from the palest rose to the deepest fuchsia. A little pinewood bed with a pink satin canopy sat under the window, through which I could make out the drab, fog-shrouded façades on Rue Fondaudège.

"Oh," I said instinctively, "don't you know you're never supposed to put a child's bed under a window? Imagine the little thing standing up, pounding the window with her tiny fists, falling through it, ending up three floors below..."

My ex-husband's eyes widened in terror.

"That's true, you're right," he mumbled.

I realized he was having to force himself, for his dignity's sake, not to move the little bed away at once.

"Shall we move it together?" I heard myself offer, astonished at myself.

And so we found ourselves hoisting our granddaughter's bed, meant for this Souhar I'd never met, so we could move it next to the wall without marring the carpet, which really was very luxurious, lustrous and thick.

"That will take care of the little princess," said my ex-husband, happy and relieved. "What do you think?"

Pity, as well as a lingering trace of affection for this man I'd so terribly hurt, stopped me from answering that I found his decorative choices appalling, from the posters of naked babies in fields of flowers or cabbages to the relentless pink everywhere you looked, and so I merely asked him, in a slightly pinched voice, "Where did you find the money for all this froufrou?"

"It cost me everything I had," said my ex-husband, so unguardedly that I was sorry I'd carped at him.

After all, I asked myself, what business is it of mine? And then, in my pocket, my fingertips grazed my son's crumpled letter. A surge of anger made me feel almost sick to my stomach. Oh yes, I snarled to myself, how easy it is to claim you're broke when you've thrown away all your money!

I stomped out of the room, sickened by such vulgarity, such mindless materialism.

"I'll bet you're going to buy her her own television," I barked.

"Yes, that's next on the list," said my ex-husband, with the same almost beatific simplicity as when he talked about the child.

I heaved a very audible sigh, noting that he seemed to have forgotten all about his move to Spain. We were back at the apartment's front door. Just then I heard a rustle coming from my old study, a little room overlooking the courtyard, where I used to prepare my lessons and grade my students' papers. How I loved that study, I remembered with some sadness. I slipped past my ex-husband before he could stop me. I threw open the door to my study, hearing his frantic cries behind me.

And now I'm standing in the lobby of our building, wondering: Am I going to tell Ange what I saw in that room? Or would he not understand that sight's implications, maybe not even care, in his deep indifference to anything that concerned my ex-husband? Oh, it's not like it used to be, I tell myself, I can't confide in Ange about anything—I have to worry about his health and be wary of him at the same time—there's nobody left I can talk to. (So he was the only one? Yes, that's exactly right, and didn't that make us proud, as if our arrogant conjugal seclusion, our longstanding habit of hearing anything we were told with a deliberately inattentive, deliberately closed ear, so that no one's little personal problems would linger in our memory, as if that cozy isolation had been won from some heroic struggle or expressed some special grandeur, when in fact, I suddenly say to myself, it might have been nothing more than a failing disguised as a choice!)

No, I sadly think, I won't be telling Ange that I saw Corinna Daoui after all these years, and especially not that I found the Daoui woman in a place I never dreamed she might set foot, never imagined she might dare, yes, to display her revolting, seedy, defiled self: the pretty, sober little room I once used as a study, off-limits to everyone when I was away, even to my ex-husband, such that our son long referred to it as "my mother's sacred study."

Can you imagine? I would ask Ange if I could. All those years went by and I never once thought about Daoui, never felt a single sordid memory of Corinna flit past my mind, of Corinna or more precisely everything she represents in my Les Aubiers memories, and then all of a sudden I find her ensconced in my own apartment, on Rue Fondaudège, where I never, ever thought a Corinna Daoui might have the nerve to venture, so widely—when I lived there, at least—did the people of Les Aubiers fear and loathe the city center.

Do you understand? I'd say to Ange, who would shake his head in honest denial. No, he would say, I can't understand why the sight of this woman should upset you so, since very rightly you've never wasted your time wondering what sort of life your ex-husband was living, and who with, and in what room of your apartment. He would probably give me the same little smile he always does, kindly but distant, unintentionally condescending, when I bring up my childhood in Les Aubiers, he who grew up on Rue Vital-Carles in central Bordeaux and who takes a very plain, unquestionable, ineradicable pride in being a "true Bordelais." I made sure never to take Ange to Les Aubiers, though he never asked. For him Les Aubiers simply doesn't exist, no more than any spot outside the old city walls could claim to be part of Bordeaux, and to Ange that conviction has the serene, confident inflexibility of an article of faith, so he never tries to convince anyone of its truth, nor to discuss it in any way: he merely cracks an indulgent half smile and raises his eyebrows, superior and vaguely amused, whenever I unthinkingly speak of my "Bordeaux" childhood—you can be whatever you like, he seems to be saying, except, most certainly, a true Bordelaise.

No, no, I tell myself, paralyzed in the dark lobby, not yet ready to go upstairs and face Ange, there's no point bringing that up with him, no point even mentioning that I recognized Corinna at once, even after all these years, precisely because of the expression on her face, the look in her eyes, which, to someone like Ange, without his even knowing it, would immediately rule out any pretentions to Bordelais status. I'm sure he sometimes sees that same expression on my face, that same look in my eyes, I'm sure he can spot them, unconsciously sense them, I'm sure he goes right on seeing them when I myself am convinced that, by dint of experience, habit, and assurance, I've rid myself of them forever.

Today I'm a respectable middle-class woman, always carefully dressed, coiffed, and made-up, and my speech is fast and slightly high-pitched, with only the briefest of pauses between sentences. But to Ange, I know, I'm not fooling anyone, and I also know he doesn't care, since, despite his innate fondness for distinguishing the true Bordelais from the rest, he's no snob—snobbery is in fact a vulgarity he despises. And so he could easily take a liking to Corinna Daoui, might even find her attractive or funny. But he would never forget where Corinna comes from, and that difference would be one of those differences that definitively separates two distinct species.

To be sure, Ange loves me, he chose me, we're married. Still, I've often thought he married me because he already had a marriage behind him, because his children had been conceived and carried by the right sort of woman, and so, his duties fulfilled, he could now permit himself to marry the woman who simply appealed to him, knowing there were no consequences to fear. It was about pleasing himself, nothing more—not a family, a neighborhood, a whole race of authentic Bordelais. I also know Ange has no idea he feels like this. That way of thinking is the very stuff he's made of. And so Ange is always kind, because he's at peace with himself.

Oh, is Ange really kind? Isn't what he is the very opposite of kindness?

Sitting at a computer, Corinna turned her ruined face toward me.

"Hello, Nadia!" she cried, in a burst of unfeigned pleasure.

She stood up and quickly took me in her arms, an American-style hug, professional, brief, and distant, accompanied by a very light pat on the back. She gazed at me, smiling, her head tilted a little to one side.

"Say, you're looking pretty good, you're as plump as a little baby."

She had that Les Aubiers accent I know so well, the piercing voice, the jagged pronunciation, the unflowing, unmelodious way of putting the words together, the uneven, excessive highs and lows. It had been so long since I last heard that accent so close to my ear that it made me flinch, like a revolting smell. Even my ex-husband stopped talking that way once we left Les Aubiers together and moved to Rue Fondaudège.

"You're wondering what I'm doing here, aren't you?" said Corinna.

"No, no," I murmured, horrified at the thought of Corinna Daoui telling me one word about herself.

I backed toward the doorway, though I couldn't help taking a quick look around. And, I would tell Ange (but I'm not going to tell him anything at all, there's no point), what really drove a knife through my heart was that my study was still just as I'd left it, with nothing to betray the presence of a Corinna Daoui, even though, as my ex-husband told me a little later, she'd moved in long before. Daoui had quietly taken my place, discreetly curled up in my armchair, bringing with her only a computer and the almost physical brutishness of her accent. Daoui's face was worn, she was painfully thin. She was wearing a sort of mauve satin dressing gown, with a dragon on the back. My ex-husband gave me a nudge and nervously said to me, "All right now, we should get going."

Unkindly, just to needle him, I changed my mind.

"Wait a minute," I said, "there's no hurry."

I went to Daoui, now sitting at her computer again.

I asked, "You're working?"

"This is how I set up my appointments," said Corinna.

With a wink that wrinkled one whole side of her face, she went on: "You know what I do? Did he tell you?"

I turned to my ex-husband. Miserable, sheepish, he mumbled, "She's a sex worker."

"Still? At your age?" I cried.

"Hey, we're the same age, me and you," said Corinna gaily. "Besides, that's not at all what I used to do."

I sniffed resolutely, in the manner of someone who knows better. But deep down I had no wish to get into a debate about whether Daoui's activities back when we all lived in Les Aubiers were strictly speaking sex work or not, particularly because at the time I found it entirely reasonable that Daoui should do what she had to do to get by, given that she'd never had much luck in school.

"I can't accept that you brought her here, that's all," I said to my ex-husband on our way down the stairs.

He stopped, a faint smirk on his lips, and murmured,

"So what am I supposed to live on?"

"You're living off of her?"

I couldn't believe what I was hearing. Not taking the time to think, I indignantly added, "I don't want one more month's rent from you, if you were ever thinking of sending it. I don't want any money from…from Corinna Daoui's ass."

"You didn't always feel that way," he answered.

"Oh, that's ancient history!"

I was so outraged that my words came out in a screech.

Because we used to be friends, Corinna, my ex-husband, and me, back when we were teenagers, and since Corinna, who'd dropped out of school, was the only one with any money (*and because she's also a considerate and devoted and good-hearted person*), she thought nothing of paying for our outings to the pool (*she has a young boy's narrow, long body and slender, strong limbs*) or skating rink. And she might have given us presents, too, she might well in fact have lavished all sorts of clothes and trinkets on us, and even books, even spiral notebooks and pens, since unlike her we were still in school. We accepted these things with pleasure but without gratitude, because we felt no real esteem for Daoui. Where did she get that money? She didn't have to tell us—we knew. It would have been unthinkable for the reserved teenagers my ex-husband and I were to talk about such a thing with anyone, and Daoui herself never brought it up.

We didn't grasp the depth of her kindness, we were too young. We felt no real esteem for Daoui, no. Today, now that I can appreciate her thoughtfulness and stoicism, I can be sorry for our dismissive condescension toward that very young woman, our blind, selfish, high-school stupidity, yes, I can look back on all that with remorse. Which, I'd like to explain to Ange, in no way implies that I have to see the fifty-year-old Daoui, scrawny, cheaply dressed, probably a smoker, living in my apartment on Rue Fondaudège, as anything other than the sordid incarnation of a thing I'll have to flee for as long as I live, a thing I must never surrender to, not even out of compassion, a thing I must even trample underfoot should it, should that detestable past, ever dare cross my path.

"You managed to get away, and now here it is coming back to haunt you," I said to my ex-husband.

"You're mean, Nadia," he answered quietly.

He asked if I'd ever met up with Corinna in the thirty-five years or so since Les Aubiers.

"No," I said, "this is the first time."

"You sure about that?" my ex-husband prodded me.

I didn't answer. He then told me what Daoui had told him, that we'd run into each other six or seven years before, as she was on her way out of La Rousselle station, where she'd been locked up for a day and a night, and I, Nadia, was on my way in, presumably to call on Lanton (explained my ex-husband). And according to Daoui she felt so bereft at the time, in such physical and emotional pain, that she couldn't help clutching my arm and begging me to take her to a café somewhere, or at least, since I immediately refused, to give her a little money, because she didn't even have the bus fare to get home. I pulled away (as Daoui put it, nonjudgmentally) and hurried into the police station, giving her no clear sign that I'd recognized her, but she felt certain I had.

"Is that true?" asked my ex-husband. I admitted to nothing. I merely said it was possible, I couldn't be expected to remember my every chance meeting with some long-ago acquaintance in Bordeaux (which actually never happens, since I live in the heart of the city where not even my brothers and sisters, not even my elderly parents, ever venture from their distant outskirts). But in fact I do remember that encounter, yes, and Daoui's poor, grimacing face, which I later saw again several times, terrified, in my dreams. Even if she promised not to say a word, not to tell me a thing, it would have been beyond my abilities to drink a cup of coffee before such a face.

But why didn't I stuff a ten-euro bill into her hand? Too miserly? No, no—so why? Obviously to avoid prolonging the moment, even minutely, to avoid creating any bond between Daoui and me and so run the risk, for example, that she might try to find me on the pretext of paying me back.

How, after that, how I feared I might find Corinna waiting for me outside the school! Latching onto Ange, striking up a friendship, wangling an invitation to our apartment, and then explaining to him, why not, just how much I owe her, Corinna, who made my life in Les Aubiers so much more comfortable! *Corinna would have said no such thing, because she had no sense back then that we owed her anything at all.*

Or else, thinking she was doing the right thing, she would bring up my parents, those two old people living out their lives where they always had, and so Ange would learn that they weren't dead at all as I'd claimed, and to be sure he wouldn't give a damn that those people were still alive in their Les Aubiers project, but he'd fault me for my lie, and then I would seem a strange and ignoble person.

Because I never think about them, I've forgotten their faces, I've almost forgotten their last name, which hasn't been mine for so long, thanks to my marriages.

"I don't want to talk about Corinna anymore," I told my ex-husband as he walked me homeward down Rue Fondaudège.

But I couldn't help it. The words came out of my mouth, impossible to hold back, as if pushed out by my troubled heart, my jealous heart.

"Doesn't it bother you," I said, "that Corinna's doing her work right next door to the princess's little bedroom?"

My ex-husband didn't deign to answer. I sensed his embarrassment and unhappiness. A suspicion came over me.

"She's not playing grandmother, I hope?" I said. "I'm assuming she never so much as comes near the child?"

"Nadia, that's none of your business," my ex-husband answered.

He was holding my arm. I could feel his anger vibrating in my flesh.

"Don't worry, I won't say a word about Corinna to Ralph," I said. "I'm not going to tell him you have an old girlfriend turning tricks just through the wall of the bedroom where you so lovingly look after your granddaughter."

I could see that his lips were pinched and white from the effort he was making not to answer me. More gently, I asked him, "Incidentally, remind me what Ralph's wife's name is? The child's mother?"

"You don't remember?"

"No," I said.

"Yasmine."

"So who's Wilma? Do you know her?"

He thought for a few seconds.

"Wilma, no, no idea," he said.

I let out a little "oh" of surprise.

He didn't notice. That was when we caught sight of Noget under the fog-shrouded linden trees on the Place de Tourny.

19. We'll probably never see each other again

I spend the last night with Ange, in our bed. Although his wound seems to have stopped oozing, it's badly infected, and the infection is beginning to spread all around. Not one inch of Ange's flesh seems untouched. His body is deep red, his face pale, faintly gray. A painful bedsore was forming, so I helped him onto his side, and he now stays that way at all times, which complicates his eating and drinking. He doesn't care. As a bedpan, Noget brings him a little bowl from his apartment downstairs, but Ange rarely urinates or defecates.

"He's only had one bowel movement this week," Noget told me.

Nonetheless, Ange feels obliged to eat everything Noget puts before him, and the portions are huge for someone who never gets out of bed. But he's still as thin as ever, if not thinner. He almost never speaks anymore. The air in the room is unbreathable. Noget comes and goes, ever cheerier, youthfully carefree. He's shaved that old beard of his, and he now seems so different, so renewed, that my feelings toward him have little by little gone from hostile mistrust to a sort of reluctant affection. He really is a different man. I have no parting instructions for him. Whatever has to be done he will do, and he'll do it better than me.

It's true, he'll liquidate Ange better than I ever could.

I only tell him how to go about sending Ange to come join me as soon as he's fit to travel. After extensive calculations, I leave him three thousand euros in cash.

"Keep trying to convince Ange to let Doctor Charre have a look at him," I say.

"Ange is exactly right not to want that dangerous old cretin anywhere near him," he answers, with an inappropriate twinkle in his eye.

I immediately ask, "What do you know about Doctor Charre?"

"Only what I have to know," says Noget. "That he hates people like you."

With a sort of puzzled curiosity, he adds: "Do you even try to keep up with things?"

"No," I say. "Ange and I don't read the paper. We do listen to the radio, but only the music stations, jazz and classical."

"Which is why you don't know anything about anything or anyone," says Noget reproachfully.

"Our society is too well informed as it is," I say.

Noget reaches out and pats my belly.

"So, is there a baby in there?"

"I told you, it's menopause! You're such an idiot."

Noget bursts into a loud, heartfelt laugh.

"I don't believe a word of it," he says.

Suddenly he turns serious.

"In any case, don't go see your Doctor Charre, he'd get rid of the fetus and never even tell you."

When I wake up by Ange's side early the next morning, he's still asleep. Noget is already there, standing at the foot of the bed in the dark. He tells me my breakfast is waiting.

I kiss Ange's hollow cheeks, his hot, dry lips. I dissolve into tears, to my great embarrassment, since Noget's still in the room.

"We've never been apart before," I say quietly.

All of a sudden Ange opens his eyes wide, gives me a vacant stare, then closes them again, as if exhausted from this close study of me.

"Farewell, Nadia," he murmurs. "Whatever you do, don't come back."

"You'll be coming away, my love," I say, racked by guilt.

Ange would never abandon me—or would he? Hand me over to a stranger, even though I was ailing, leave me deep in the slow suffocations and insidious, inexorable constrictions of a city gone bad, contracting to cut us to bits? So I should have stayed back in Les Aubiers, close by those two old people and the rest of the family? Is that where I'm supposed to be? Far from the murderous heart of the city?

"If only you'd let yourself be treated," I whisper in his ear, suddenly almost hopeless. "Oh, darling, then we'd be going off together..."

He wearily shakes his head on the pillow. Then he

struggles to raise his lips to my cheek.

"So you're going to have a baby, Nadia?"

"No, no," I hurry to say, "what a ridiculous idea! My period has stopped, but that's normal at my age."

"Glad to hear it," says Ange.

He's far too weak, I can see, to say anything more. A tear trickles from his right eye, soaks into the pillow. His skin is so hot that the damp trail immediately dries.

I stand up and ask Noget to leave the room so I can get dressed.

"Be quick about it," he says. "The toast will get cold."

Clenched all night in the squalid warmth of the bedroom, my lungs relax and dilate painfully when I step through the doorway. I give Ange one last look. He's drowsing, frowning severely, his lips moving slightly, as if he were scolding someone in a dream.

"This is much too much, I can't possibly eat all this," I say when I walk into the kitchen.

I see that Noget's so-called toast is actually scones glistening with melted butter, accompanied by little fried sausages and scrambled eggs. There's also a salad of fresh fruit crowned with whipped cream and the madeleines Noget bakes himself, deliberately letting the edges darken just a little.

"For the road," he says, with a benevolence so expertly feigned that I feel forced to choke down everything he's laid out for me, and it's all so good, despite the queasiness filling me.

When I'm done, I feel listless and bleak. I dread going out onto the cold street. I ask Noget for a second cup of coffee, then a third. Finally I pull on my cardigan, now too tight to button.

But where my son lives it's hot, so unendingly hot that once I get there I'll just roll up that cardigan, stick it in my suitcase, and forget about it.

"Are you taking the tram?" asks Noget, very amiably.

"Yes, it's the only way," I say.

A rush of heat turns my face bright red. I can feel the sweat trickling between my breasts, beneath my undershirt. I busy myself to hide my fear.

"It's the only way, right?" I say again, with a little laugh, as I fasten my purse and put on a dab of pink lipstick.

"Yes, you certainly mustn't take a taxi," says Noget.

"I'm not in the habit of splurging on taxis," I say.

But Noget can see through me. He knows it's simply out of caution that I'm not calling a taxi; he knows I'm afraid I'll end up with a driver who immediately throws me out of the car or drives me into the depths of mysterious neighborhoods, where I would be lost forever.

I take my suitcase out to the landing. I extend a hand to Noget, my fingers slightly stiff, slightly cold.

"Well, goodbye."

"Goodbye," says Noget.

Just as his hand touches mine, my chest quakes with one single sob, dry and violent.

"Save him," I say. "I'm begging you, Monsieur Noget…"

"It's a little late for that, don't you think?" cries Noget, suddenly angry. "If you hadn't looked down on me so…"

"I'm sorry, I'm sorry," I say, very quickly. "I do regret it, you know."

We stare at each other, awkwardly. I pick up my suitcase

and start trundling down the stairs. Noget doesn't offer to help. I hear him close the door behind me almost as soon as I've turned around.

20. The tram's playthings

Rue Esprit-des-Lois is dark and silent. The white glow of the few streetlights meant to illuminate it is immediately swallowed up by the fog.

I pull my suitcase along by its handle, and the rattle of the casters on the uneven sidewalk seems loud enough to wake the whole street, but the soot-colored façades show no sign of life. I've put on my high-heeled ankle boots for the trip. The sound of the heels on the concrete is the kind that foreshadows a crime. That click-clack, so feminine, so tempting. I hurry along as fast as I can, my chest tight. But then the frantic hammering of my heels expresses my fear, and so makes it worse.

I can't go on living in this city. It scares me, it's killing me a little at a time. Let me at least get away before it can clutch at my heels to pull me down!

I'm completely breathless by the time I reach the Place de la Bourse. There, the orange-tinted lights are so plentiful and so powerful that they cut through the fog and cast a bright blaze over the vast square, over the cold splendor of the restored, magically white façades. This excess of uncanniness makes my head swim. An empty square so brilliantly lit—oh, to what end? I ask myself.

My footsteps resound even louder on the new white

paving stones. Nowhere could one be more obviously in the center of the arena. Dragging my big lurching suitcase, I scurry across the square to the tram stop. I see the tram coming from the Place des Quinconces, or rather I sense it, an incandescent mass, as if white-hot from its own lights, which liquefy the fog all around it.

I step toward the tracks. I gracelessly raise my hand, all the while telling myself there's no need, that the tram surely stops at every station.

It races by, so fast that the rush of cold air makes me stagger. I take a step back. He must not have seen my hand, I tell myself—I was too half-hearted about raising it. *He or it? The driver, whom I didn't even see, or the tram itself?*

I sit down on the bench, shivering. For all I know that tram wasn't in service, for all I know the cars were all empty. It came up too fast, wreathed in a light far too dazzling for me to see anything inside.

In front of me, beyond the street and the quay, the river is steaming with fog. I can smell its silty breath, the malodorous cold rising up from the black water.

The hiss of another oncoming tram makes me jump to my feet. I reach out, shake my hand—again the tram zooms right by me, again its extraordinary speed and the pallid blaze of its windows leave me dazed. Soon a third, then yet another glide by, right before my eyes, ignoring my signals—none of them stop at the Place de la Bourse.

I'll miss my train if I wait any longer, so I decide to stop trying. I set off down Quai Richelieu, pulling my suitcase behind me. The night is still pitch black. Many trams go by, in both directions. After a hundred yards or so I cautiously turn around and see a tram at the stop I've just left. A handful of passengers are getting off, glowing like torches under the lights of the square.

Don't all the trams stop at the Place de la Bourse?

I'm not making much progress. The train station is still far away, my legs are limp. For the first time in a long while, I feel violently humiliated.

Because just when I was placing all my faith in the tram, all my hope, that very tram rejected me.

Suddenly I just want to give up, turn around and go home, back to Ange, lie down at his side and slip with him into mindless slumber, interrupted only by Noget's furtive appearances to stuff us with food. And yet I keep walking, knowing I'll go on even when contrary ideas urge me to turn back. I still love life, stupidly, brutally. Oh no, I'm not tired of living, and isn't that what now repels me most about my dear, my very dear Ange: his untellable, avid, disgruntled traffic with death, the way he's giving his body over to decay? I never want to see that again.

Finally I turn away from the quays and onto Rue Domercq, which leads straight to the Saint-Jean station. Several times the tram goes by, filled with passengers clearly bound for the station, since that's the last stop on the line. Approaching a stop just as a tram is slowing down to open its doors, I wonder if I should try one last time to get on, encouraged by the sight of the little knot of people in the shelter, shielding themselves as best they can from the damp cold of the fog. No malign force will spot me among all these people, I tell myself. For that matter, I think I see several faces and shapes just like mine. In the old days, I would never have noticed that those two women, and maybe that man too, had the first thing in common with me. Now, inspired by a new, subtle sense, I can see it. Just as I can immediately tell the difference between two smells I know well, or two familiar tastes, I can distinguish the people I look like from the crowd I once thought I belonged to, who have with perfect sincerity stopped seeing us—Ange and me and others—as in any way their equals.

If those three dare to assume they'll be let on the tram, I tell myself, if they feel sure enough of it to voluntarily wait in this clammy, almost fetid cold, why on earth shouldn't I? I come closer, pressing my suitcase to my leg. The last few steps to the shelter I walk backward. Just as the tram opens its doors, I change my mind and hurry away, almost running, amid the breathless clamor of my high heels and the suitcase casters. You idiot, you simpleton, I furiously chide myself, do you really think it's enough just to hide away in a crowd, just to go unnoticed for a few minutes? That's childish, it's stupid. You'll never be able to get on. And if they can, that's because for them things are somehow different. Maybe you're worse than they are, or at least your punishment's more severe. Or you're just worse, yes, why not?

I shudder with fear and anguish as I imagine the spectacular obstacle that would have stopped me this time, so close to my goal, from boarding the tram. A vicious blow, a terrible fall, something painful and humiliating—how moronic, when I'm only five hundred yards from the station!

The tram glides close by me with a mocking little chirp. Pressed together in the back of the tram like the flowers of a tragic bouquet, a sad, dark nosegay destined to be crushed underfoot, my fellow-creatures' three faces look out at me in sorrow, in pity—poor woman, having to walk, and so fat, too, so ungainly, red with cold and fatigue! That forlorn fellowship makes me angry and ashamed. How ugly they are, how wretched and defeated, I tell myself, dismayed to think those same words might come to their minds when they look at me. But are they, like me, also thinking: I want nothing to do with all that?

21. What does she know about me?

I just make the train to Toulon. I somewhat timidly sit down in the only seat left, beside a young woman I question with a glance, doing my best not to look too imploring. She gives me a quick, slightly desolate smile. I sink comfortably into my seat.

I feel joy in my heart. This woman is so different from me, but she's perfectly willing to have me beside her, unavoidably close. Sharing the central armrest, our forearms touch lightly. She doesn't seem to notice. I'm so happy that a triumphant giggle escapes me. And still she doesn't react, she stays turned toward the window, her fist under her chin, showing only her slender, severe profile, her thin lips peppered with little bits of dried skin she sometimes absentmindedly pulls away with her teeth. Her blond hair is tied behind her neck with a black velvet ribbon. Her skirt, her thick sweater, her hose, everything is black. Her eye is round and blue and underscored by a dark circle that twitches in time with a throbbing vein.

The thought that this unambiguous, dominant young woman (she could have scornfully shot down any suggestion of my sitting beside her, and I wouldn't have dared appeal to anyone to make her let me: who would ever have spoken up for me?) seems to be in the grips of some listless sorrow secretly cheers me. She's suffering, I tell myself, oh, how she's suffering! Maybe even more than me—is such a thing possible?

She doesn't move, simply stares unseeing at the expanses of plowed earth racing by outside the windows. When the conductor asks for her ticket, no part of her reacts but her hand, which slowly drifts toward her purse. He has to ask twice, because she doesn't hear him at first. He doesn't ask me for anything, doesn't even seem to notice I exist. I nap tranquilly, my hands crossed over my swollen stomach, with Noget's food, I imagine, roiling and fermenting inside it. Occasionally half opening my eyes, I see holes appear in the fog, which soon turns to rags as we put the Gironde behind us. A little before Agen, I see the sky for the first time in months—a dull, pale blue sky, but the sky all the same, free of the cottony veil that's settled over Bordeaux and trapped my beloved city beneath a damper of frightening thoughts and poisonous dreams.

Eyes closed, I fall into a vague daydream of one day returning in triumph, delivering my city of its…its miasma? Its poisonous fixations, its grim vanity? Oh, I can't remember anymore.

I wake up in Montpellier, roused by a smell that reminds me I'm hungry, voraciously hungry. The train is almost empty now. My neighbor is nibbling at a hard-boiled egg, indifferent to the little bits of yolk falling onto her skirt.

How hungry I am! Why didn't Noget make me a sandwich, maybe tuna, or cheese?

She rewraps the egg in its foil, almost untouched. I can't stop myself. Surprised at my own audacity, I ask, "May I have the rest of your egg?"

And that question, which I would once never have dreamed of asking, confirms my feeling that I've fallen even further than I thought. Realizing that I've become a figure of loathing, I no longer strive for irreproachable decency and honor, allowing myself to mumble or cackle audibly in public, asking my seatmate's permission to place my teeth in the imprint of hers in the cooked egg white's delicate metallic flesh. How abject, I tell myself, asking for such a thing, particularly when you're a woman as portly as I am!

My face has turned deep red. I add: "I'm sorry, I can't think what came over me, asking you that."

In response, she gives me her taut little smile, which pulls back only one side of her mouth and does nothing to lessen the fierce sadness lodged in the blue of her eye, small and round as a bird's. She holds out the ball of foil.

"Go ahead, I'm not hungry anymore."

Then she rummages in the purse at her feet with a sudden haste and what seems almost a fear of disappointing me, and she pulls out a beautiful, very yellow banana, unspoiled by the tiniest black spot, and adds, "Eat this too, I don't want it."

She delicately lays it on my tray. In an overpowering surge of weakness, tears come to my eyes. I free the egg from its foil. And I look at the grooves left in the white by my neighbor's uneager, sorrowful teeth, and I bite into the egg, taking care to keep my own teeth in those tracks, scrupulously hewing to them, in a superstitious expression of my gratitude. And at the same time, I wish that were enough to chase the dull despair out of her bright little eye. For this woman's despondency no longer brings me the slightest joy.

Doesn't she see anything about me to make her shrink back in horror? Or are her own torments so distracting her that she's forgotten...all vigilance, that her vision is clouded or she's lost all interest in the world around her? That she feels no fear of the terrible fate that might be piled atop her present sorrows merely from my mouth clamping down where her own mouth clamped down?

The train is stopped in Marseille. It's late afternoon. Everyone has gotten off but my neighbor. The warm, red sun casts a scarlet glow over the station's glass roof, and at the same time inflames her emaciated face through the window, all at once giving her the illusion of an ardent, almost joyous demeanor.

"You're going on to Toulon as well?" I say.

"Yes," she says.

"And then," I say, my heart quivering, "I'm catching the boat to C."

"Me too," she says.

I let out a grunt to hide my delight. Any expression of pleasure in the face of such pain would seem obscene.

The train doesn't start off again. No one boards. We're alone. And night falls, sucking away any semblance of animation from the woman's cheeks, returning the deathly livid cast to her bony forehead. Suddenly she stands up, stumbling over my knees and, before I can move, straddles my legs to step into the aisle.

"Don't you think it's odd that we're still in the station?" she asks, worried.

"Yes, I do," I say.

And as I speak I feel the fear incubating in my consciousness beginning to hatch.

She can't be late for Toulon, she tells me, she can't miss that boat, and I see her long, slender legs pacing back and forth, lashing the fabric of her skirt with a sound like a sail flapping in the wind—and that wind, oh how we begged it to come up at last and make the sails of our catamaran snap and swell when we set out, Ange and I, on the bright, tranquil waters of the Arcachon basin, seeing the villa Ange inherited from his parents growing ever smaller in the sparkling summer-morning light, back on the bright, tranquil shore we'd just left, *and I said to myself, even in the very heart of that bliss, am I really this woman who has no other divinity to implore than the wind, the pleasure craft's friend, and if so how did I turn into her, and is it right, or should I regret it, and should I feel sorry for abandoning the dreary, unyielding religion of my scolding old parents, who, unbeknownst to Ange (his pretty purple cap with the transparent visor, his mirrored sunglasses, his healthy, sweet smell), are at this moment languishing in their Les Aubiers housing project, not knowing they're dead, not knowing I claimed that they were, but perhaps now and then feeling—in their necks, to which they abruptly clap an astonished hand, or in their chests, or in their bellies—the mysterious bite of that curse, who might well be wasting away, withered by an unseen torment and silently supposing that that pain comes to them from the daughter who went away, who never visits or calls, not once in thirty-five years*, and then I realize that she's talking to me as she paces up and down the aisle on her long, stiff, stork-like legs, her sad, bitter face just barely lit by the bluish ceiling lights and the glow from the station, sudden shadows running across that pale, bleak face in time with her strides, bringing out the bones beneath.

I'm angry at myself for missing the start of what she was saying. I struggle to recall what I must have heard but not listened to, not realizing she was talking to me, and so I lose the thread of what she's saying now. I drift back into a daydream, back into aloneness—and none too soon, I tell myself, because don't I dread and loathe the mere idea of hearing the intimate details of other people's lives? Oh, it's not the same at all with her, this woman who was willing to let food touched by her mouth enter the dark place that is mine. But I'm lost all the same, and now I can't follow or even understand anything she's saying. A few scattered words—fire, far away, remains—that I can't connect to anything at all. But I do feel the weight of an unhealable sorrow. That shapeless burden is already settling onto me, weighing me down. Still, how I wish I could come together with her grief, try to distract it with good thoughts. But now that cold, hard mistrust I know so well is freezing my uneasy heart, now I'm secretly relieved to know nothing of this woman's sadness, even if my gratitude to her is far keener than my relief is to me, or my icy mistrust.

How can I fight back that reflex? I sink further into self-loathing, into a horror of what I am and can't help but be, until in a blinding flash of almost cosmic understanding (the deceptive, unbounded enlightenment that sometimes comes with an excess of alcohol), I finally see and accept and endorse the cause of our tribulations, Ange and me and all the others just like us—like us not so much physically as in the depths of their self-centered souls.

Now the woman is silent. Her emotion has left her slightly breathless. I look down—she thinks I know her now, she doesn't know what a louse she's bared her soul to! What's happened to her, what secrets has she been telling me? I wish I could know, in just a few precise, dry, impersonal words.

Night has fallen. The woman asks my name and I tell her, not daring to ask hers, thinking she might already have said.

"My name's Nathalie," she murmurs, raising her arms to retie the bow in her hair.

She adds: "I don't think this train's going to go any farther, shouldn't we be getting off?"

I hoist myself out of my seat.

"But now how will we get to Toulon?" I ask, in a voice made sharp and plaintive by anxiety.

An aged conductor in a white uniform walks past on the deserted platform. Stepping off the train before me, Nathalie stops him and imperiously asks where the train for Toulon is.

"There aren't any more trains tonight, you'll have to wait till morning," he answers, as if surprised at our ignorance.

Then, after one look at our two shocked faces, he breaks into a run, the tails of his jacket bouncing off his voluminous buttocks, and when Nathalie begins to jog after him, calling out, demanding information and explanations, he speeds up and disappears from view.

"I think he was scared of us," she says, with her gloomy, misshapen little smile.

I want to test her.

"You're right, and why would that be?" I ask.

"I don't know, it doesn't matter," she says after a few moments of silence.

She smiles her tragic, one-sided smile again and looks me straight in the eye, as if defying me to make her say anything more, or to placate me, the way you might smile at an old lady or a little child, but, far from placated by that bright, round eye suffused with inconsolable sorrow and also with the sort of trust and closeness she finds in the thought that she's told me her story, far from reassured, I look away, my gaze wandering this way and that. All of a sudden I find something worrisome in that face of hers.

It's too strange, I tell myself, the contrast of that round eye and that gaunt face, of sorrow and authority, of her beauty as a whole and the almost ugliness of the details; that pointed noise, those hollow cheeks, that sparse hair. It's too strange, I tell myself again, not only that she doesn't push me away but that she seems eager to draw me to her and keep me close. Because rather than give me a wave and go on her way, now she's saying in her beautiful, vigorous voice:

"Come on, we'll rent a car."

"You think?" I say, startled.

"It's that or miss the boat," she says.

"I can't miss it," I say, on the brink of tears.

"And neither can I, right?" she says, staring at me.

And with that the melancholy darkness absorbs every

trace of blue in her eye, and, desperate for something to do, I reach for my suitcase, hating myself, almost drunk on that hatred. I follow her down the platform, not daring to walk beside her. *Because I might be a nuisance, because the fleeting glance of some passerby might unjustly associate her with me. But we run into no one on the platform.* It's barely eight o'clock in the evening, and this whole huge station seems to be empty.

"My ticket does say the train goes to Toulon," I grumble.

"Yes, that's a shame," she says after another brief silence that makes me think she's weighing her words to keep from hurting my feelings or worrying me *or because she wants to lull me into complacency*.

"I'm going to ask for my money back for the Marseille to Toulon part," I go on.

"Don't do that."

"Why not?"

"What good can it do to complain?" she says quietly, still walking on. "You may not be in any position. And it'll only end up being your fault anyway. They'll show you you were mistaken in one way or another."

"But what about you, didn't you make the same mistake? You were planning to go on to Toulon, weren't you?"

"Yes, yes. In my case, there was no reason why the train shouldn't take me to Toulon," she says hesitantly.

"It stopped in Marseille because of me?"

She doesn't answer. At first I'm shocked, then simply befuddled. Panic pushes me toward her until I'm clinging to her heels. She's carrying a big black purse over her shoulder, and nothing more.

"Why do I never know anything?" I croak.

"Don't you watch television?"

"No, my husband and I are opposed to television," I say, this time with some firmness.

But the image of Ange slowly dying in our bed sends a piercing sorrow coursing through me. The words I was about to speak on the subject of television stay stuck in my throat.

Once in the meagerly lit lobby, Nathalie heads straight for the Europcar counter. Vast pools of shadow submerge the corners of the room in a vagueness that seems aswarm with activity, though I can't see a soul, and I tell myself that this darkness must hold the ghostly, agitated, unhappy trace of everyone who's passed through here all day, and then I wonder if they might still be there and I simply don't see them, so I look away, my eyes fixed on Nathalie's back, resolving, since I must make a choice, to put myself entirely in her hands.

I hear her speaking quietly to the clerk, the only person in sight, to my eyes at least, in the lobby. She holds out her credit card.

"I'll pay you back," I say.

"Don't worry, it's fine," she says.

And I'm relieved, and, all at once, ignobly cheerful.

22. Death at breakneck speed

And now, like an eel in the mud, I'm emerging from a viscous torpor, my lips sticky, my eyes heavy, my bladder intolerably full.

"I have to go to the bathroom," I murmur hoarsely.

My jaw is so numb that I palpate it cautiously, almost expecting to find it shattered by some fist's mighty blow. But no, I feel only the sticky spume of sleep on my lips. I hear Nathalie's voice as if from a tremendous distance, muted and slowed, struggling to make its way through the clouds—which I'm convinced I could touch, if only I had the strength to raise my hand—of my somnolence.

Is it a little strange that she should use the very same words as Noget? She asks, almost declares, "You're pregnant?"

"No," I say, furious.

But my mouth is still filled with plaster, and only a gurgle comes out. Embarrassed, I clear my throat.

"On the contrary," I say irritably, "the only reason I haven't had my period in a while is that I'm menopausal, and it doesn't mean you're pregnant just because you have to go to the bathroom, right?"

And with this a sensation of great speed begins to run through my numbed muscles. *Did someone hit me? Have I been drugged?*

My fingers rub the coarse fabric of the seat beneath me, too small for me, I think, feeling my thighs hanging over the edges. I carefully turn my head in the direction Nathalie's voice seemed—with a slight delay—to be coming from.

I've never fallen asleep so suddenly anywhere. In this dim light, I can scarcely make out her sharp profile, her downturned mouth. Her hands are holding a steering wheel. *Oh, a Twingo, like the one Ange and I used to drive.*

The night is deep, the road deserted. Nathalie is driving so quickly that the tiny car skids and squeals at every curve.

"Slow down a little," I say.

Several long seconds go by before she curtly shoots back: "I don't want to miss the boat."

Through the windshield I see only a silent, absolute darkness, unpierced by so much as the fleeting lights of a house now and then. Are we in the country, are we by the sea, are we driving through an industrial wasteland?

The road is in terrible condition, and the car lurches this way and that. Nathalie screeches to a halt beside a hedgerow. I quickly get out. My thighs are already damp with a few drops of urine. It's so invigorating to empty myself, a warm breeze fanning my buttocks, that, protected from the darkness of the night and the darkness of all the invisible or nonexistent things around us, I forget my embarrassment at doing this in front of Nathalie. Far below me, I hear what seems a faint splash of breakers, the soft knock of smooth stones gently stirred by the waves. I take my time. My lungs swell in tranquil joy.

When I get back in the car, I find Nathalie turned to one side, looking out the window as if to make clear that she wanted to spare me the discomfort of imagining her seeing and hearing me pee.

"Thanks," I say, cheerfully.

She starts off again. She's panting and puffing in a weird way. Her hair's come undone, and now it's hiding her forehead and cheeks. She's not the same as before. She has a strong smell all of a sudden, not unpleasant, but like nothing I know. Silently, too fast, we drive through the unbroken darkness.

Shouldn't there be villages, shouldn't there be supermarket parking lots with big glowing signs?

"Nathalie," I say.

With a quarter-turn of her head, she looks toward me. I scream, I close my eyes. Then I open them again, staring resolutely straight ahead.

A dark, fleshless face, the head of a decomposed corpse, topped with a blond wig someone put there in a spirit of ridicule or the intention of causing terror.

My lips and hands are trembling. Nathalie is dead, I tell myself. How can that be? How much of all this is real?

And her wide, lipless mouth showing irregular yellow teeth, ready to clack together at any moment in a comical chatter, that's why she's not saying anything, why she can't say anything ever again.

I'm far too afraid to dare look at the hands on the wheel.

Powerful hands strewn with little red hairs holding an identical wheel, Ange looking as if he'd been crammed into a toy, but today it's a different pair of hands, though the car is exactly the same model and color.

Nathalie's dead, I tell myself, and I'm alivc, and yet she's the one driving, and she's been dead for a long time, and I didn't realize it because I didn't look at her closely enough. I'm so ashamed, and so afraid! Where is she driving me, then? Where could this specter I was stupid enough to take for a friend possibly be taking me? Unless my place now is to be a friend to shadows, and to nothing and no one else?

23. I don't want to know her anymore

Eventually, to my great surprise, we drive past the Toulon city limits sign, signifying the endpoint of this furious race through an invisible landscape.

"We're going to make it," says Nathalie.

And since her voice is soft, tranquil, and human, I steal a glance at her. I see the woman from the train again—her sharp profile, her eye like a marble pressed into her flesh, her anxious mouth. I look at her hands and see long, fine fingers gripping the wheel. Deeply relieved, I let out a laugh.

And then, all at once, we're half blinded by a wild riot of lights, a carnival fairyland. Nathalie parks in the lot of the port. We both sit and blink for a moment before we get out. I don't dare look Nathalie's way too often, for fear I might find her horribly transformed again, and I'm not sure how aware she is of these spectral mutations, so I wouldn't want to upset her with displays of fear or mistrust. It simply seems to me—and I note it with sadness and rage—that there's no way I can like her now, because she inspires a latent, inexpressible horror inside me.

Slightly intimidated (even her!), we amble toward the glittering hulk of the ferry boat, a towering façade of flashing lights emitting a soft, saccharine music. The last passengers are just getting on. I take out my ticket, and Nathalie immediately sees I'm in first class.

"Oh, too bad," she says, "we won't be together."

She seems genuinely disappointed.

"Are you going to be all right?" she asks, and so much solicitude touches and alarms me at the same time.

I don't trust her anymore. *What more does she want to show me, in what state is she sorry I won't see her, what torments of the soul? Does she realize I wasn't listening to a word of her outpouring of grief? Does she realize that, in a certain way that doesn't rule out shame, I'm not sorry I wasn't? Was she hoping to make me pay for that by exposing who knows what, even worse horrors if through some stroke of luck we'd been assigned to the same cabin?*

Mumbling, I tell her I'll manage, there's no reason things should go badly for me now.

"Still, be careful," Nathalie whispers. "It's so hard for people like you, it's so unjust..."

"What do you mean by 'people like me'?" I ask.

She slowly shakes her head with a sad little smile, either because she doesn't take the question seriously or because she refuses to let the answer cross her lips, to defile her mouth, and offend my ear.

"I must tell you, I don't quite understand what you're talking about," I say with a certain haughtiness.

I feel a sudden surge of hate for her. She shouldn't say such things, I tell myself, not even to be nice.

Then the disparity between our two tickets forces us into two separate lines as we enter the boat through a gap in its side, like a vicious gash in its radiant, glimmering flesh *made by a wood chisel or some other such tool, puncturing and then rooting around in my husband's tender human flesh to be sure he can never recover and come to understand just what he is or what he's done and be filled with the idea that he deserves the evil thrust into him, and so end up resembling that evil.*

24. Finally a little fun!

The table is laid with a lavish array of delicate dishware that seems meant more for decoration than for use.

"Imagine daring to eat off such beautiful things!" I say to someone, slightly giddy.

In a luxuriance of bright lights and amber gleams (vast mirrors reflecting the gold of the frames, the crystalline glassware, the shining silver), I'm sitting across from that thin, austere man, the captain, by virtue of the custom that the ship's master distinguishes between his passengers according to their prosperity and invites those in first class to share his table and the honor of his presence.

Oh, I tell myself—happy, lighthearted, almost untroubled—isn't it nice to be favored, and how long has it been since any sort of privilege was bestowed on me?

Because the captain sees me. We're sitting face-to-face, and he regularly sees me and smiles, the same formal rictus he shows all his guests, and so, I tell myself, almost drunk with relief, it's as if other rules prevailed at sea, rules that don't include recoiling in disgust from people like me, and who knows, maybe rules that don't include bothering with or even knowing about the kind of codes that have governed Ange's and my existence in Bordeaux all through the past year.

Because the captain sees me. I don't look like anyone else at this table, but here I am, and those aged heads nod at me when our eyes meet, and I nod my drunken, laughing head back, my astonished, eager head. The profusion of lights hurts my eyes. Sometimes I close them to give them a break. And when I open them again nothing has changed, not the senseless extravagance of the countless dazzling lights, not the captain's cold cordiality, not even the little nods of my tablemates' heads, their pale faces sagging with excess, quivering, wrinkled flesh, discreet salutations making clear that we're members of the same clan.

I have money, I tell myself, and here that's what matters, it erases everything else. Isn't that wonderful? Isn't that simple and just? How I now hate Nathalie with her pity and her rigid ideas about "people like me," how amiable I find these old tourists around me, who judge nothing but the presumed abundance of my means. And so, I tell myself, whatever it is I'm supposed to be isn't inevitably and everywhere visible, and a luxury cabin on a Mediterranean ferry can blind people to it, whatever it is that I still don't see myself!

I feel slightly lost. A waiter sets a mayonnaise-slathered half lobster before me. The captain tells a joke. Everyone laughs. I can't help blushing, my cheeks are hot and damp. I wish he'd give it a rest, but now he's on a roll, and basking in his success. No one's looking at me in particular, that's not where the danger lies.

But my heart is uneasy, *the side of my heart that's still decent, appalled, and humiliated, but meek, so very meek.*

I swallow some mayonnaise, and unlike Noget's it tastes bitter and salty, like a concoction of tears and snot. Everyone around me is still laughing, their flesh heaving, excited. The captain tells a joke. It has to do with grotesque and odious people, intolerably ugly and stupid, and it's about Ange and me, and my ex-husband and Corinna as well. The punch line is feeble, the humor crude. Oh no, it's not funny at all.

Is Ange being punished for marrying me? Is he marked because he ended up becoming like me, just as people take on the traits of the evil thrust into them, which doesn't frighten them, which they even take for a good thing?

It's not funny at all, I'd like to shout, pounding my knife on the table. The captain keeps up his banter, so amused at himself that he bursts into laughter before he's thrown out a new quip, leaving the crowd hanging on his every word, quivering with impatience, the forks in midair, the lobster forgotten, and sometimes the pent-up laughter rebels against its confinement in their jowls and erupts before its cue, in little belching blurts. My eyes fill with tears. But I'm here, protected by my money, anonymous in this exuberant illumination—I'm here, elegantly made-up and properly coiffed, and yes I'm too fat and slightly sweaty in the heat of the lights, but aren't we all, around this table, overweight, sweating, and worn? I'm here, and delighted to be here in spite of everything, and then I suddenly hear myself adding my forced laughter to the salvo that greets the captain's latest sally, and then my laughter strengthens, swells, dries my eyes. Mouth agape, bent over the table, I laugh so hard my throat feels ready to rip open.

I see Nathalie walk past the double doors that separate us from the ordinary dining room, left open because of the heat. She hesitates, then stops for a second, poised on one leg. I see her looking at my cackling face, my jutting teeth. Paralyzed by my demented joy, I'm incapable of acknowledging her in any way. Oh God, I ask myself, did she hear that last joke?

25. I hold her close

And what a surprise, later in the evening, to find the cleaning lady sitting on my bunk, her back slumped in sorrow, the woman in the navy blue uniform with little gilded buttons who readies the cabins for the night, turns down the beds, checks the supply of soap and towels in the bathrooms.

Right now she's not doing any of that. Overpowering grief is rocking her shoulders back and forth, and beneath the dark fabric of her jacket I can see the very sharp, protruding line of her vertebrae, and it's as if she feels so profoundly sad and lost that she doesn't care that in that bony ridge she's baring a fragile and intimate part of herself.

"Here now, here now," I say.

She looks up, her face crumpled in despair.

"Is there anything I can do for you?" I say, slightly uncomfortable and afraid.

"It's nothing," she says, "it's not me."

"What do you mean, it's not you?" I say.

This woman and I are about the same age. I sit down close by her on the bunk, unsure what to do.

"There's this lady," she says.

A tragic grimace deforms her mouth.

"Oh," she says, "it's so horrible, I can't stop thinking about it."

A shiver runs down my back as, from the brief description she gives me, I realize she's talking about Nathalie, whose cabin she's just seen to.

"What was she like?" I say. "Was she..." (I choke back a nervous titter) "normal?"

"Normal? Well, of course she was, but," says the woman, "how normal can you be when you've been through such a tragedy—you don't know what happened to her?"

"No, I don't," I say firmly.

I try to stand up, but an inertia holds me down, something resigned and defeated inside me, something remorseful and weary, and I lower my head, trembling, *my nape exposed, accepting the blow and the awful weight of the axe, the fearsome jolt of the inevitable end.*

"Her husband," says the woman, wringing her hands on her clenched thighs, "and her two little children, she showed me their pictures, a boy and a girl and the husband, all wearing big smiles, a beautiful family, you know, and he took the children away on vacation to a house they'd rented, and she wasn't there because she was going to come join them later, she had work, and the house caught fire in the middle of the night and the little boy was burned but he got out, and then the husband tried to get the little girl from her room and it was too late and they both burned, the father and the child, can you imagine? Burned to death, you understand. The boy's in the hospital, third-degree burns, that's why she's going there, to see him. There were four of them and now there's just the two, the little boy in such terrible pain under his bandages and her, the mother, all alone. She told me all about it but she never cried, and I don't know why, I'm the one crying...I don't know why..."

So devastated that my whole face is frozen, my jaw locked, I feel obligated to mumble, "It'll be all right..."

My voice is breathy, inaudible. The woman collapses into my arms, her head on my breast, overcome with emotion.

Through the graying roots of her red-dyed hair I can see the ice-blue skin of her scalp. I see my own tremulous hand clumsily smoothing that two-toned hair, clumsily massaging that exposed, shining skull, cold as a polished gem. The woman sobs gently, submissively. No doubt she can hear my pounding heart, I tell myself, my shamed, sorry heart, she can hear it, and what does she think of it?

Now patting that stranger's damp brow, my hand has taken on the regular rhythm of the ferry's rocking. It's been a long time since I last held someone in sympathy, with no disgust getting in the way, as it did after Ange was attacked. Wasn't it my father and mother I last pressed to my shoulder, the day I left Les Aubiers, with all the compassion that came with my certainty that I'd never come back, and their having no idea, such that even then, even as I was lying to them, telling myself I would never come visit them and they'd never dare, with their hesitant faces and imprecise, jagged speech, never dare venture into the city in hopes of seeing me, even then I felt infinitely sad for them?

26. Too late

First it's an old man in pajama bottoms who opens his door, and I beg his pardon and knock at the next one, which is answered by a young man, and so on all down the second-class corridor, very oddly, since there's nowhere Nathalie can possibly be if not here, in one of these cabins.

I want to tell her I understand her grief now, and I'm sorry for her—I don't think I could go on if there were no way of telling her that. That vital necessity, that frenzied, violent need to find the woman I'd hurt with my silence, my seeming indifference, keeps me scurrying up and down the corridor even after it's become perfectly clear Nathalie isn't here.

But, I say to myself, how could she have gone on being so thoughtful and kind, how could she have seen my disinterest in her story and gone on offering me her help, the support of her efficient, practical will? I certainly couldn't have… Oh God, oh God, I have to kneel at her feet, nothing less… Maybe she thought there was no point expecting so much from a woman of my kind? Did my rudeness and heartlessness simply fit in with her idea of the way people like me typically react, people she takes pleasure in protecting, as it happens, because she's a charitable, tolerant soul? In the end, it doesn't matter, it's unbearable, it's unthinkable that she should be somewhere on this boat, asleep or awake, with no idea of the things I must tell her and show her—that she should be living and breathing so close by, bearing the scar of that unforgivable insult…

And I remember the few words I'd recalled on the train when she was done talking to me, I remember the fire and the children. "My God, my God," I mumble, staggering over the corridor's floral carpet.

Where is she, what does she look like now? I haven't seen her—or maybe I didn't recognize her?

Just then, at the far end of the hall, I see the cleaning woman disappearing into the stairway that leads belowdecks, the woman whose tear-soaked cheek was pressed to my bosom not long before. I call out, I run to the stairwell.

I frantically ask her for Nathalie's cabin number. And when she tells me it's 150, I don't dare contradict her. I don't quite remember who answered when I knocked at cabin 150, but I know it wasn't Nathalie. Could she be with someone else?

I go back to the door and knock loudly. Nothing. Or is there? I think I hear a quiet rustle that someone is trying and not quite managing to silence. I knock again, I whisper, "Nathalie!"

I press my ear to the door. And I strongly sense the echo of another ear on the other side of the door, just next to mine, and I hear what sounds like a bated breath and a quiet moan, and ill-contained sobs, but it could well be nothing more than the night wind, I tell myself, not believing a word of it, *just as I tried to convince myself it was nothing other than the wind that was calling me, and the wind's breath I was hearing, when, long ago, the telephone used to ring and there was nothing on the other end, no voice, only breathing, muted, sorrowful, afraid, and ashamed, paralyzed by anguish and uncertainty, which I answered with silence or a few sarcastic words meant to hide that I knew perfectly well who it was, who it was that couldn't speak a word to me but couldn't resist the need to hear my voice, even for a moment, I knew it wasn't the wind but my father's breath, or my mother's, or maybe both at once, and how clearly I could picture them clutching the receiver and giving each other ever more desperate glances, urging each other to speak some word that wouldn't come out, a word that faded and died as soon as it was born amid that ever fainter, ever faster and more hopeless breath*, but it must be the night wind, I tell myself, pulling away from the door Nathalie won't open because she doesn't want to let me see her this evening. And

I trudge back upstairs, telling myself that for all my life I've failed everyone and every situation it's ever been my lot to experience.

27. It's him, that's my son

Now I'm trying to spot Nathalie in the crowd of passengers, posted by the top of the gangplank, the sunlight still pale and opaque but already almost blazing, the early morning air vibrating with the threat of an infernal heat to come.

I who so yearned to see my son again, now I find myself hoping he'll be late, or maybe even have forgotten or neglected to come meet me at the boat, so desperate am I to see Nathalie first.

How I'd like her to drive me to my son's house in a rented car, and this time I wouldn't be afraid I might suddenly see her face change before my eyes, I wouldn't be afraid of anything she might say or do, and I could unambiguously redeem myself and at the same time ask her what it is she thinks—or knows?—I am. And then beg her to forgive me, I who took care not to hear a word that she said, and promise her I'll find some way to be a better person than I've been.

But, she might say with a charming and generous smile, no one expects any sort of humanity from you.

No, she'd never say such a thing. What she'd say is:

"Go see your poor parents in Les Aubiers; let these newfound aspirations to goodness take that form for a start, with a well-deserved visit to those people who've done you no wrong."

"No wrong?" I'd say roughly. "But wasn't it wrong, and very gravely wrong, to try to bind me up in the mediocrity of an existence completely enclosed in the boundaries of a neighborhood and austere rituals and incomprehensible, unyielding mistrusts of anything that wasn't in our ways? I'd rather die than see those faces again—faces mine must look a little like now that I've aged some—I'd rather die than feel the pity the sight of abandoned, rejected old people always inspires, a pity mixed with remorse and nostalgia, because don't all old people, quiet and unassuming all their lives, have a bereft or pleading look that can make your heart ache even when they've never done one thing to deserve your indulgence?"

But the flow of passengers slowly thins, and Nathalie isn't among them.

Half numb with despair, I walk down the gangplank myself. I'm already hot in my black clothes, and my scalp stings and itches.

In just the few minutes since the boat docked, the intense paleness of the sky has succumbed to the invasion of an azure so elemental that the paving stones on the dock and yellow-and-white façades beyond the port seem tinted blue by it, as if no surface could resist absorbing such vigor.

Perhaps because my eyes are burning as well, I violently collide with a man at the bottom of the gangplank. My head crashes into his shoulder, my glasses fall to the ground. He lets out a little cry of pain, my teeth having jabbed him in the collarbone. I shout, "Careful, don't step on my glasses!"

I bend down to retrieve them, and as I'm standing up again—my gaze climbing from the white-espadrilled feet up the long, hairless, oddly slender tan legs of this man in his wide-legged khaki shorts, a pair of pink-and-white striped briefs very visible inside them, as is even, I believe to my deep discomfort, the soft, shiny hair of the loins (and I think I detect a warm, intimate smell, clean, soaped, perfumed)—a long-ago memory of two little legs, skinny but powerful, clasping my hips and encircling my waist with such stubborn force that I had to put on an angry face to get him to loosen his grip and drop to the ground, back when I came home to the Fondaudège apartment at the end of the day and my son leaped on me like an anxious little monkey, the brutally precise memory of those limbs, warm and strong but so slight, leaves me speechless and trembling. Oh, I recognize those grown-man legs, I made them myself.

With one hand I push my glasses back on, with the other I touch my son's thigh. He leaps back.

"Ralph, it's me," I say, standing up all the way.

But when I do my son's beauty grabs me by the throat. Gasping, I put one hand to my chest. He was a very appealing young man before, but in a slightly slovenly, almost moony way. And now I see that boy with his diffuse charms, his ever-presumed but rarely displayed gifts, transformed into the archetype of glorious manhood, even more incredibly handsome than his father, my ex-husband, and I know Ange and I would once have sneered at such splendor, automatically associating it with a kind of idiocy, but, either because this is my son or because Ange's jeering influence is waning now that I'm far away from him, Ralph's newfound beauty awes me, intimidates me, and also saddens me terribly.

Frowning, he peers at me. He's taken off his sunglasses

to examine me more minutely. A shy, surprised smile bares his teeth.

"Mama? Is that you?"

"You don't recognize me?" I say, feigning levity.

He can't help looking me up and down, as if in search of some piece of me that might prove I'm the mother he remembers. It's been so long since we last saw each other, so long. And I look back at him, not hiding my admiration or the twinge of melancholy I feel forcing my mouth into an ugly, stiff smile.

I take an awkward step forward to embrace him. And he steps toward me, a tiny reluctant step, and bows his head to let my lips graze his cheek, but he doesn't touch me or return my kiss. Certainly, this man who turns out to be my son is a figure of stunning physical perfection, but...

A shapeless unease enfolds me, clinging, subtle, ungraspable, as if when I stepped toward my son I'd ensnared myself in a gigantic spiderweb.

What is it about him, I ask myself, that isn't quite right?

We're the only two left on the dock. The sunlight rebounding off the white paving stones forces my eyes into a tight little squint, and I can feel my flesh recoiling from the relentless assault of the suffocating heat. My breath is quick and unsteady.

What is it about my son's appearance that's not right?

"You've gotten so fat," he says bluntly.

"And that bothers you?"

"As a doctor, yes," he says.

"And as my son Ralph?" I say.

"A little, there too," he says with a quick, flustered laugh.

"I'm going through menopause," I say, "although some people refuse to believe it and insist on thinking I'm pregnant, how ridiculous."

"It's not hard to find out," says my son.

He looks away, likely troubled by the intimate turn our conversation has taken.

He's wearing a white linen short-sleeve shirt, strangely tight, so stretched over his broad, flat torso that the little metal buttons seem about to pop off. All that—the trim, muscular figure, the narrow waist, the thin, chiseled face, the lush, curly black hair, the brown eyes rimmed with long, thick lashes—I remembered all that before, and I recognize it now. But what about the rest? The thing I can't put my finger on, can't yet put a name to, but whose strange source is somewhere in my son's gaze, what is that? He's Ralph and not Ralph at the same time, he's my son, but my son as if with someone else's eyes. And that someone else seems a coldly righteous man, animated by an unyielding fervor, a hermetic passion that overflows, just a little, through a discreetly but implacably dogmatic stare.

Oh, it's mystifying, because what once defined my son's personality—to the point, often, of obnoxiousness—was the very opposite of what I see here today: it was an unremitting, tedious irony applied to everything indiscriminately, a limp, disdainful distance he inevitably put between himself and anything that happened. I remember, for instance, the remote, vaguely sardonic look on his face as he told me he was leaving Lanton, the way he watched me, waiting to pounce at my first sign of distress (because I was so fond of Lanton, so fond) and viciously mock it, as if it were unseemly and grotesque, rather than exceptional and praiseworthy, for a mother to dote on her son's lover instead of her son himself.

And now there's no trace of ridicule left in the eyes of this man poised on his shaved legs, boldly offering his face to the merciless sun—there's only something severe and intransigent, almost brutal.

I open my purse and take out Lanton's letter.

"Here," I say, "I don't want to forget this, it's from Lanton."

He takes it from me with a steady hand. He crumples the letter into a ball, looks around as if in search of a trash can. Evidently failing to spot one, he stuffs the letter into the pocket of his shorts.

"You have to answer him," I say anxiously, "or he'll think I didn't give it to you."

"Who cares?" says my son.

"But if he thinks I didn't obey him, he'll avenge himself on Ange," I say softly.

"Don't believe everything he tells you," says my son.

And his hard, categorical tone is meant to announce that the question is closed.

He picks up my suitcase. With that, his lips begin to tremble. He stammers, "Oh, Mama..."

A moment later he gets hold of himself. He purses his lips, turns his back to me, and starts toward the parking lot with my suitcase in his hand. And I watch him walk off, resolute, ever so slightly solemn, my son who used to shamble aimlessly in tennis shoes, slouching and slump-shouldered, along the sidewalks of Bordeaux, adrift on his own boredom. How straight and tall he stands now! How this arid land has hardened him!

I walk after him, feeling the fiery paving stones through the soles of my ankle boots.

A tall man whose face seems familiar, wearing a baseball cap with a transparent visor, comes walking toward us. He passes by my son without a glance, but he stops when he reaches me. The faint shadow of his visor tints his cheeks and forehead violet. Seeing me keep walking, he leaps straight in front of me. Now I have no choice but to stop. My legs are rubbery with fear. In a shrill little voice, I call out: "Ralph!"

The man lets out a contemptuous laugh. I can't help thinking I should know who he is—should and would, if I weren't such a coward.

"Ralph!"

But my son is already far ahead, and doesn't hear.

"Ralph!"

Isn't that anger I now hear in my voice, the same blinding, dizzying anger, feeding on its own energy, that used to take hold of me, and afterward leave me deeply troubled, when my son was slow to loosen the little legs firmly clamped around my waist after he'd bounded into my arms, and that anger made me forget my strength and not see the excessiveness of my reaction, because sometimes I pushed him off so roughly that he fell backward in the entryway of the apartment. And one day his skull must have struck the floor in a worrisome way, that must have happened at least once, immediately snuffing out my senseless rage, throwing me to the floor beside him to take him in my arms and rock him, wretched, silently praying that he might forget this scene and tell no one of it, and never hold this one memory of his mother in his mind.

The man spits at my feet, a dry, unproductive hack. He blurts out a word I don't understand, hearing only the end: "yer." I shout in terror. He walks around me and stalks off, jumps over a chain barring access to the boats, and disappears behind a freight container.

28. Everything we hated, everything we condemned

Catching up with my son by his car, I can feel his impatience, almost annoyance. I say nothing of the encounter I've just endured. He gestures toward the backseat.

My son's car seems extremely luxurious. It's white and huge and must be brand-new. It gleams so in the sun that my gaze can only skim its surface. I open the remarkably thick, weighty door and let myself drop—or be sucked, it almost seems—into the low, yielding black-leather seat.

Oh, the things Ange and I used to say about people who buy big cars, the fierce contempt, the furious hostility we unleashed on them, we who proudly and virtuously squeezed our ample bodies into our cramped little Twingo, smugly reflecting that we could well have afforded such-and-such a sedan whose surpassing comfort and power we saw extolled on the billboards of Cours Victor-Hugo (there and nowhere else, since we didn't watch television), and we looked at the price and howled at the appalling stupidity of spending such sums just for that, and it thrilled us to know, and to know the other knew, that had we so chosen we too could easily have granted ourselves that mindless splendor, that vulgar embellishment of our discreet success.

And now, I tell myself, deeply pained, now I find my own son feeling the need to display himself in just such an obscene vehicle.

And those two old people in Les Aubiers who happen to be my parents, how they ran to the window when their practiced ear told them an expensive car was pulling into the parking lot! How proudly they delighted in the sight, showered with glittering sparks of that good fortune, almost honored to live in a place where such a car deigned to park for ten minutes, and not jealous, never envious, too docile for that. How I wish I could stop thinking back to that moment, how I wish I could eject them from my memory!

"Delighted to meet you," she says, in a grave, mellifluous voice.

Sitting in front, she reaches back between the seats.

"Mama, Wilma," says Ralph laconically.

I extend an uncertain hand. She brushes hers against it, not squeezing it, and I shiver at the touch of a warm, tender skin, telling myself that my own dry, dimpled, frightened little hand must make her feel like she's touching a lizard.

"Good trip?" she asks.

But she's already turned around, uninterested in my answer, or even whether I answer, and so I say nothing, impotent and desolate, feeling my capacity for reflection and judgment and perspective being drowned by the tidal wave of unconditional admiration and painful obeisance that hasn't washed over me for so long, protected as I was by Ange's assurance, he who could never be made to feel reverence for anything or anyone.

Now I'm just a naked body, vulnerable, piteous, ripped from its shell or its armor, and so white.

I have no work, I'm alone. There's nothing left to save me from the sense of my own pointlessness. And—just as in my unarmed younger days, when I first met Ange's daughters Gladys and Priscilla for example, or when I faced a certain type of mother at school, at once snooty and winning, full of scorn and innocence—this unknown Wilma, who to the best of my knowledge has no official grounds for being here beside my son like a wife, need only turn toward me with the faintest tinge of unintentional arrogance and offer me her face in three-quarters profile, her beautiful tanned face, smoothed by a liquid base whose subtle orange tint can only be detected by its contrast with the matte, lighter skin on her neck, yes, this miraculous woman, conventionally but strikingly elegant and nearer my age than my son's, need only appear, like the fusion into one visible person of all the invisible, supreme people in this world, to make me surrender to the authority I've granted her, to make me stop striving for a freedom of mind and an independence of soul that I once thought I prized above all other things.

Oh, such weakness I have in me, such weakness. What's going on with this Wilma, I ask myself, and what sort of relationship am I meant to forge with her? As Ralph's mother, am I expected to demand some special deference?

My son starts up the engine, and I lean over slightly in my seat for a better view of Wilma's profile. The air conditioner whirrs. It's almost cold.

The things Ange and I used to say about air-conditioned cars and the people who buy them, the things we said about even the little I've seen of the life my son leads...

Her light chestnut hair nearly matches her skin; it's shiny, straight, carefully pooled on her shoulders. A fine dark down covers her upper cheeks. Her eyes are black, like my son's, and magnified by mascara and eye shadow.

This woman put on full makeup for an early-morning trip to the port to pick up her mother-in-law. Her plump, wide lips are an ardent, glowing shade of red. She's wearing what looks like a beige linen pantsuit. I give a little cough, then ask, "Where's Yasmine?"

My son is absorbed in the delicate task of maneuvering out of the parking lot and back to a wide, dusty road. I see a frown on his face. Meanwhile, the woman smiles vaguely.

"What are you talking about?" says my son, in a tone of repressed fury.

"I'm talking about Yasmine, your wife," I say.

A warm, heavy breath mists my ear. I feel a hairy tickle on the back of my neck. I snap my head to one side. A dog's gaping maw has just appeared by my face, as if threatening to rip me apart should I say one more word. That dog must have been sleeping in the far back—is it obeying some unspoken command from my son, surging up just when I ask him a question?

I pull away, pressing myself to the window, as far as possible from that monstrous beast.

"I didn't know you liked dogs," I say, slightly breathless.

"He's a Bordeaux mastiff," says my son.

"His name is Arno," says Wilma.

"Ah, Arno," I say, discreetly giggling to myself.

How horrible, how horrible, Ange and I used to think, those middle-class young people who show off by buying the biggest, scariest dog they can find and then saddling it with a human name, how horrible they are!

Unfinished houses line the road on both sides, rusty metal rods protruding from bare cinder blocks. And now the sun is high in the sky, and I think I can smell the scent of the morning's new, hopeful heat through the glass. I bend forward until I'm almost touching my son; I bathe the back of his neck with my mouth's warm breath, since, I say to myself, he's so fond of dogs now. And I also say to myself, in a burst, a fragment of a dream: My little boy's fresh-scented neck!

I murmur, "So, what about Yasmine?"

My son violently slaps the center of the steering wheel. He cries, "Will you shut up?"

I wasn't expecting such aggression. Tears come to my eyes, reflexively, with no sadness. I see Wilma's hand appeasingly pat my son's bare thigh, and when she pulls it away her handprint stays behind, damp on his amber skin. She gives me a neutral, diplomatic look, appraising the forces in play here.

"You have no idea how to behave," says my son, through his teeth. "Mother, you make me ashamed. How dare you ask such a question in front of Wilma? That's not done and you know it, it's simply not done."

"Never mind, it doesn't matter," Wilma murmurs calmly.

"It *does* matter," says my son, slightly strident.

"I'm sorry, I'm sorry," I say, distraught.

I'd like to ask for news of the little girl in hopes of smoothing things over, but I still can't bring myself to speak her name, that terrible "Souhar," which to my ears sounds like a provocation, a sneer, an obscenity, even a vicious offense. Has Wilma noticed?

"Ralph and I live a very tranquil life," she says, as if imploring me not to speak of anything that might upset the stability of that existence.

"Yes," I say, "Ralph's father said...said our granddaughter was a very quiet baby."

My last words drop into a heavy silence, snatched up and swallowed by that wordlessness, unbroken even by the breath of the two strangers sitting in front of me, as if they were holding it so we would share nothing, least of all the chilled air of the car. My grating breath alone fills the air, accompanied by the quick, damp, congested panting of the animal in back.

Less because I want to hear the answer than hoping to disrupt the rhythm uniting my breath with the dog's, I ask, "Is she doing well? The baby?"

Again that silence, virtuous, accusing. At a loss, I turn my face to the window. What did I say that was so out of place? Are they mad at me for not saying "Souhar"? But that can't have so struck them that they should immediately come together in this punitive silence, unless...unless they know everything, understand everything that's troubling me...but that seems so unlikely, so unlikely...

The SUV abruptly turns away from the road and the still sea, which looks as if it were shielding itself from the blue sky and sunshine behind the row of new or half-built villas.

"That sea doesn't shine," I say.

My son scoffs.

"Is that the poetic style you teach your students?" he says, in a voice dripping with sarcasm. "No wonder they didn't want anything more to do with you!"

"I thought," I said, exasperated, "I thought you'd turned into such a kind man, and you were determined to love me in spite of everything, just as I do you!"

"That's true," says my son, immediately calm and gentle despite the fervent undercurrent that forever seems to run through him, making his voice vibrant and intense.

Now we're driving along a very steep gravel road that twists and turns at impossibly sharp angles. So my son lives in the mountains, I tell myself, with some foreboding.

As the car climbs, ever more laboriously, through dark, dry clumps of arbutus and short pine trees with black trunks and bare, blackened branches, the sea shrinks to an opaque blot and finally disappears from view. And then we cross to the other side of the ridge, the shadowed side, and my heart cowers in my chest.

The shadow is vast, stretching for miles all around us, over the forest of charred pine trees, over the deserted valley, the dark, meager river at the bottom looking from here as if it were frozen in place, paralyzed by dark ice. My son turns off the air conditioner.

Suddenly it's cold. The silence surprises me. Even the dog has stopped panting, as if saving its strength. My son turns on the heater. And still we climb, onward and endlessly onward, at a crawl, and it seems to me that every moment that goes by takes me further from Ange, and closer to deserting him forever, since now it will take so long to go back down to him.

29. This is how they are

My son and this woman, this Wilma whose age, poise, and beauty affect me more than I dare admit (I have no hold over her, no possible sway, I can't even imagine having any, nor could I try to win her over as I did Lanton, who was young and as it happened had no mother of his own, since that woman had so many times remade her life and replaced her husbands, so many times diverted her affection onto new children, that the paltry share left to Lanton had in his eyes long since gone stale), live in a vast stone house built on the mountainside, in the village of San Augusto.

I have to describe all this with the deepest detachment, since there's nothing I can change. But this is not, not at all, what I was expecting to find.

I'd so dreaded having to face my granddaughter's name, having no further pretext, however tenuous, to protect my mouth from it, so to speak. And perhaps even more than that, I dreaded *how can I say this, how can I admit to this* having to realize, as I looked at the child's face, at her eyes, the darker or lighter irises contrasting starkly or not with the whites, at her skin, creamy or otherwise, that my son had perpetuated the indignity of our bloodline.

I couldn't bring myself to ask my ex-husband, that innocent, good-hearted, ignorant man, what our granddaughter looked like in that way, which was in all honesty the only thing I cared about. He wouldn't have understood if I had.

I never watch television, I tell him. My mind isn't like yours, it's not clouded by all that foolishness. I learn a lot from television, says that simple man. He could say to me, he would have every right to say to me: Nadia, you know far more about evil than I do, you're far closer to evil than I am; abstaining from TV hasn't protected or purified you, no, by forgoing TV you haven't leaped into some great cleansing fire; you might have, I don't know, dived into a fetid swamp. Myself, I'm the same man I always was, deep down, however fond I am of television, he might tell me, that upright ex-husband of mine.

But I haven't had to examine Souhar's little face, whatever it looks like.

"Where's your daughter?" I asked Ralph almost as soon as we reached his house.

Everything was spinning; I had to lean on the car not to fall. All those twists and turns had left me dizzy. My stomach was churning. My son grumbled a few unintelligible words, scowling with a rage that might at any moment erupt to smite his poor mother in her mire of ignorance and incomprehension.

Once it was I who could terrify him with one frown; I could bring him to tears with the tiniest hint that I might lose my temper—when was it, how old was my son, when the fear moved from one side to the other? My loving little boy was so afraid of angering me, couldn't bear to see me upset with him for any reason at all, and then the young man he turned into was so nebulously oversensitive that I took to weighing every word I dared speak to him, even then never quite sure I wouldn't incur his wrath, and at such times I was like some of my students, whom I see taking a desperate leap into the void when I ask them a question, no doubt praying that their fall will be as lazy and endless as a fall in a dream, and that my face too will go on hovering unchanged, ever patient and gentle before their own tortured faces, until the end of time.

I found the courage to ask, "She's not here?"

"No," said my son, very sharply.

The house that my son and this Wilma now live in looks over the valley, its back turned to the road, and it's such a tall, austere house, of solid gray stone, that you can see it from far down the mountain, even from miles away.

"I'm so disappointed," I said. "I was hoping to meet my granddaughter at last."

"Well, you're not going to," said my son.

And I'd so steeled myself for the sight of the child that I was sincerely unhappy and even distraught that she wasn't here, not simply relieved, as I would have expected.

Raising a questioning, surprised eyebrow, I tried to attract Wilma's attention. But she looked away, like a discreet wife who knows how to mind her own business, and so I learned beyond all doubt that she wasn't the child's mother Yasmine. Because in the car it had occurred to me that this Wilma might be Yasmine, that Ange and I might have misremembered his marrying a Yasmine, or that she might have changed her name, decided to go by something else, *as I myself would most certainly have done if my name were Yasmine.*

So maybe it's all very simple, I'd told myself, so reassured by that idea that I almost laughed out loud.

I'd never seen a picture of this Yasmine. My son had hurriedly informed me of his marriage, one day when I ran into him on Rue Sainte-Catherine, refusing to tell me anything more of his wife than her first name, Yasmine (or did he say Wilma?).

My son wouldn't tell me about his wife because I had, in his words, appropriated Lanton when he was still with him—I'd stolen Lanton away from him, even cuckolded him with Lanton, he'd said. "Symbolically, which is worse," he'd added, seeing the disbelief on my face. Now he wanted to be sure I left his wife Yasmine in peace.

"But," I'd protested, "what on earth could I do to your wife, what are you afraid of?"

He was afraid I... How can I say this without trembling? He was afraid I might teach his wife shame and self-loathing, under the cover of affection and interest.

"But when have I ever done such a thing to anyone?" I'd cried, desperate tears spilling from my eyes. "When have I ever done such a thing?"

My son simply gave a cruel laugh and raced off, merciless and hateful. How anyone could possibly inspire such hatred in a son, an only son, once so loving, I couldn't begin to understand. I later learned that my son had gone off to live and work in San Augusto, taking his brand-new bride Yasmine with him, and then the little girl was born.

"You see," Ange had told me when we got the birth announcement, "he's not holding a grudge, since he's telling you you're a grandmother."

"Yes," I'd said, happy at first.

But then the baby's name leaped out at me, and I found myself thinking my son had sent me the announcement for that reason alone: so the six letters of the name "Souhar" would make a point that would pierce straight through my heart.

Now that I'm here in my son's dour house, I've stopped caring about that awful name. My nerves are on edge. Where are the child and her mother? Before, I dreaded the prospect of seeing them (even as I was hurt that my son had never introduced them to me), but now I'm deeply afraid for them.

My son and this Wilma live in what seems the biggest house in the village, which is otherwise only a handful of modest gray dwellings huddled around the plain little church. Set away from the others, but close enough for the inhabitants of those shabby houses to know everything that goes on in it, my son's enormous abode displays three rows of narrow windows on the other side of the road, and completely hides the valley from its neighbors, unless it's shielding them from that melancholy view, in whose depths the gaze soon grows lost—the woods ravaged by recurrent fires, the motionless river, the cold shadow draped over it all.

The fearsome sun only strikes the other slope, facing the sea. There's no trace of that blazing heat here, but it gives off an invisible vapor that makes the air shimmer all the way to San Augusto. That faint vibration of the atmosphere can cause mirages, Wilma told me. Sometimes, she said, an expanse of water seems to be floating over the village, and if that happened to me, if I thought I could even see a reflection of palm trees in that illusory lake, then I should simply close my eyes, and the vision would be erased.

My son had helped the dog out of the luggage compartment. He was about to let go of the collar, to set the dog free, because neither of them likes to keep it tied up or on a leash, my son and this Wilma had told me.

"Arno's a sweetheart," my son had said in a slightly menacing voice, as if he expected me to openly dispute it or provoke the dog simply to prove it was vicious.

Doesn't he know I don't care about dogs? That for me dogs don't exist? That any word spoken about a dog bores me to tears? But just when he was about to let the dog go, my son suddenly pulled it back with an angry, surprised jerk. Arno was about to lunge at me.

"That's odd," said my son. "Do you have a dog back home?"

"Certainly not," I said, still trembling at such hostility.

"Well, he must be smelling a male dog on your clothes," said my son, musingly.

"There's no other explanation," Wilma insisted.

"I'm not hiding anything," I said.

All three equally irritated, we dropped the question of the dog and its feelings toward me. My son and this Wilma seemed irked, almost saddened, at not understanding the reasons for Arno's behavior. That wounded pride and affection showed me the depth of their love for that dog.

Don't they have a child they should be loving like this, or is that little girl not enough for them, is she a disappointment, is she ugly, or is there too much that's troublesome about her appearance?

Wilma stroked the dog's broad reddish flanks, as if seeking its forgiveness for something. She kneeled down before it, her magnificent face touching the dog's muzzle, and said, "Go on, boy, go on."

And the dog licked this woman's cheeks, nose, and mouth, this Wilma who lives with my son and who so painstakingly made herself up to come meet me this morning. The dog's long tongue wiped away her base, her blush, her lipstick, even her mascara, and she laughed with what seemed a slightly overplayed joy.

Then my son wanted the dog to lick his face in turn. They playfully struggled for a place before the dog's mouth, competing for that benediction. Wilma stood up, proud and fulfilled, her face bare, white, and downy. And there was a kind of challenge in that display of her naked face, still glistening with the dog's saliva (I could smell it, strong and sour, I could imagine the stickiness of her skin), as if this primped and preened woman were daring me to find her any less alluring like this.

I turned away. I walked toward my son's front door. I had no wish to see my son *my little boy who was once so madly in love with me, has anyone ever loved me like that* stand up covered in his dog's spittle, displaying that same repugnant delight. My God, how lonely they must be, I told myself, to be so humbly offering themselves for Arno's affections, even if it means having to beg.

The cold was mild and dry. A vast shimmering blue sky encircled my son's house and, across the road behind us, the little houses clustered around the church, silent houses that I might have sworn were deserted had I not seen, at the windows, their impeccable white curtains.

On the doorstep, Wilma reached into her purse for a big key ring and waved me aside. My son took the dog in first, pulling it by its collar. Knowing I was behind it, the dog insistently looked back, growling, refusing to go on. A furious foam covered its pendulous black jowls.

"You must smell like dog, there's nothing else it can be," my son exclaimed with a sort of rage in his voice.

"Arno is very dominant," said Wilma.

"Maybe he senses you're not entirely happy to have me here," I said, as a joke.

"That could be," said my son, perfectly serious, even grave, with no sign of cruelty or malice.

It was a shock to see that my son had apparently lost his sense of irony, once so highly developed that he could often be tiresome, not to mention difficult to understand, since at times it wasn't quite clear if he was deliberately saying the opposite of what he was thinking or if he should be taken at his word.

Today, in San Augusto, on my son's territory, I no longer doubt the meaning of what he says. The rigorous intensity that sets his every word in a clasp of absolute literalness distances him from the son I remember more than plastic surgery ever could. Having thought that, I look at my son's face and I'm not sure I recognize it after all. I'd be happier to hear him speaking with the strong, harsh San Augusto accent, I tell myself, than with this high-minded solemnity and earnestness he once systematically mocked, when he thought he'd heard it in some pedagogical pronouncement from Ange's mouth or mine. He accused me of always taking everything literally, derided what he called my cluelessness at any sly provocation.

How did my little boy, my gentle, sensitive, tender little boy, ever turn into that young man I couldn't love?

Never once, on the other hand, did he show the slightest impatience with my ex-husband, his father, even though that man was perfectly incapable of grasping our son's sense of humor, his perverse turn of mind.

Because Ralph had sensed or realized that his father's simple goodness inevitably implied a deafness to derision, and Ralph respected him endlessly for that, and maybe he was sorry he lacked that innocence himself, and maybe, too, he resented me for—he must have thought—infecting him with a talent for seeing things from two sides, and nonetheless I hated his taste for sarcasm, his joyless laughter, and I found myself hating him too, when his jeering went on too long.

I should be happy to find my son delivered of that maddening bent. Why am I sad, why does it trouble me? Because he's still as pitiless as he ever was? Because in his pitilessness and inflexibility and fierceness I see something even more dangerous for me, in spite of his furious striving for goodwill? I'd like to tell him: You'll never be like your father, it's too late, and that's not how you are. Oh, I wish I could also tell him, in disgust: Don't you see where your hapless father's trusting heart got him? Shamelessly living off Corinna Daoui, shamelessly living in an apartment that's not his, shamelessly redecorating a ridiculous bedroom for a little girl he must see at most a few times a year, and then, still shamelessly, showing the world and Bordeaux a kind of face he can't understand everyone hates.

My son disappeared into the house with Arno. Then he came back and told me he'd closed the dog up in his consulting room, and I remembered my son is a doctor. Never having seen him practice, I forget that now and then.

I only knew my son as a student, so long in school that I'd vaguely decided school was an end in itself for him, not a way into the medical profession, which he'd chosen on Lanton's advice.

With a gentle shove to the small of my back, Wilma ushered me in. The entryway is cold and dark. The stone walls are hung with masks made of wood and leather, along with pelts stretched over wooden frames, and a vast collection of stuffed wild-boar heads.

"I've taken up hunting, with Wilma," my son proudly told me as I stared at the heads and imagined what Ange would have said of that carnage.

There's no breed more despicable than hunters, Ange used to say.

"So you've learned to shoot?" I asked weakly.

They turned their two shining faces to me.

Every hunter in this country should be executed, Ange used to say.

"Of course," said my son, "Wilma showed me."

Their two faces glowed palely in the dark entryway, lit from within by pride and desire as they recalled, I imagine, their hunting trips in the scrubland, armed with the powerful weapons I later saw in their bedroom, pursuing a lone male or a frantic sow hurrying her piglets before her, reeking of terror with Arno's snout close behind, and I later wondered if that black beast's fear was the spice in the homemade terrines my son served. Is it horror that brings out the full flavor of meat?

And how surprised I was, later, to find that my son had become an avid cook, with a fondness for red meats, and even, it can't be denied, a certain taste for blood.

I tried to admire the masks and heads, since my son

and this woman were my hosts.

"Very beautiful," I murmured, noting that Ralph immediately beamed with joy.

He couldn't repress a smile, a smile like the old days, at once broad and hesitant, happy and anxious, the smile he had as a little boy.

Didn't he smile exactly like that when he submitted a piece of homework for my verdict, or a drawing, or even a present he'd hand-made just for me, didn't he smile just like that when it turned out his mama approved, when, for example, he introduced dear Lanton?

Then his face hardened into ardent austerity again.

"I'll show you around," Wilma said to me.

"Yes," said my son, "show her around."

And then he asked Wilma to examine me at the earliest opportunity.

30. What did she see?

Lying on the examination table in Wilma's consulting room, I think of my son, who didn't come along as she took me on a tour of the huge, dark house he's been living in with this woman for I'm not sure how long—weeks, months, more than a year?

I got the impression my son never ventured upstairs, which was even colder and darker than downstairs, and divided into many rooms, all virtually empty. The only furniture in mine is a bed, a writing desk, and a chair. The bed is draped with a pink chenille coverlet, and I was so dismayed by the sight of that fabric, something I wouldn't even put on a dog's bed, I told myself, that I couldn't help blushing.

Wilma noticed.

"This was all here when we moved in," she told me. "We never have guests, so we haven't redecorated the upstairs."

Taking advantage of my son's absence, I casually asked Wilma, "Where's the baby's room?"

"What baby?" Wilma carelessly answered.

Her cheeks turned faintly pink. She bent down and dragged my suitcase into the room so she wouldn't have to look me in the eye.

"Well..." I said.

But the child's name, that cursed "Souhar," adamantly refused to cross my lips.

"You know who I mean," I said, my voice almost desperate. "Please, please, stop pretending! My granddaughter..."

Has there been some decree that I must be punished whenever I seem to sidestep that hideous name?

"Talk to Ralph," she interrupted.

We came back down the imposing stone stairway. In the front hall, Wilma opened a door with her key and ushered me into her consulting room.

"Are you a GP like Ralph?" I asked.

"No," said this woman, "I'm a gynecologist."

Then, in a gentle, professional voice: "Get undressed, mama, and lie down on the table. I'll be right back."

I never saw a doctor's office in Bordeaux as modern and well equipped as Wilma's in this humble village of San Augusto. From the rug to the armchairs, everything is fuchsia and white. The desk is a long sheet of glass on four fuchsia legs. The computer, a Mac, is the same color, and so is the pad on the examination table, and every lamp, every cabinet.

The windows look onto the deep, dark valley on one side, and the houses around the church on the other. There are no curtains. If I raise my head a little I can see the neighbors' windows, and I imagine them seeing me too, looking at me lying naked on the table in this Wilma's office, this gynecologist who lives with my son. Unless those houses are empty and abandoned, and there's no human life in San Augusto but us.

Wilma comes back, now wearing a white smock, her hair tied behind her neck, her delicate face carefully made up again. I'm very uncomfortable having her see me this way, bound up in all the unhappiness of a body too long neglected. I cover my eyes with one hand. I murmur, "You know, this feels very awkward..."

"Don't worry," says Wilma, "I'm a doctor, nothing more."

"I used to be pretty," I say, suddenly powerless to shut myself up, "but, I don't know how it happened, I lived my life, my mind was on other things, and my body, how can I say it, my body went its own way because I wasn't bothering with it, it led its own little independent life, and of course I looked at it every day, but honestly, I didn't see anything..."

"Relax," says Wilma soothingly, "I'm not paying any attention to that."

I turn my head so she won't see my damp eyes.

The house is perfectly silent. What's my son doing? Is he watching us? I vaguely sense other breaths than our own stirring the air in this room.

This Wilma woman comes and goes, pulling on her gloves, laying out her instruments, and I notice her beautiful plum leather pumps, and—below the hem of her violet skirt, half concealed by the smock—her oddly stout calves and thick ankles, and it moves me to see them, slight as she is in every other way. I whisper, "Isn't my stomach strangely swollen?"

"We'll see," Wilma murmurs.

Her voice sounds suddenly different, heavy with foreboding. I put my feet in the stirrups, feeling my thighs wobble and jiggle. My skin isn't fair, but varicose veins meander very visibly beneath the surface.

Wilma gently spreads my legs, slowly pushes the speculum into my vagina.

"That's very cold," I say, flinching slightly.

Wilma doesn't answer. I raise my head a little and our eyes meet. Hers are filled with panic and perplexity.

She quickly gets up from her stool. She thrusts her hands deep into her pockets, goes to the street-facing window. She comes back, sits down, looks into the speculum again. Turning a wheel, she widens the opening. I groan in pain. She immediately turns the wheel back the other way.

"So," I say, "what do you see?"

She doesn't answer. I ask again. Stubborn silence.

I look past her shoulder, toward the window, where a little white chicken is now standing on the outside ledge, poised on one leg in anxious but focused attention, seeming to observe me with an implacable eye. I ask, "You have chickens?"

For a moment Wilma doesn't understand, but then she glances over her shoulder.

"Yes," she says, as if relieved at the change of subject, "but we don't have time to look after them, we don't even collect the eggs. You can, if you like."

"I've never done that," I say, faintly insulted, "and I don't know that I'll have time either. I've got to go back to work. I have to find a school here."

"That's not going to be possible, with what you've got in your belly," cries Wilma, in a strangely horrified tone.

She yanks out the speculum, drops it into a little metal pail, shoves back her stool. She stands up and tears off her gloves, almost furiously.

"Who did you make this with, mama? What have you done with your life?"

Slightly sore, I pull myself up and sit on the table, my legs hanging over the white and fuchsia checkerboard tiles. I shiver in terror.

"So… Tell me what's wrong with me," I say, my voice strident.

With a sigh, I add: "And what am I guilty of now?"

Wilma's long brown eyes seem to soften in something like pity. With a slow, graceful gesture, buying time, she pulls the elastic band from her hair.

"After all," I say, "menopause isn't a crime."

"Oh, mama," she says, "that's not what it is at all!"

"So why has my period stopped?"

She shakes her head, at a loss for words.

"In any case," she says, "you're not sick. There's just… something that doesn't look like things we know."

Suddenly I can't bear the thought of her saying another word. I gracelessly plop down from the table. I can feel the thing in my stomach caught off guard by the sudden movement, I feel it lurch just above my pelvis, then settle back into place and grow still.

I hurry to get dressed. Meanwhile, Wilma takes off her smock. Beneath it she has on a tight violet angora sweater. The dusky skin above her breasts is slightly slack, though her face is taut as can be. *This woman who lives with my son might well be far older than I am.*

Not looking at her, struggling to button my pants, I ask, "Will my stomach get any bigger?"

"Yes," says Wilma, "I think this is just the beginning."

"There's no way to get rid of it?"

"This isn't the usual kind of thing, mama. I can't take the risk. We'll just have to see."

"But," I murmur, "it's not...demonic, is it?"

"Yes, it is," says Wilma.

She forces out a chuckle to hide her dismay, as if it were still possible to inject a little levity into our words, or at least as if this feint were necessary, not as a mutual deception but simply as a way of going on without falling into numb horror whenever we're together, our mouths agape in disbelief.

I have one last question for this gynecologist who lives in my son's house and who, I say to myself, may in some way be holding my son captive.

"Could food have caused this thing?"

She raises a surprised eyebrow.

"Of course not," she says, "it has nothing to do with food."

31. Bad cooking at my son's

The three of us are together for dinner in the cold, gray dining room my son and this woman have made a permanent exposition of their hunting exploits. The stone walls are covered with framed photographs of one or the other in hunting garb, holding a pheasant or crane by its legs, or standing with one thick army boot pressed to the bloodied breast of a wild boar or roe, always smiling the broad, martial, joyless smile of someone who kills not for survival or pleasure but in the firm belief that it has to be done for the common good. Wilma's smile is wholehearted, sharp, with no sign of regret or constraint, but the grin on my son's beautiful, bowed lips seems slightly forced, with a very faint hesitation, a hint of a quiver.

We sit down at the oak table, brown and massive like all the furniture in this room. The dog Arno barks from inside my son's office, with only a door standing in its way.

"He's used to being with us, he doesn't understand what's happening," says my son, tense and irritable.

"You talk about that animal like it was your child," I say.

My son's face contracts and closes. The night is dark outside the narrow windows. Between barks, the silence is absolute.

My son has put a dish of dark meat in wine-colored sauce on the table, and now he's doling out a generous portion, blushingly telling me he spent many long hours cooking this game—oh, how proud he is, I can see, to be regaling me with a dinner he cooked himself.

How can I now hope to undo what I spent twenty years

creating, how can I deliver my son of his anxious, angry eagerness for his mother's judgment—what do you care about my pronouncements, I wish I could tell him, they're no better than any others!

My son gives Wilma a helping even more plentiful than mine, and then parsimoniously serves himself.

"You were nagging me about being fat," I say loudly, struggling to make myself heard over the dog's protests, "but how do you expect me to lose any weight if you give me so much to eat?"

My son looks at me. I see compassion in his eyes.

He murmurs, "Wilma explained; now I see why you looked pregnant, forgive me."

I waggle a frantic hand at him, retreating. I categorically refuse to talk about the thing I have in me.

I begin to eat. The strong, complicated taste of the meat and sauce immediately startles and exhausts me. My jaws are heavy with fatigue; all at once I find it impossibly arduous to chew and at the same time focus on what I'm tasting so I can come up with something to say about it. I can only tell my son it's very good, I'm too tired to say anything more.

In reality it isn't good at all, it's heavy and gristly and aggressive. Is this supposed to be some sort of test?

My son casts me a wary glance, and then, as I look back at him with a steadfast affection, his whole handsome face suddenly glows with happiness *and I see the child I loved to see looking like this, a child who is still alive, then, beneath the features of this resentful, tense adult, this resentful, vindictive adult who's a stranger to me, so hard to like, so different from Lanton with whom I felt a kinship the first time we met, whom*

I loved, yes, more than my son, so much so that his death would have left me adrift in despair, which my son's wouldn't have, it might even have come as a secret relief, ridding my life of the burden our resentful, unquiet relationship had become, and no such name as "Souhar" would have infected my tranquility, but if, when my son's face suddenly lights up like a lamp, I can once again see the child I loved, then can't I also learn to love the man he is now, just a little, a man whose resentment and unquiet rancor so imperfectly conceal the child I loved, but did I really love him, did I love him as I should…

I put down my fork, wipe my lips. My stomach is thrashing. No one can see it under the table.

"Ralph!"

My son jumps. The dog stops barking, and silence encircles us.

"You have to answer Lanton's letter," I say. "You absolutely must."

"Do you know what he wants me to do?" says Ralph, icily.

"No," I say.

"So how can you demand that I answer him," says Ralph, "if you have no idea what he wants?"

He moodily pushes away his plate. Wilma reaches out and strokes his head. Trying to calm himself, my son takes a deep breath.

"All I know," I struggle to say, "is that you're putting Ange's life in danger if you don't answer Lanton."

He stands up, furious.

"You see what a monster he is," cries my son, "and it seems like you're still protecting him!"

"It's not him I'm protecting," I say, "it's Ange."

"But there's no hope for Ange," says my son.

He slowly sits down again. I close my eyes, my ears ringing. Suddenly my son's rage subsides, and he murmurs, "He wants me to come back to Bordeaux, he wants us to get back together."

"Yes," I say, despairing, "he still loves you."

I begin to weep.

"So what about my poor Ange?"

"Apparently he's doomed anyway," says my son.

I ask, "Who told you that?"

"Richard Victor Noget," says my son.

"He's the one who's killing him," I say.

"No, I don't think he is," says my son. "I think it's you, Mama."

Anger dries my eyes. I shout, "I have never, do you hear me, never done anything to hurt Ange!"

"You didn't know you were doing it," says my son, in a soothing tone that frightens me more than anything, "but you led him into something you shouldn't have. In the beginning, he should never have had any problems, he was innocent."

He turns toward Wilma, as if to explain a situation to someone who can't fully grasp it:

"Mama's husband Ange came from a good family, had a good upbringing, never felt unworthy."

"That's true," I say. "What's that got to do with anything?"

"He never should have married you," says my son, "unless you moved away, far away from Bordeaux."

"Ange would never have wanted to leave Bordeaux," I say.

"Well, he's never going to leave his beloved city again," says my son, with wrenching sadness.

In my torment, I pointlessly repeat, "Lanton... He still loves you..."

And we say nothing more, and in that silence I almost wish the dog would start barking again.

His chair screeching on the tile floor, my son gets up to bring in the dessert, a chocolate mousse. The evening is cool, but he's still wearing his shorts. His smooth, slender, slightly awkward legs could easily be a teenager's.

I lay a hand on my belly, feeling another, chaotic life moving inside it. I'm not hungry anymore. All this dark food disgusts me. But my son's eyes shine once again with that tortured, almost hateful hopefulness as he sets a full bowl of his chocolate mousse before me, so I have no choice but to eat it and let out little *mmm*s of pleasure to appease him. Every mouthful is torture. I'm not hungry! Just one more spoonful, all the same, and then another, crammed deep into my throat, until I'm about to gag—I can't choke this mousse down... I swallow and it's gone, sliding down, just two spoonfuls to go, they seem so enormous, insurmountable...

My son looks on excitedly, happy to see me eating.

And what about the thing inside me, is every mouthful bringing it new strength?

"You should have left Ange in peace," says my son all at once, "you shouldn't have thrown yourself at him like you did."

"Thrown myself at him?"

"You never should have…"

My son struggles to come up with the right word, then lets out a little laugh, a hard yelp.

"…seduced him, driven him into marrying you. If you hadn't got your hooks into him, he wouldn't be in this state today."

"You're still mad at me for leaving your father, at your age!" I say.

"This has nothing to do with my poor father," says my son calmly. "It has to do with your husband, and you know exactly what I'm talking about."

For something to do, I scrape at my bowl, now determined not to leave behind any trace of my huge helping of chocolate mousse but too angry to care about my son's feelings. I'm stuffed to the gills, I could burst at any moment.

And if I did, what would that thing look like when it came out, what manner of thing would it be, and how monstrous?

"I thought the food would be lighter and healthier here," I whine.

"Don't you worry about that, mama," says Wilma, "We're going to take good care of you."

Is there a grain of truth in my son's accusations? Why, I ask myself, heartsore, why must this ancient history be brought back to life, these ancient regrets and missteps, can't it all be forgotten after so many years of irreproachable behavior? Why should that grace be refused me? How can that suspicion still linger in a corner of my son's memory, a suspicion he quietly nursed at the time because he was mad at me, and then threw in my face because I was divorcing his father and he thought it wrong—the suspicion that I'd turned to Ange only to better my standing and cleanse myself of my blood?

Oh, I wish I could say to him, such a foul broth you're stewing in!

"So what about your daughter? And her mother, this Yasmine," I say, "why aren't they here, tell me that?"

I feel an ugly sneer on my lips. I have no real confidence in this counterattack, and my voice shakes. My son drapes himself in disdainful silence, he doesn't even bother to turn his head.

But he wasn't there when, it's true, I began to deploy all the classic moves for snaring a man, when I began to dance around Ange until I caught him in the net of my carefully practiced charms; my son wasn't there, so what can he know of my feelings, my love for that man, that colleague I wanted and vowed I would have? You didn't love him, my son would say, but what does he know? You didn't love him, my presumptuous son would tell me, you only wanted to erase where you come from and who you look like—but what can a son know of his mother's feelings for a man who isn't his father?

"You don't know the first thing about love," I say. "You ran out on Lanton..."

"I don't want to hear another word about that bastard," my son shouts.

Wilma goes out. After a moment she comes back with a long, heavy metal box and sets it down on the end of the table. It came just this morning, she tells my son, and it's everything they'd been hoping for.

My son lets out a cry of joy, and in spite of myself

I remember him crying out just like that on the many Christmas mornings we spent on Rue Fondaudège, and while my son's whoops brought a tender, gentle smile to my ex-husband's lips, I myself could only scowl, incomprehensibly jealous of my son, whom I nonetheless gave everything he wanted, telling myself: I never had such a lavish Christmas, almost wanting to see him disappointed as I'd so often been at his age, before one single, sad present, ineptly chosen.

Wilma carefully extracts an array of metal parts from the box and assembles them into a hunting rifle. She hands it to my son, who gauges its heft, lovingly strokes it. How happy he is!

He playfully aims at my chest. And, playfully, I raise my hands.

"Don't shoot!" I say.

My tone must not have been lighthearted enough. Shamefaced, my son lowers the gun.

32. What's going on between them?

My first night in my son's house is a very painful one.

As if Wilma's examination had granted the phenomenon inhabiting me a new confidence, even brazenness (or was it a growth spurt, I ask myself, set off by that dish of game in sauce?), my body is racked by spasms and what feels like a clawing from inside, savage and unrelenting.

"A whole litter of cats closed up in a bag," I say to Wilma when, unable to take any more, I finally drag myself out of bed, deep in the night, in search of aid or consolation.

I knocked at the door to their room, and after the briefest moment Wilma opened it, still fully dressed. The room is lit by the gentle glow of a night-light. I can see many gleaming metal weapons hanging on the wall behind Wilma. My son's brown-haired head sticks out from under the sheets, motionless. He's sound asleep.

"I can't give you anything right now," Wilma whispers, "I'm going to have to come up with a special treatment for you, mama."

"But I'll never get to sleep," I say.

She shrugs in impotent sympathy. Then she turns away. Together we look at my son's tousled hair, as if meticulously arranged on the pillow, undisturbed by so much as a breath—why, I ask myself, do I feel as if this woman is watching over him like a jailer?

"This Lanton of yours," Wilma murmurs, "Ralph never stops thinking about him—he says his name in his sleep."

Pensive and sad, she adds, "Ralph still loves him too, it's clear..."

"Lanton's a very powerful man in Bordeaux," I say. "He could easily hurt Ange if he wanted to."

"Well, what can you do, right?" says Wilma, roughly. "Good night, mama, and try to get some sleep anyway."

A hairy shadow growls from the bed where my son is lying still as a stone. The dog Arno jumps to the floor, its claws scraping the wood. Wilma closes the door.

This same intimidating woman suggests to my son that he take me along on his rounds. My son happily consents.

The early morning is bright and frigid. You've absolutely

got to eat meat at breakfast, my son asserts, or you'll never get through the long hours to come and the cold of the drive down. He brings out a terrine of wild rabbit with pistachios. Seeing Wilma cut a hefty piece for herself, and finding nothing else on the table but bread and a potful of coffee, I accept the slice of terrine my son hands me with his encouraging smile. Another strong dish, slightly overwhelming, but the quiet, unafraid happiness that relaxes my son's face as I eat it, feigning hunger and pleasure, more than compensates in my mind for the difficulty of choking down wild game first thing in the morning.

Wilma eagerly takes a second helping, almost pounces on it, wolfing down her rabbit terrine without bread, spearing it with her fork, taking long swigs of black coffee between bites.

I hope this isn't your child we're devouring like this, I'd like to tell my son, as a joke.

But I don't. I can't help thinking he's unhappy to see me witnessing Wilma's voracity. Still, she's beautiful, elegant, very delicate in a mauve silk peignoir, and impervious to the cold. When she asks me to go with Ralph on his rounds, her voice is soft but commanding.

Does she want someone keeping an eye on him at all times?

In the entryway, Ralph lays a fur jacket over my shoulders.

"You've got to cover up," he says.

I instinctively shrug off the wrap, and it slides to the tile floor.

"I'm sorry," I say, "but I hate fur!"

He picks it up, smooths it, as if to comfort it.

"Well, like it or not," he says, "you're going to have to get used to it."

"What do you mean by that?" I say.

He silently heads for the door, carrying his medical bag, wearing a long deep-red leather coat.

"Wilma told you what she saw with the speculum, is that it?" I ask.

He adamantly shakes his head to tell me he's not going to answer.

"All right, Mama, off we go," he then says, so amiably (and with something close to tenderness in that *Mama*) that my lips begin to tremble, ready to stammer out something that nonetheless doesn't come, whose very sense and intention I don't yet know.

A handful of women are waiting on the sidewalk in front of the house, huddled in the glimmering cold, all of them stocky like me, very dark-haired and dusky, with Wilma's long, tapering eyes, jet black, slanting high toward their temples. They cast curious, tittering glances my way.

In a whisper, I ask my son who they are.

"Wilma's patients," he says.

He adds that they live in the little houses clustered around the church, on the other side of the road.

"Go look around sometime," says my son. "They make leather masks, like the ones we have in the front hall."

I ask what I could possibly want with a mask. My son falls into a hesitant silence. He reaches out and unlocks the car doors from a distance. Then, for what feels like the first time, he looks me straight in the eye.

"You can have them reproduce your loved ones' faces,"

he says. "That way they'll be with you, hanging on the wall, they'll see you coming and going."

My son puts the bag in the trunk and sits down at the wheel. I whirl around and scurry back to the house. The women watch me with laughing eyes—is it the sight of my open cardigan flapping every which way, now that I can't button it over my stomach? I hear my son calling. Not turning around, I shout, "Just a minute, I'll be right there!"

I hurry into the house. My heart clenched, *a heart that's not so old anymore, my old heart now young again, stupidly beating in time with what inhuman heart?*, I go to the two masks I'd seen in the entryway, facing the boar heads. They're made of a fine, smooth light-brown leather. One shows a young woman's face, the other a tiny girl's. The first is grave and somber—the mouth is downturned, the black glass eyes full of an indefinable sadness. The second, the child's, though its shape and its features are much like the other's, is merry and joyful.

So they're here, I tell myself—but only here?

A quiet rustle turns my attention toward the staircase. Wilma is watching me, motionless on the bottom step, her arms crossed over her smock. Such bulky calves for so slight a figure, I reflexively think. Shc seems angry, on edge. With a quick flick of her wrist, she seems to drive off my presence, erase it from reality.

"You're going to make Ralph late," she says. "You should be with him!"

"Because he's not supposed to be alone?" I say.

"Usually I go with him myself," says Wilma.

And that, I then understand, is what's irritating her: not

that I looked at the masks but that I left my son unattended.

I go back outside. *Wasn't Ralph alone yesterday, when Wilma showed me the room, and then when she examined me? No, no, he had the dog with him, Arno was keeping an eye on him.*

A cowardly relief then comes over me: my son is here, he's waiting for me in the car, the engine purring. Should I be helping him escape Wilma's control, should I wish I hadn't found him so obediently waiting? Oh, I say to myself, I don't know, I have no idea what my son wants in all this.

I climb in beside him, sinking into the deep seat, which smells discreetly of wild animal. My son starts off at once. A little vein is throbbing spasmodically on his temple.

"Wilma certainly likes meat," I say.

Ralph snaps back, "Don't say one word about Wilma, I don't want to hear you start finding fault with her. Wilma's your host, you have no right to do that here, Mama!"

"I'm not finding fault," I say, "I'm just saying that woman likes meat like...like a predator."

"Not one more word!" cries my son.

Suddenly he's covered in sweat. He turns down the heat. I murmur, "You almost seem like you're afraid."

Slowly we drive down to the sea, leaving the cold shadow behind us, the icy, bright sky, the fearful, gray little houses huddled beneath the church.

Little by little I feel the heat hitting the metal of the car. It works its way inside, ever more insistent. My son parks on the shoulder, frees himself from the seat belt, takes off his coat as he sits, with the precise, mechanical movements of someone who does the same thing in the same order every day.

"I'd like to know," I say, "is it true that you came to Bordeaux this year and saw Ange?"

"Yes," says my son. "He told you that?"

"No," I say. "He didn't tell me a thing."

Humiliation and sadness weigh on me. I feel stupid and bitter, ill-treated. *And yet Ange and I never kept secrets—oh, did I ever love him as much as I said, how can I be sure? And would I have loved him if he hadn't given me a chance at a good Bordeaux life, respectable and superior, how can I be sure?*

My son stops the car in a hospital parking lot, in a little seaside city with low white houses and palm trees so tall their slender summits lash back and forth in the burning hot wind. A stiff breeze slaps our faces as soon as we open the doors. My son is dressed in Bermuda shorts and a Hawaiian shirt. I wonder if I should take off my cardigan.

I'm marked, I tell myself, with the very visible sign of something ugly and loathsome, even if it doesn't have a name. In the end, I leave my sweater in the car. I catch up with my son in the hospital, then follow him up to the children's ward, where, he says, there's a little patient he visits every day. He opens the door to a room, shows me in.

And from her chair by the bed, not standing up, Nathalie gives me a smile, or rather, her white chapped lips briefly open in a sign of friendly recognition, almost immediately erased by her usual sorrow.

To one side, I glimpse the vague shape of a child's bandaged—oh, I'm not ready to look at that yet.

My son takes Nathalie's hands in his.

"So, little man, how's it going this morning?" he then

says toward the bed (and he bends over the child with such outright tenderness that he could easily be the boy's father).

Nathalie rubs her forehead, pushing aside her pale hair. The child doesn't answer, and she quietly tells my son that it's not going well. Then she turns her limpid, red-rimmed eyes toward me. Grief has bent her lips into a stiff little smile, like a smirk. I slowly take the three steps separating me from her chair, which she seems helpless to stand up from, held down by sorrow or weariness or trepidation (maybe he won't die as long she keeps her eyes trained on him?), and just as slowly, gracelessly, I kneel down before her and lay my forehead on her thighs.

A few seconds go by, and then I stand up, my hands now replacing my forehead on Nathalie's thighs to push myself up. Did I put too much weight on her muscles? She grimaces in pain.

I back toward the door—oh, I make very sure not to look at the bed.

Embarrassed, my son pretends not to notice. He talks to the child in a comforting, lighthearted voice, but he did see me prostrate myself, and it made him uncomfortable, maybe even irritated and ashamed. I stammer out a goodbye and flee. The door slams behind me, making all the others shudder.

33. A little golden bag, a little silver bag

Back in the parking lot, by my son's car, I realize there's no way I can wait for him in this heat.

I circle around the hospital and start down a shady

street lined by the tall whitewashed walls of houses whose courtyards or gardens are tucked away out of sight. The few women I meet are short and brown-haired. They greet me with reserved but benevolent nods, and sometimes a word I don't understand, in a language nonetheless close to my own, as if the heat and humidity had dilated that language's sounds, opened its vowels, slowed its pace.

As I walk past a half-open door, something stops me in my tracks—a faraway melody, a reedy singsong that part of me recognizes, the other part remembering nothing and telling me to keep walking, my feet of two minds, one crashing into the other.

I listen closely. The coolness of the room beyond this half-open door is suffused with a smell I think I know—or do I?

I feel myself shiver, cold sweat trickling over me. I want to get away, but I stay where I am, watching for something.

I can hear the song more clearly now, and the voice, a very old woman's voice, a timeworn voice, but still steadfast, tenacious—I know that voice, oh how I know it, just as I know the words:

Come dance, my little golden bug,
Come dance,
God stands over all,
Come dance to the sound of the balafon,
Little white hen, come dance!

Didn't I once struggle to repeat those very words after the woman who sang them to me in the voice I now hear, however weakened and wavering with age—a patient, happy voice, stubborn beneath its seeming humility?

Come dance, my little silver bag!

No, there's no song I know as well, as profoundly as this one, even if I've forgotten I know it, even if I took great care never to sing it to anyone. Suddenly the voice goes silent, as if it knew someone was lurking and listening.

I start off again down the warm, mild street, terrified that at any moment I'll hear footsteps behind me, that a gnarled but still vigorous hand will land on my shoulder and, in that harsh, jagged accent—in my own language or another I tried hard to forget but which I'll understand all the same—the old woman will say, "Is that you, Nadia? How fat you are!"

And how will I answer? Feign surprise, deny all knowledge of Nadia, using the slightly sharp, racing voice I can so easily adopt, and a few high-flown, precious words this illiterate old woman won't understand, which will drive her back as efficiently as a bullet to the chest?

But this is ridiculous, I tell myself, that can't be her, it can't be my mother.

Come dance with the woman who's all alone,
Fragile thing, I'll go and dance,
God stands over all!

From the moment they came to Bordeaux, my parents never left Les Aubiers projects, where my father worked as a groundskeeper, two people perfectly united in their fearfulness, slinking through the streets as if they were sought for some terrible crime, in everything they did acting as if they'd done something wrong—could those cowering people, who could have been accused of any misdeed without so much as a thought to defending themselves (and they would have helpfully held out their wrists for the handcuffs, apologizing for being a bother), could they really be here, so far from home, serenely singing *My little golden bag*? And singing it for whom, for what little ears, in what little head will those words take root forever, words I wrongly thought had slipped from my memory: *Little black hen, come dance to the balafon*?

It's ridiculous, I tell myself, it's ridiculous.

No hurried footsteps have come up behind me, no hand has snagged my shoulder. But the terror is still in me, physically materializing as an urgent need to empty my bowels.

"But where, for pity's sake, where?" I can't help murmuring aloud.

I hurry onward with clenched little steps, fearing catastrophe.

Go back to the house of the little golden bag, beg them to let you use the toilet, and if your aged mother really is there, she surely won't turn you away...

The street leads to the seafront avenue, where it ends. The hot, dry wind blows skin-lashing, eye-stinging sand through the air.

Desperate, about to give in (and in my exhaustion almost yearning for the unstoppable warm spurt to begin), I sprint into a bar on the street corner. And the tears in my eyes are almost tears of gratitude when a moment later I find myself sitting in the privacy of the bathroom, repaid, respectable again.

I hear a quiet hum of men's voices from the bar. Some of them stand out now and then, a higher pitch, a quick laugh, an exclamation. And among them... Still perched on the toilet seat, I lean toward the door. Someone tosses out a joke in that language I can't understand, met with a round of friendly, indulgent laughter—and then that same man speaks again.

I know that mellow voice, even with this gaiety I've never heard in it before...freed of its tremulousness...its excessive, unwholesome humility... And he seems to be telling jokes, which would be extraordinary...

Just when I'm about to stand up, a fresh bout of diarrhea drops me back onto the seat.

It's him, how can I go on doubting it? Could they really have afforded to move here on his paltry groundskeeper pension?

I put my forehead to the door, close my eyes. I'm trembling and shivering. My swollen stomach rests on my knees, awaiting its moment.

Exactly which of my crimes is this thing meant to punish, this coming abomination?

Now, a bit later, I'm out on the little street again, slowly walking back the way I came, resigned to passing by the house of the little golden bag. The mellifluous-voiced man must have gone home to that house by now, that man who is my father, my elderly father, beyond all possible doubt, whom I didn't see in the café when I finally emerged from the bathroom.

It must be noon. The smell of meat fried with onions and spices has settled onto the street.

How eagerly, how happily, with what an untroubled conscience I climbed the stairs toward that smell when I came home from school for lunch, and how in later times I fled it, careful not to make any dish that would confront me with it again, turning my heels in disgust if I happened to stroll past a window or door it was coming from, or one like it, or a memory of it!

My mouth is dry with hunger, a fearsome hunger. Now I've almost reached my parents' house. The door is open, I see. I don't slow down. But a sudden dizzy spell blurs my vision, and to be sure the noontime heat is overpowering and the noontime sun fierce, but that's not what's blinding me, and I know it.

I stop and wait until my vision clears. Then I walk toward the wall opposite my parents' so I'll be as far away as I can when I pass by their door, and that moment soon comes, the moment when I'm straight across from the open door to my poor, aged parents' new house, the parents I declared dead to Ange's face without a blink or a shiver though I knew it wasn't true, though I knew, how could I not, that my silence and tacit disownment and mute, groundless hatred would surely hasten their actual death, and somehow or other I would hear of that death, but I could never tell Ange, and so that death would become a shameful secret in the ugly depths of my heart.

I look intently into my parents' house. And I would be willing, and I would be ready, should my eyes meet with the most fleeting glance from either one of them, to ford the gap between me and the door.

And I'll simply walk in, and I'll greet them as if nothing had happened, very normally, with no show of emotion, which would only be awkward for all three of us.

From here, across the narrow street, the sunlight's so bright that the room seems very dark. I can make out a table, a cupboard, a sink.

My son is sitting before a full plate at one end of the table. He lifts a spoon to the lips of a tiny girl in a high chair. She opens her mouth, then closes it tight, and my son lets out a loud laugh. He turns the spoon toward his own mouth, takes a dab between his lips, then holds it back out to the child, who immediately eats.

Two old people are sitting before them, a man and a woman, and even from here, from behind, I recognize my father and mother. They're sitting at the table, arms touching. My father's hair is sparse and white. My mother's is covered by a yellow scarf.

Suddenly my son looks up, and for a few seconds we stare at each other. A gleam of merriment lingers in my son's eyes, on his parted lips, but I see it slowly fade as he realizes I'm there and I've seen him.

34. What have I done to that boy?

I hurry back to the hospital parking lot. My son's car is still sitting in the blazing sun.

Someone comes running behind me—it's him, it's my son. We wordlessly climb into the car, in our usual seats. It's so hot inside that I can't hold back a groan.

I sense anger in my son, not the guilt I was expecting. And I also realize that the raging resentment I'd long felt toward him, ever since he left Lanton and maybe even before, maybe from the very beginning (*did that really never happen, my too brusquely repelling his embrace, the anxious, devoted child he was on Rue Fondaudège falling back and hitting his head on the tile floor, did that really never happen, my picking him up, more afraid for myself than for him, and desperately pressing him to tell no one? Oh it's true, how can I deny it, and I hated that he was forcing me into such acts, such a loss of control, and into making him my accomplice in secrecy, because everything about him filled me with muted irritation*), that resentment is gone from inside me.

I'd like to lay my hand on his thigh and tell him, but that would mean admitting the anger I once felt, and so I keep quiet, sitting motionless at his side, in that silence heavy with his anger and annoyance.

He starts back up the mountain road. The soothing shadow envelops us. Very quietly, I ask, "Why did you bring them here?"

My son shoots back, "Who?"

"Your grandparents," I say.

"Because they were dying of sadness back in that horrible apartment, that's why," says my son in a hard voice.

"But you didn't know them," I say. "I never took you to see them when you were little."

"So?" cries my son. "They're still my grandparents, aren't they? Besides, that's the whole problem, I never met them, thanks to you, and it's hard to have a natural, relaxed relationship when it started so late."

He stops the car at exactly the same spot where he took off his leather jacket earlier. He puts it on again, buttons it up, as—amazed to hear myself speaking so freely—I ask, "The baby, that's Souhar?"

"Yes," sighs my son.

"She lives with them?"

"Yes."

"She's pretty," I say, "she's already got beautiful hair."

My son has started off again, back up the deserted, silent road, which pushes us deeper into a hostile winter with every passing yard. His jaw has hardened, his lips are tucked back into his mouth. He's not going to say another word.

And no, I never told him my parents were dead, I simply never said they existed, never spoke their name, never described my life as a little girl in Les Aubiers, so he would understand and accept from his earliest childhood that no question on that subject would be tolerated, and wasn't I hoping he'd get the idea that even thinking about them was forbidden in just the same way?

Breaking the silence, my son says to me stingingly, "You never knew it, but the day I turned twenty I went to see them in that filthy project where you were letting them die."

"So you had their address," I stammer.

"I got it from Papa," says my son, "poor Papa."

I wasn't blind back then to my son's father's weaknesses and forebodings, no, I wasn't blind—I kept a close watch on that man, vulnerable as he was to emotion and apprehension; I suspected he might seize any occasion to flout the rule that we must never, no matter what, tell my son of my parents, but I knew all about his failings and fears, and I knew what he thought: that one day some act of providence would avenge my parents for the way I'd treated them, without a trace of reverence or piety.

Again my son stops the car. He covers his face with his hands, and I hear him sigh. Because he's thinking of his father, my ex-husband? Or because he'd spoken of Souhar?

A surge of affection for my son rushes to my face, making my cheeks hot and damp.

I think I can say your daughter's name now, I'd like to tell him: Souhar, Souhar!

I give the back of his neck a quick, light stroke.

"I saw your father not long ago," I say. "He's doing all right."

My son shakes his head, rubs his eyes, turns the key again.

"I'd like to bring him here too," he says, "but he doesn't want to come."

"He's moved a horrible woman into my study," I blurt out, immediately sorry I did.

"I know," my son answers softly. "He doesn't want to leave her, he says he owes her so much."

I can't help but laugh in derision. But immediately that laugh makes me ashamed.

"If you could only answer Lanton!" I say.

My son taps his fingernails on the steering wheel. Between the flaps of his leather jacket I see his thigh twitch, bare, golden, smooth, and slender, as if, I tell myself, an eternal youthfulness were preserving my son's lower half just as it was when he was fifteen, while, to compensate, an excessive maturity fills his gaze with the earnest gravity, the lofty dourness that yesterday made me almost doubt that this man, this fanatic, could possibly be my son.

But a fanatic for what cause, what faith? The attainment of his own moral perfection? Oh, I would tell him, you're not a naturally good man like your father, that would be too much toil and pretending for a soul such as yours, is there really any point?

"I will never," says my son, "never answer Lanton."

35. He's giving a lecture

My son and I have a quick lunch with Wilma (two braised teals, with tiny spoonfuls of cabbage and carrots that Wilma doesn't touch, claiming to be full from a generous helping of teal, but clearly the truth is that this woman likes and perhaps even tolerates nothing but meat), and when, falsely casual, Wilma asks if I spent the whole morning with Ralph, I find it easy to lie and say yes.

My son doesn't correct me. Pleased, reassured, Wilma suggests we do the same tomorrow morning.

I'm very hungry, but I force myself to take only one thigh and some carrots. My son eats very frugally, leaving Wilma to devour the rest of the meat with a pleasure so excessive that you can only look away.

Afterward, they both go off for a nap. They start seeing patients again at four in the afternoon, they tell me.

I step outside. Even at this midday hour, the road is cold and damp, however clear and bright the sky over the roofs. I start off uphill on the road, which circles the cluster of houses and runs on between two rows of pine trees, first low and scrawny, then ever taller, thicker, and more vigorous, and so I soon find myself in the damp coolness of a blue tunnel, where nothing rustles or shakes.

After a multitude of inexplicable curves, with no visible reason why the road might have thought it should turn this way rather than that in this endlessness of identical pine trees, I suddenly come out into a vast clearing.

Children's shouts begin to ring out. A new-looking building of wood, glass, and aluminum deploys its sinuous, rounded forms at the far end of the clearing. Before it, a pretty paved schoolyard, now filling with a flood of children.

I come closer, already in the grips of envy and regret. I clutch the bars of the fence. The big blue and gray pine trees surround the school from a distance. All wearing brightly colored anoraks, the children run and jump in the muted light, in the eternal, polar shadow that veils this side of the mountain, but the sky is high and bright.

I immediately sense that this is a good and fine school, where nothing bad could ever happen to me. How happy I'd be to work here, I tell myself!

The tranquil joy radiating from the children's dark faces, their quiet play, everything tells me that here I'd be just where I belong, and it pierces my heart with the gentle pangs of melancholy.

I pull myself away from the fence and walk into the schoolyard. The circle of teachers immediately stretches into a line as I come near. Curious and gentle, they extend their brown, deep faces toward me, and now they're bent over me, short as I am, like tall, kindly pine trees.

Oh, I tell myself, at first struck dumb, I'm one of them!

Then my surprise falls away, my uncertainty and timidity, and I feel how positively natural and irrefutable is my likeness with these strangers now smiling at me, curious and patient, trusting in my decency and my right to walk into this schoolyard.

"I'd like to see the principal," I say, after the customary greetings.

They answer me in my language, politely, with an accent I recognize, my parents' accent, which I once so violently scorned.

Inside myself, I reflexively flinch. Reflexively, too, a very faint disdain brings a cold little smile to my lips, I can feel it, a smile quickly erased, and I cordially thank them, silently praying I'll soon be allowed into this group whose accent I might well end up taking on, I say to myself, and not even know it.

I walk to the door they've pointed me toward. No sooner have I knocked than a bright voice tells me in French to come in, and the moment I push open the door Noget's face leaps out at me.

Terrified, I pull the door toward me again. The voice on the other side exclaims in surprise. I push the door open again.

"Well, come in," says the principal.

She's a pleasant young woman, with a smile on her face. The continual twitching of her wide, protruding lips reminds me of Corinna Daoui in our Les Aubiers youth, as does a very slight veil of sadness in her black eyes, emanating from some old or indefinable pain, in spite of her smile.

She's sitting at a desk. Above her, facing the door, a tacked-up poster shows Noget's face—his beard trimmed and combed, his gray hair slicked back, his hollow cheeks no doubt discreetly touched up with pink. Below it I read: RICHARD VICTOR NOGET, AUGUST 29, 8:00, COMMUNITY CENTER.

"Noget's coming here?" I say, dumbstruck.

The principal looks back at the poster.

"Yes," she says. "Quite an honor, isn't it?"

"But why should he be coming here?"

"Well, after all..."

Now it's her turn to be surprised, and she looks at me in friendly puzzlement.

"Well, after all, he's Noget."

"And so?"

"Don't you watch television?" she asks, her voice suddenly almost mystified.

"No," I say, "my husband and I don't have a TV."

Still pleasant but cautious, a touch more distant, her gaze slips from my face to my breast, to my stomach, where it lingers musingly before climbing back up to my eyes. She gestures broadly toward a bookshelf against the wall.

"I imagine I have his complete works," she says.

I go to it, pull out a book.

"That one," says the principal, "is his first little treatise on education. I'm going to ask him to sign it for me."

I page through the volume, reading a few sentences here and there. I feel as if I'm hearing Ange's voice: "The classroom must be not a comforting womb, but a place of judicious severity and implacable justice. / My brothers, what have we done to our children? / We must bring them not milk, an abundance of milk in their earliest years is enough, what we must bring them is in a sense the opposite of soothing milk: we must bring them blood, metallic, unpleasant, and sublime."

Yes, that's exactly the sort of thing Ange liked to say, and it so put me off that I learned to play deaf when he launched in, looking at him with a vacant eye, humming to myself (come dance, my little silver bag!) so my mind would go blank and I wouldn't have to hear.

An incredulous little laugh escapes me as I turn the pages, confronted with the undeniable truth: this is exactly what Ange wrote in the articles he managed, not without effort or colossal pride, to have published in several journals, which I then couldn't get out of reading, since he would have been gravely insulted. I even think I recognize bits and pieces of certain sentences, whole phrases, a rhythm, almost a breath, I think I can hear Ange breathing!

I put the book back on the shelf, turn toward the principal. A last lingering hope makes me ask her:

"Have you heard of Ange Lacordeyre?"

"No," she says.

"He's written articles on these same subjects, he..."

"Richard Victor Noget is often imitated," the principal interrupts, with a touch of arrogance in her smile, "but he has an instantly recognizable style all his own. Still, it's true, there are some very talented plagiarists out there."

"When did his first book come out?"

"Twenty years ago at least," says the principal.

Nothing of Ange's is that old, but if he'd stolen from Noget, wouldn't he have been caught? Can't two minds think the same thoughts in the same words, a few years apart?

Recess is ending, I hear the bell. Charming as ever, the principal casts a quick glance at her watch. She speaks a few words in that language I don't know—or perhaps once knew and then unlearned, having so long cursed it—and seeing that I don't understand she grows slightly troubled, as if suddenly alarmed that she'd greeted me as a peer, as if I might be an enemy hiding behind a friendly face.

"I have to get back to work," she says, with an apologetic smile.

"Yes," I say, "of course."

My hands clasp over my breast.

"You wouldn't by any chance," I say, in a tone more pleading and desperate than I would have liked, "have something for me to do in your school? I'm a teacher, I've been teaching for years!"

She freezes, silent and uncomfortable. She looks me up and down again, very quickly, from head to foot.

Slowly, she answers, "I'm sorry, but we don't have any openings."

She shakes her head, as if to forestall any further discussion. I start up again all the same, beseechingly:

"I'd be happy just supervising at recess, and in the lunchroom at mealtimes."

"But you only seem to speak French," says the principal, very polite, very gentle. "That won't do for our children."

"I believe I'm perfectly capable of learning your language," I say.

She sighs, shrugs. She stands up to tell me it's time I was on my way. Oh, I don't want to go.

The fact is, I know your language, I'd like to cry out; I

pretend I don't but the truth is I know it more intimately than any other—won't you please let me stay!

I really don't want to go. How untroubled, how safe I feel in this clearing ringed with still, vigilant blue pines, under the friendly gaze and protection of teachers like tall, kindly pines! Wouldn't the thing twitching and scheming in my stomach have to surrender in an atmosphere so free of poisonous ruminations?

The principal lays one hand between my shoulder blades and gently pushes me out of the room. Now the schoolyard is empty and silent. Only a muffled purr of voices from the closed-up classrooms seems to faintly stir the limpid air, an air as if rock-hard in its purity.

So I have no choice but to walk out of the school, walk away from the clearing. I take one last look back before I start down the road. The principal is watching from behind the fence. She raises a hand, gives me a slow wave.

36. High times on Rue Esprit-des-Lois

Back in my son's house, I gather my courage and pick up the dining-room phone. I punch in the number of our apartment in Bordeaux.

A stagnant air fills the whole of my son's house, but here the atmosphere is heavy with death, constraint, and fear, and—I say to myself, dread washing over me—the hacking, slicing, and chopping of too many commingled meats. I think I hear Arno panting behind the consulting-room door.

The phone rings and rings. When someone finally answers, I say nothing, choked with emotion.

"Oh, it's you, Nadia," says Noget's voice.

"How's Ange?" I whisper. "Oh God, oh God... Can I talk to him?"

He doesn't answer. Everything goes quiet, as if he'd put his hand over the mouthpiece. I shout, "Monsieur Noget?"

"Yes," he says. "I'm afraid that won't be possible, Nadia. No, I can't put Ange on."

I then make out the clink of bottlenecks against glasses, bursts of laughter.

"But how is Ange?" I say desperately.

"Not so well," says Noget.

He seems distant, bored, as if I were being a terrible nuisance.

"So you're having a party at my place, Monsieur Noget?"

"*Your* place, yes... Listen, Nadia, I believe I'd best hand you over to one of my guests, I have quiches and turnovers in the oven, and those tricky little cheese croissants..."

He loudly sets down the receiver (on my little marble table?), calls someone over.

"Hello?" says the voice of my ex-husband, my son's father. "Who's there?"

"It's me, Nadia," I say in a tiny little voice.

"Oh, it's you? *Hello, hello*!" he says in English.

He's clearly drunk, and his high spirits bring a chill to my heart.

He laughs. I can clearly make out Corinna Daoui's harsh, rasping voice behind him. Meek and imploring, I ask,

"Tell me how Ange is doing?"

"Who?"

"Ange! Ange! My husband!"

"Your husband? But that's me, my love, I'm your husband!"

He laughs again, without cruelty, almost sweetly. Then the line goes dead—did he hang up? Or was it Noget?

Arno erupts into furious barking. I hurry out of the room, run to take shelter in the yard behind the house. It's untended, planted almost solely with chestnut trees. It's so dark that the trees, the dirt, the few overgrown bushes, everything seems black. The yard is steeply sloped, clinging to the mountainside. I take a few steps downhill, my feet splayed to keep from tumbling forward. With every step I stumble over what I first assume to be gravel, kicking it before me, seeing pale little shapes rolling along. I plop down on my backside.

For a moment I sit where I've fallen. My fingers dig into the dirt. I pick up one of those pieces of gravel—but it's not gravel at all, it's a bone. And then another, and another: they're all bones, an abundance of skeletal detritus in all different sizes. A groan of horrified surprise springs from my lips. I quickly stand up, dust off my clothes. So, I tell myself, they've killed all these animals, so many animals…

I turn around and climb back toward the house. The bones shift and roll under my feet, under my groping hands—they spill down toward the valley, toward the blackened pines, toward the river's dark, still waters.

On this second night in my son's house, I again get out of bed, forbidden to sleep by excruciating contractions.

Unable to stand it any longer, I go to my son and Wilma's room. Just when I'm about to knock, I still my hand. I hear a sound, the sound of a deep, superhuman breath. Could that be Arno exhaling, powerfully enough to rattle the door? But, I tell myself, Arno's not so big that he… There's an animal serenity in that breath, a wild, patient self-assurance, and the tranquil but vigilant pride of one who has laid a heavy paw on a defeated breast.

I walk away as silently as I can, now more terrified of seeing that door open than of anything else. Back in my room, I latch the door behind me and open the window, hungry for fresh air. A white moon casts its cold light over the yard. I think of the little school in the clearing, wondering if the students stay there to sleep, if they spend their whole childhood there. Oh, I tell myself, I hope they don't go home to the village! Violently, painfully, I wish I were there, in the milk-white clearing, in the friendly shadow of the pines. How well I would look after those children, wherever they come from!

Was I always fair and hospitable with the students—rare, in the neighborhood where I taught—who reminded me of Les Aubiers, was I always decent to the little girls who looked to one degree or another like the little girl I was? In all honesty, I wasn't fair or hospitable or decent, I was unfeeling and remote, even derisive, silently wanting to see them eradicated, see them fly away, far away from my beloved school, and didn't I sometimes picture them as pigeons, so multitudinous and filthy and unnecessary that they can be shot down without sanction?

But now, I say to myself, how well I would look after those children!

37. They still want to take care of their aging daughter

This early morning in my son's house goes by exactly like the one before.

"You'll go with Ralph on his rounds," Wilma tells me.

"Yes," I say, "very gladly."

And my son acquiesces, without displeasure, as Wilma cuts up big pieces of duck pâté on her plate and puts them in her mouth with her fingers, trembling slightly with what I now know to be a desire so savage and an appetite so fierce that it hurts.

And my son drives me back down to the seafront. We hardly say a word, but I sense that he's already used to my being there, I sense he's forgotten, in a way, that the woman beside him is his mother, who so filled him with rancor and rage. I myself never forget that this is my son sitting beside me.

I'm so happy to be riding with you, I would tell him if I weren't still afraid of his reaction. Was that you breathing so loudly last night? I'd like to ask. Or, I'd say, were you buried under the covers, waiting in terror for that woman to fall asleep at last?

He parks his car in the hospital lot. He's going to visit Nathalie's child.

"I'll meet you back here," I tell him, "I don't want to go up."

He gives me a long look, then silently turns away and strides off to the hospital door, his big medical bag slapping his calf just as his schoolboy satchel once did. Unconcerned that he might see me (because my son knows perfectly well where my steps will take me, he knows perfectly well, and maybe he's glad), I hurry straight back to the little street.

I'll walk by my parents' house again, I tell myself, but I won't go in, not yet. I feel my cheeks and forehead turn red. No sooner have I taken one step onto the refreshingly breeze-swept street than the words and melody of another song begin to float in the sweet, shimmering air.

I'm in diapers,
I'm in diapers,
The child wails,
Oh, how long will he wail?

Again I recognize my mother's voice, even grown piercing and thin with old age. That worn little bell of a voice won't give up, it flutters down the street, drowning out the hum of televisions or conversations drifting over the other houses' walls.

I'm in diapers and I'm hurting,
Oh Mama, how I'm hurting,
Will that child wail forever?

I've never heard that song before. But, I ask myself, almost angry, is that a song fit for the ears of a tiny little girl?

The brave, battered goat bell of my mother's voice draws me in spite of myself. I'm not far from the house. The door is wide open. Now my mother seems to be singing at the top of her lungs. My legs weak, I walk into my parents' house.

My mother stops singing. She's standing near the sink, tiny and slight in the very cool kitchen. Her white hair is gathered into a wispy ponytail at the back of her neck. She's wearing a long beige cotton dress, ornamented with arabesques.

The baby, Souhar, her fingers hooked around the bars of a playpen, gives me a slightly blasé, superior look. Then she turns her eyes to my mother, waiting to see her reaction and no doubt match hers to it. My mother seems uneasy, expectant—but, oh God, what is she expecting?

"Yes?" she finally asks, in her language.

I swallow. In a murmur, I answer, "It's me, your daughter."

"Which one?" my mother asks in French, after a pause.

"Nadia," I say.

"Nadia?" my mother repeats.

She puts her hands to her hair, as if to hide it, as if there were some rule that a daughter mustn't see her neglected old mother's hair. She glances at Souhar, looking lost. The child sees her bewilderment and grows worried, her chin quivering. My mother forces a reassuring smile, but Souhar seems not to trust her, watching for that false smile to fray, and my mother valiantly keeps it up.

"Don't you recognize me?" I say.

"Of course I do," says my mother.

"No, you don't," I say, "I can see it."

And even though I've spent thirty-five years of my life doing all I could to ensure that no one in my family, should by some exceptional circumstance I run into them in the city, would recognize my face and my manner, at least not enough to approach me and speak to me; even though I inwardly snuffed out every visible trace of my upbringing so it wouldn't leave its mark on my face or my way of speaking or standing; and even though the most glorious proof of those efforts' success, the proof that would have delighted me most, would have been that on meeting this old woman I would summon up nothing in her maternal memory, I find myself somehow disappointed, almost shocked.

"Sit down, Nadia," says my mother.

She sounds as if she's saying my name to make sure she won't forget it. I sit down at the table. My mother picks up Souhar, gives her a hug, and sits down in turn with the child on her knees. More for something to say than because I want to know, I ask, "Do you know where the baby's mother is? Yasmine?"

My mother begins to shake all over, from her head to her feet, whose flip-flops I suddenly hear clapping against the floor tiles. Her eyes fill with tears. She stands up, walks into another room. She comes back without the child in her arms, softly telling me she's put her to bed. She sits down again.

"You've seen the woman up there?" she whispers.

"Wilma? Yes."

"She was the one who took Yasmine," says my mother in a low, hissing, sorrowful voice.

I repeat, "Took her?"

But my mother presses her lips tight to keep herself quiet. She makes a hurried little gesture, pretending to toss something into her mouth.

"Don't eat any meat up there," she mumbles, quick as she can. "If they try to give you some, say no. You haven't eaten any, have you?"

"No," I say, frantic, sensing I'd be expelled from my parents' house at once if I told the truth.

My mother reaches out, strokes my hand.

"I think I do recognize you now," she says, "but you've gotten so fat, what could have made you put on all that weight?"

"It's menopause," I say.

"Yes," says my mother, "that happens, my little girl."

The sound of my father's footsteps comes from outside the door. He's heard our voices, and he's wondering if he should come in.

"Look here, it's Nadia," my mother gaily cries in her language, "your daughter Nadia, she's come back."

My father lets out a loud shout.

A little later, in the kitchen grown quiet again, as if itself again, with Souhar still asleep, my mother confides, "Ralph brought the baby here so that woman wouldn't take her too. He was afraid."

My father nods vigorously. The glances he gives me are still shy, but now they're filled with joy.

"That's right," he says, "he was afraid for the little one."

"That woman," says my mother, "she put a spell on him."

There's no hatred in her tone, no revolt, only the acceptance of something fated, an acknowledgement of bonds that can't be undone. I then catch my father staring at my forehead—ardent, blissful. So, I tell myself, he loves the unlovely woman I've become, he still loves her…

"Don't go back there," adds my mother. "She'll take you next."

"Oh no," begs my father, "don't go back!"

"Stay here, we have a room for you," says my mother.

I whisper, "You don't feel any rancor?"

They look at me blankly, vague smiles on their faces. The meaning of that word escapes them.

"My poor son, my poor Ralph," I say, "so I have to leave him alone in that house, with her..."

"There's no fighting these things," says my mother.

38. Everyone's better now

Noget spots me straight off in the crowd that's come to hear him at the community center, and when he speaks he's speaking only to me, even if his quick little eyes flit over the audience's heads as he intones the clear, ringing words of his lecture.

He's clean, properly dressed in a suit and tie, but inelegant and even slightly indecent thanks to his paradoxical, nebulous flesh. I slip into the line of readers waiting their turn for a dedication. Sitting behind a table, he greets me with a sly smile. I bend down, my mouth very close to his ear.

"Monsieur Noget, I'm ready to hear it now... Tell me... Is Ange dead?"

"Dead?" he cries, feigning indignation.

He bursts into a mocking laugh.

"Nadia, Nadia! I don't believe Ange has ever been better."

"Is that true?"

I almost collapse in relief. Noget digs into a shoulder

bag at his feet. He pulls out a wallet, and from the wallet a photo.

"Look," he says, "this is Ange with his new girlfriend, maybe two weeks ago. We were all out at a restaurant."

The man in the photo looks almost nothing like Ange. On the other hand, I immediately recognize the woman: Corinna Daoui. They're sitting side-by-side, smiling, in fine spirits.

"That's nothing like Ange," I say dubiously.

"Yes it is," says Noget, "look closer."

I hold the photo up to my eyes. The forehead, the straight nose, the full lips—yes, that could be Ange, thinner, younger, but it could also just as well not be.

"I'm happy he pulled through, I really am," I say, handing the picture back to Noget.

"All it took was you going away," says Noget coldly.

The readers behind me are beginning to lose patience. Just as I'm leaving, Noget clutches my arm and pulls me back.

"So, Nadia," he purrs, "your stomach's much smaller now, did you deliver my child?"

"No, of course not," I say, "it was menopause."

I giggle nervously, uncomfortable to be talking of such things with him.

"You're lucky," he says.

He lets go of me, waves me off to make way for the people waiting behind me.

I leave the community center, take a few steps down the sidewalk. A tall man bumps my shoulder.

"Excuse me," he says.

He has a baseball cap pulled down low on his head. In the mauve shadow of the visor, he gazes vaguely into my eyes for a moment. Then he races off, as if he were afraid I might try to hold him back.

At my parents' house, I find my son paying his daily visit to Souhar. The little girl is delighted to see him, and she covers his cheeks with kisses as he cuddles her and half sings endearments into her ear. My father and mother are there too, sitting side-by-side, slightly slumped, tired.

When my son looks up from Souhar's shoulder, I see that his face is glistening with tears.

"Papa's dead," he tells me.

Stunned, I ask stupidly, "Papa?"

I walk my son back to his car. Sitting down at the wheel, he says to me, "It was Lanton, your dear Lanton, who gave me the news. He called me."

"You see?" I say.

"Somehow or other he killed Papa, I'm sure of it," says Ralph. "He seemed so triumphant."

He slams the door. As usual, he gives me a little wave. I see him wipe his eyes as the car turns away and drives off. Through the window I can still make out the back of his head, his delicate nape, and the distance accentuates the feeling I always got from my son, that in his oversized car he's not a man but a lost little boy trying to put on a good front, and like every day I feel a pang of commiseration in my heart—my benign, gentle heart, my old, placated heart.

Slowly I walk back to my parents' house. I can feel the dense heat of the paving stones through the soles of my sandals. And already I can hear my mother's shrill, shaky voice as she sings for Souhar.

The hurt is gone, gone from inside of me,
And now I can dance.
The hurt ran away, quick as lightning,
I can dance!

Every day my mother, that stubborn old woman, makes a dish of buttered semolina and grilled chicken or fried fish with eggplant or tomato. I eat that food without a trace of doubt or fear, I swallow it gratefully. And when I come into the kitchen and smell the butter melting in the piping-hot semolina, I can't help but think it was this, this semolina crumbled each morning by honest fingers, that helped rid my stomach of the thing that had taken it over.

Because, I say to myself, where could that thing—that black, glistening, fast-moving thing I saw slide over the floor of my room one night as I was undressing for bed—possibly have sprung from if not my own body? A quick, black, glistening thing that left a faint trail of blood on the floor, all the way to the door.

If, I say to myself, if someone forced me to tell of it as precisely as possible, if I had no choice but to tell of it and describe it, what would come to my mind as a way of comparing that quick, black, glistening thing to something familiar is an eel—a short, fat eel, though the thing might have been hairy, its fur smoothed and stuck down by something wet, blood or mucus.

That elusive thing left a faint trail all the way to the door.

I immediately scrubbed down the floor with a sponge. And, assuming my parents, still watching one of their favorite shows at that hour—a show about desperate people trying to locate missing loved ones—never turned their eyes toward that fleeing thing when, as it must certainly have, it crossed through the kitchen, then no one saw it, no one could later prove any link between it and myself, and set out, for example, to bring it back to me.

My parents laugh heartily at the television, like children. Sometimes, too, they're moved to the depths of their souls. They wish I would watch that show with them—but how could I ever do such a thing?

My husband and I never had a television, I almost told them, with a touch of arrogant aggression.

Happily, those words never crossed my lips.

After lunch, seizing the opportunity of naptime, I call Lanton. The sound of his voice throws me into such disarray that at first I can't speak.

"Hello! Hello!" he says, annoyed.

Finally I whisper, "Lanton…"

"Oh, it's you, Nadia," he says, his voice suddenly quiet and tense.

He says nothing more. I can hear his breathing, heavy and fast.

"I miss you terribly," he then says, "terribly. You know, I think…" (He forces out a little laugh to hide his discomfort.) "I kind of think I can't live without you," he says. "I can't live a good life without you."

"Lanton," I say, struggling over my words, "did you do something to hurt Ralph's father, my ex-husband?

Ralph thinks you did. Is that true, Lanton?"

"That nobody," says Lanton, "he dared to come back and see me about his stupid ID card. I got rid of him, that's all."

"Got rid of him," I say, "what does that mean, Lanton?"

"I don't want to talk about that guy, please don't make me," says Lanton, almost breathless. "Nadia?"

"Goodbye, dear Lanton," I say.

I hang up and sit for a long time, unable to move, prostrate on my parents' little stool by the telephone.

Naptime over, I take Souhar out to the beach, pushing her stroller along the boardwalk. I half sing her name as I walk, Souhar, little Souhar, do you want a little golden bag or a little silver bag? Bent forward, her back to me, looking all around, the child nonetheless tells me by her nodding head and shivering shoulder blades that those words fill her with joy, even if she doesn't yet fully understand them.

And now she stretches out one arm to show me a sight that amuses her. A man and a woman are running along the beach, holding hands, leaping and bounding like two young goats. But they haven't been young for a long time, you can see it from here: the man is gray-haired, the woman wizened and ropy. They throw themselves onto the sand, roll around, stand up again, so happy they seem unhinged. They come toward Souhar and me, and we watch, standing still in our tracks.

I know them. Oh, I tell myself, I know them well.

The man is Ange, and the woman, in a short turquoise dress, is Corinna Daoui. Ange is wearing a white T-shirt and a linen suit. His face is fresh and healthy, he has a vacationer's tan. Even Daoui has lost the blue-gray tint decades of cigarettes and poverty had given her.

Neither surprised nor embarrassed to have run into me, they each give me a kiss, one after the other, two identical noisy kisses on my cheeks, like family. I shift my weight from one foot to the other, clutching the stroller handles. Both at the same time (immediately laughing out loud at having spoken together), they ask, "So what's new with you?"

I wave away the question with a vague gesture and a forced smile. I look deep into Ange's eyes—but there's no covert message inside them, and they return to me only an expression of well-being and a perfectly untroubled conscience.

"Let's go have a drink," says Daoui.

"Yes," says Ange, "or a quick coffee."

"I can't," I say, "I have to get home with my granddaughter."

Daoui then exclaims over the beauty of the child, her marvelous black curls. In a muted voice, I quickly ask Ange, "So you're better now?"

He looks at me with a vague, slightly perplexed eye, as if he were searching his memory for some clue to my meaning.

"Oh yes," he finally says, "of course, yes."

He pulls up his T-shirt, puts his finger to a pink scar on his side.

"Corinna's never been ashamed of anything," he says serenely, pulling down his T-shirt, seeming to mean this as an answer.

Daoui puts her arm around him, kisses his neck.

"And…what about work?" I say, breathless.

"I've got my class back again," says Ange, "and Corinna will be working at the school as well, helping the children who have trouble keeping up."

"We go home the day after tomorrow," says Daoui. "You sure you don't want to come for a drink?"

I weakly shake my head. Daoui takes my hand and presses it to her heart. Ange lays an impersonal little kiss on the corner of my mouth. Smiling, cordial, they walk off, arms around each other's waists.

I start off again, pushing Souhar homeward.

My mother's voice greets us as soon as we turn onto the street, her little-bell voice, wafted along on the warm, tremulous air.

Mama, so many problems,
Some people know things,
I don't know anything,
So many problems, Mama!